"Grace, I'm still mad," Luke said. "I only hope you won't pull another stunt like that."

She heard him take a deep breath.

"Right now you can tell the FBI you had a breakdown and lost touch with reality, and that's why you took off with the boy. I know that's bull, but at least the law would have to consider it. But if the feds get wind that you were out trying to destroy his birth mother's credibility, you can kiss the nervous breakdown story goodbye. They'll throw the book at you. For the time being you're the innocent victim in the public's view. You don't want to fall from…grace," he said, "If you'll forgive the pun."

"That isn't funny," she said with a catch in her voice.

He frowned. "I can't take it when a woman cries."

"I'm not crying."

"It's okay. You tried to help. I overreacted. Come on, Grace."

She let him enfold her in his arms, and suddenly nothing mattered. There was only Luke and pure sensation flowing through her veins. She tried to focus on the hurt he'd caused her, on how close they were to their goal. Her little boy…soon, soon, her little boy would be safely back with her.

But at the moment there was only Luke and her hopeless, spiraling need….

Dear Reader,

We first learned about a situation identical to the one in *Fugitive Mom* from an article in a newsmagazine. However, in real life the story had an unhappy ending when the foster parent was required by the courts to return her baby to the biological mother. A year later, one of our close friends underwent a similar ordeal, and our hearts were touched.

This is why we write books—we can solve these thorny problems and create happy endings. But we certainly do enjoy putting our protagonists through the wringer on the route to success. And wouldn't it be wonderful if the heroine fell in love on her journey?

We hope you enjoy *Fugitive Mom*, and please visit us on the Harlequin Web site.

Best wishes,

Carla and Molly
(*Lynn Erickson*)

Fugitive Mom
Lynn Erickson

HARLEQUIN®

TORONTO • NEW YORK • LONDON
AMSTERDAM • PARIS • SYDNEY • HAMBURG
STOCKHOLM • ATHENS • TOKYO • MILAN • MADRID
PRAGUE • WARSAW • BUDAPEST • AUCKLAND

ISBN 0-373-70973-0

FUGITIVE MOM

Copyright © 2001 by Carla Peltonen and Molly Swanton.

Visit us at www.eHarlequin.com

Printed in U.S.A.

Fugitive Mom

CHAPTER ONE

COURTROOM C OF THE Boulder County Justice Center looked just like the other courtrooms in the sprawling building: blond wood, industrial blue carpet, judge's podium, jury box and spectators' benches in a kind of faux Danish modern style. But to Grace Bennett, sitting at a prosecution table in front, Courtroom C was the worst hell on earth.

"'In the case of minor Charles L. Pope, he is remanded to the permanent custody of his biological mother, Kerry Ann Pope,'" the Juvenile magistrate intoned, reading his decision. "'He is to be removed from the care of his foster mother, Sally Grace Bennett, in four days' time. The State of Colorado and the County of Boulder thank you, Ms. Bennett.'" His gavel thudded dully on its block.

Grace heard the young woman at the other table say something: "Oh, wow! Thank you, Your Honor."

The words were spoken by Kerry Pope, in her early twenties, thin and pale, wearing worn jeans and a sweatshirt that said CU, out of prison six months ago, out of her halfway house only two months ago. Rehabilitated, according to the legal system. Charley's biological mother. A joke! It must all be a stupendous joke, a bad dream. Kerry had never taken care of Charley. Never!

Grace put her head in her hands, elbows leaning

on the blond wood table. She fought tears, felt desperation fill her to the brim and spill over.

The clerk of the court scribbled busily; the court stenographer tapped the judge's last words into her machine. There was no jury to comment upon the decision, to murmur or gasp, but there were onlookers, mumbling in a monotone behind Grace, probably talking about their own cases, not hearing or knowing or caring....

No, Grace wanted to scream. *You can't do this.* Charley, handed back to his so-called *mother.* Her Charley, whom she had cared for since he was three months old. *Her* son, for God's sake.

"Grace," her lawyer was saying, "come on, Grace, we have to go."

She raised her face up to the woman who'd represented her at this hearing. "They can't do this, Natalie. They can't just—"

Natalie Woodruff took Grace's arm gently. "We have to leave. The judge has ruled."

"But can't you...can't we appeal this? There must be *something* we can do."

Natalie's eyes were full of sympathy—not that it would do Grace or Charley any good. "Not now, Grace. It's over. We have to go."

Slowly, Grace stood up. Her knees felt weak, her stomach knotted. Her heart pounded sickeningly in her ears. *Charley, Charley.* Automatically, she reached for her handbag and stepped away from the table. She glanced at the Juvenile judge again; he was reading a file the clerk had handed him, peering at it over half glasses. He'd already forgotten Grace and Charley—he was dealing with another case. *Oh, God.*

"Grace," Natalie said again.

She moved shakily toward the double doors at the back of the courtroom, following Natalie. She prayed Kerry Pope wouldn't say anything to her.

Natalie was pushing the first set of doors open; they closed behind Grace with a whoosh, then the second set opened and the world rushed back—the crowded corridor of the Justice Center, the front entrance not far away, summer sun spilling through, the security guards on duty.

"Come on, Grace, let's get out of here," Natalie was saying, but Grace felt so weak for a moment she slid down onto one of the long benches against the stark white wall.

"Ms. Bennett," she heard, and looked up. A young woman was standing in front of her. Vaguely familiar. A little heavy, a worried frown between her eyebrows. Wearing a rumpled gray suit that showed her dimpled knees.

"Yes?" Grace said faintly.

"My name is Susan Moore. I'm with Child Protective Services. I...I know about you. I heard the decision."

Grace adjusted her glasses and gazed at Susan Moore.

"I'm sorry," Susan said. "I'm so so sorry."

"Thank you," Grace whispered.

"Here," Susan said, pushing something into Grace's hand. A scrap of paper.

Grace stared at her hand stupidly. "What is this?" she asked.

"Help," Susan said. "A phone number. Call it."

Grace raised her eyes. "I..." But Susan was walking away through the crowd.

"Who was that?" Natalie asked.

"Oh, an acquaintance. Telling me how sorry she was." Instinctively, Grace lied. She had to think, go home and pay the baby-sitter and hug Charley and think. What did Susan Moore mean? *Help.* What kind of help? Who...?

"Do you want me to drive you back?" Natalie was asking.

"No, no, I'm okay. Honestly. I'll make it." Grace tried to smile.

"Sure?"

"Yes, I'm sure. Thanks, Natalie. I know you did your best."

"I'm afraid," her lawyer said, "the courts are prejudiced in favor of the biological parents these days. We knew that going in."

"Even when the parents are drug addicts or abusive...yes, I know. You warned me."

"We made a good try," Natalie said, squeezing Grace's hand.

"Not good enough," Grace said sadly.

"I'll file an appeal," Natalie said.

"Yes, an appeal."

"We can try again. If Kerry does something outrageous, if she puts Charley in danger, well, we can bring it to the court's attention. The judge might review his ruling in that case." Her voice held little conviction.

Grace stopped short and put her hand on Natalie's arm. "She will, you know. She'll do something terrible. You know it and I know it and the judge should have known it. Think of Kerry's history. Drugs, rehab, more drugs. You think she's really rehabilitated? For God's sake, Natalie, she's going to slip again. She was abused as a child, and you know what that means. You know..." Her voice clicked off.

"Take it easy, Grace. Social Services will send someone to check on her."

"Oh, please, don't patronize me." It was the first flare of anger she'd felt, and it was satisfying. Better than hopelessness.

"I'm sorry, I didn't mean to."

Grace ran her hand through her dark-blond hair; it was held back by a clip, causing her bangs to stand up in spikes, but she didn't care. Glamour was not one of her strong points. "No, I know you didn't, but you can't expect me to trust the *system,* not after what the court just decided was in the best interests of a minor."

"Calm down, Grace."

"I've always been calm. I've always done the right thing. Look where it got me. And Charley."

"Listen, I'll go back to the office and work on the appeal. I have all those psychological studies you gave me."

"The ones they didn't allow into evidence," Grace said bitterly.

"I'll send them to the judge."

"And maybe he'll read them. *Maybe.*" She'd worked so hard, looking up studies on drug addicts with a history of child abuse, recidivism. She was a psychology professor, after all. She knew about addicts. She knew about Kerry Pope. She'd had many therapy sessions with Kerry four years before as a volunteer at the women's shelter where Kerry was staying while she had her baby.

That was how it had all started. She'd only been trying to help the women in the shelter, the beaten-down ones, the hurt and lost and abused ones. Kerry had been one of those refugees, a nice young kid, still a teenager at the time. Kind of innocent, pregnant by a boyfriend turned violent, sort of pretty in a washed-out way. Blue eyes, stringy blond hair. Skinny with an incongruously big belly. In those days Kerry cried a lot and was terribly frightened about caring for a baby. She was just out of high school, for God's sake. Grace felt sorry for her, and she had broken the therapist's first rule of thumb; she had become emotionally involved with her patient.

When Kerry had given birth, Grace had visited her in the hospital, brought a present, held the infant.

"Charles Leon Pope," Kerry had said. "I like that name."

Grace had stared down at Charley, his waving arms and tiny clenched hands, his pale, vein-etched eyelids, the blond fuzz on his head, and although she hadn't realized it at the time, she'd fallen in love.

"You okay, Grace?" Natalie was asking.

"No. But I'll manage. I better go home." She smiled grimly. "The baby-sitter."

She drove back carefully, aware that she was distracted. Pulling up in front of the half of the duplex she owned, she turned the car off and sat for a moment, her head resting on the steering wheel. Then she straightened, got out of the car and walked up the path to her front door. Familiar, comforting. Geraniums in pots, Charley's plastic fat bike on its side on the grass, his old fire truck there, too, a muddy spoon and bowl from the kitchen sitting on the front stoop. What had he been doing with *that?*

Inside, the television was on—afternoon cartoons. Grace didn't like Charley watching too much TV, but

Ellen had probably been happy to let him. She was a sweet kid, lived down the street, and Charley loved her.

"Hi, Mrs. Bennett," Ellen said, popping up from the couch. *Mrs.* Bennett. No matter how many times Grace had told Ellen there was no Mr. Bennett, the girl called her Mrs. She'd given up correcting her.

"Hi, Mommy," she heard, and Charley appeared over the back of the couch, jumping up and down. "Hi, Mommy, Mommy, Mommy! We're watching cartoons!"

Mommy. Charley knew no other mother. He didn't remember his first three months with Kerry's post-partum depression, her inability to nurse him or hold him or provide him with more than perfunctory care. The word tore her heart out. *Mommy.* The court had negated four years of motherhood and declared an utter stranger his mother.

She paid Ellen and watched her walk out, then down the street to her house. She was trying hard not to show her inner turmoil, but she doubted her own acting ability. She was a straightforward person, a plain, ordinary, law-abiding woman. Her talents were few but enough for her own fulfillment. She was a good mother. No. Better. She was a terrific mother. And she was a darn good teacher. Her classes at the University of Colorado always had a waiting list: Psychology 101, Abnormal Psychology and a graduate course in Behavior and Therapy.

"Come here, Charley," she said, sitting on the couch and holding her arms out.

He ran to her. His eyes were blue like Kerry's, but he had darker hair. A dirty, healthy four-year-old. He was going to have a substantial nose when he matured. His father must have…

"Mommy." His grubby fingers played with the collar of the suit she'd worn to court. A plain navy-blue suit. Several years old and not very stylish. The skirt was too long and sagged around her hips. But she'd wanted to look respectable. God, she might as well have worn jeans like Kerry.

"Yes, sweetie?" He was warm and solid on her lap, and smelled like dust and little-boy sweat.

"Can we go out for ice cream after dinner?"

It was his favorite outing—walking along the Pearl Street Mall in downtown Boulder and licking an ice cream cone.

"Not tonight, Charley."

"Why not, Mommy?"

She took a deep breath. *Because I can't, because I'm done in, because I don't want to see anybody.* "Not tonight, okay?"

He sulked. But she knew he'd get over it. Charley had a sunny disposition and didn't hold grudges long. He was independent, though. Stubborn and willful and wonderfully bright. She held him until he wiggled, burying her face in his hair.

Four days. She was only his mother for four more days. How was she going to explain that to him? The enormity of the mistake, the injustice, overwhelmed her once more. Charley was her *son.*

"Mommy," he whined, wriggling off her lap. "I'm hungry."

Grace could only go through the motions, fixing him a snack. Despite the routine, her mind raced, searching for a way out. An appeal might work. Natalie had said she'd write one up. But not in time, not in four days. Should she call the judge at home? What was his name? Fallon, yes, Judge Henry Fallon. Call him and explain, beg, throw herself on his mercy?

Ridiculous.

What, then? Hand Charley over as if he were a stray dog from the pound? *Here you go, Spot, a nice new owner for you. Oh, don't worry, you'll get used to her after a while.*

As a psychology teacher, she knew full well what this kind of disruption could do to a child. It could leave Charley with a profound distrust of adults, a possibly severe incapacity to trust, to form relationships, to love. It was worse than a mother's death—at some point even a small child could accept a parent's death, but to a child abandonment appeared to be a deliberate act. Punishment. Oh, God.

She sat at the kitchen table, watching Charley crawl on the floor, pushing a Tonka toy car.

"Broom, broomm," he was saying. "And now he passes the blue car, faster and faster. Around the corner. Screech, he turns over!" He flipped the car and spun it around. His fingers left sticky peanut butter prints on his toy.

Charley.

Her life had been perfect. Her son, her teaching, her research, her friends in the wonderfully liberated atmosphere of Boulder, Colorado. Everything under control, no need for messy relationships or men. She'd been perfectly happy.

"And he spins and, *crash,* into the wall!" Charley said.

She'd just finished the paperwork for Charley's legal adoption. She had needed the release from Kerry Pope, that was all, a simple, easy signature. Kerry hadn't signed. Instead, she'd petitioned the Juvenile Court for permanent custody of Charley. After four years.

At first Grace had figured she herself was a shoo-in. Nobody would remove a child from a loving parent who'd taken care of him since birth and return him to a convicted felon who'd abandoned him years before.

Natalie had warned her, but she hadn't listened. Not that it would have done any good.

Charley was lying on his stomach, twirling the wheels of his race car with a finger. He turned his face up to her and smiled. "We won the race, Mommy. Did you see?"

"Yes, I saw. Congratulations."

Then he was up and running around the kitchen table, his sturdy legs pumping furiously, his elbows tight to his sides. "Broom, broo-o-m! Faster and faster! Watch me, Mommy."

And then, at that very moment, Grace knew that she could never give Charley up.

What to do? What were her options?

Charley was in the living room now. She could hear him talking to Hazel and Whiskers, their two cats. The animals had ventured downstairs for their suppers, running the gamut of Charley's overexuberant play. "Nice kitty," she heard him croon. "Here, play with my car. Broom, broo-o-m!"

She needed help.

Help.

Susan Moore, the look in her concerned brown eyes as she stuck the scrap of paper into Grace's hand. Help. A phone number.

Where was that piece of paper? She must have put

it in her pocket. Yes, the pocket of her suit jacket. She hurried into the living room and grabbed her navy-blue jacket from the chair where she'd tossed it when she'd gotten home, felt in the pockets. Nothing in the left pocket. The right one, yes, a crumpled scrap that she'd jammed in there when Natalie had spoken to her.

She flattened out the paper with shaking fingers. There was a phone number scrawled on it, a Denver number. If she called it who would answer? What kind of help would be offered? But at least it was an option, a possibility.

She lifted the cordless phone from its base and punched in the numbers, quickly, before she lost her nerve. The line rang, once, twice, three times. Oh, God, she'd probably get an answering machine, and then what would she do?

Someone picked up at the other end. Grace's heart lurched.

"Women's Assistance." A female voice.

Grace couldn't think of what to say.

"Hello, can I help you?"

"Uh, yes, I..."

"Are you in an emergency situation?" The question was put sharply.

"Uh, yes, well, no, we're not in immediate physical danger, but we..."

"Okay, relax. Tell me what your problem is. We're here to help."

"Who are you?"

"I'm afraid I can't give you specific names. Just as I don't want to know yours. We are an organization that aids women and children in danger of any kind."

"Yes, I see. I...my son, he's four. He's my foster

son, actually, and the court has ruled that his biological mother should have custody. In four days. I have four days. His biological mother is…she's not able to take care of them. Drugs, prison. Oh, my God, I know she'll hurt him. I can't…''

''All right. Is there a father involved? Your husband?''

''No, neither.''

''We have a way. We call it our underground railroad. But you must understand, you can leave no tracks. You simply disappear. You end your old life. A clean break. You tell no one.''

''Yes,'' Grace whispered.

''It's up to you. It's a big decision. If you feel your son is in enough danger to warrant such a drastic step, I can give you an address. No questions will be asked. You leave now.''

''Now?''

''Tonight, as soon as possible.''

''Oh.''

''And please destroy any records—this phone number, for instance. Memorize it if you must. Memorize the address I give you. We have to be able to trust you.''

''Of course. I understand.'' Grace's heart hammered. Should she do this thing? She and Charley— a vanishing act. Did she have the guts? The alternative was too awful, though.

''Are you still there?''

''Yes, I'm here.'' She took a deep breath. ''Please, give me that address. Will it be far away?''

''No, not far. And you'll receive another address when you leave there. You'll need to decide where you're headed.''

"Can I make up my mind later?"

"Sure, that's up to you. Only the person who gives you the new address will know."

"Okay, I'm ready." Grace found a pencil in her junk drawer, held it poised above the pad she kept for her shopping list.

The voice recited an address. It was in Denver. Good, not too far. She could get there easily by tonight. It was only thirty miles away. Thirty miles, but a gulf so wide she could never leap back across it.

"Memorize the address."

"Yes, no paper trail."

"Will you be all right? Get as much cash as you can. A credit card can be traced. Do you have a car?"

"Yes."

"All right, good. But be warned that an APB could be put out on your car, on your license plate number. Also—" the voice hesitated "—if you leave the state with your son, if your action is declared a kidnapping, be aware that the FBI will be called in."

"Oh, my God."

"Weigh the consequences. We've had success, but we've had a few failures, too."

"Yes, yes, I see." Her voice quavered.

"Anything else you need to know?"

"I don't think so. Oh, wait, is there a...a charge for your help?"

"No. If you're able to leave some money at your stops, feel free to do so."

She hung up, trembling, staring at the address she'd written down.

"Mommy, what are we going to have for dinner?" came Charley's voice.

"Dinner, well..." She tried to sound lighthearted.

"Charley, sweetie, I have to go out to run some errands, so let's go to McDonald's. How about that?"

"Cool, McDonald's. Can I get the Kiddie Meal?"

"Sure, anything you want." She was distracted, her brain going at full speed, planning, figuring.

Cash. After McDonald's she'd go to the ATM at her bank, take out as much as she could. Gas her car with her credit card—no one could trace that any farther than Boulder. She had four days before the alarm would go out. Four precious days.

Ask Stacey next door to feed the cats. Buy cat food. How long would she be gone? Days, months, years? Her career, her life, her friends, her uncomplicated, comfortable existence—all gone. She'd be a fugitive.

Pack. Clothes, toiletries. Charley's favorite toys. Some groceries to take in the car. A pillow and blankets for Charley.

The car. A gray Volvo station wagon, nondescript except for her license plates. But she had four days before she had to worry about that. Maybe she'd sell her car or rent one. No, no, she couldn't rent one; that always required a credit card.

She stopped and drew in a breath, needing to calm herself. Then she moved around the house, getting suitcases, trying to think. It was too hard. Images kept flying at her out of the blue—her friends' faces, the lecture hall full of her students, the women at the day care where Charley went to preschool. The courtroom again, Kerry Pope's big triumphant smile when the judge had ruled. Charley, Charley in his crib, Charley in his new bed, all his toys, her cats, the basement stacked high with file boxes from her classes.

Her whole life was here.

Somehow she managed to pack, even remembering

coats in the event they were still on the run when fall arrived. Towels, one set of sheets—just in case—pillow, blanket, toy cars and plastic dinosaurs and Charley's favorite books.

"Charley, let's go," she called out.

At McDonald's, Charley got ketchup all over his T-shirt. She could hardly eat—a chicken nugget or two, a Coke. Her heart raced and her hands trembled.

The pickles slid out of Charley's burger onto his lap. He looked up at her guiltily, but she didn't care, just wiped the mess up with a handful of napkins.

"Charley," she said, "guess what?"

"What?"

"We're going on an adventure tonight. A trip."

"A trip. Where, Mommy?"

"Oh, nowhere special, we'll just visit friends for a while. We'll drive wherever we feel like it."

Ketchup smeared on his face, dribbled down his shirt. Her beloved baby. She had held and rocked him, sat up with him when he had colic, gone through the ear infections and ampicillin routine. Read stories to him and taken him to *Bambi* and *Lion King* and *Snow White*. She was his mother, she thought fiercely.

By six o'clock that summer evening her car was packed, Stacey given her key and shown the twenty-pound bag of Cat Chow.

"And could you collect my mail? I'll get it from you in a little while. Maybe you can send it. I'll call."

"God. You're sure in a hurry," Stacey said.

"Uh, yes, my dad is sick. My mother called. An emergency."

"Oh, I'm sorry. I hope he gets well soon."

"Yes, we all do. Thanks, Stacey."

She took one last look around her side of the duplex. Her home. The only home Charley had known. But she had to be strong and leave it behind. For her son.

"Come on, sweetie," she said, and they went out the front door together. Grace let it lock behind her, walked down the path to her car, put Charley in the back seat and fastened his seat belt.

She drove away, down the familiar tree-shaded street, past her neighbors' houses, past the large red-roofed, sandstone buildings of the University of Colorado, out to the Boulder Turnpike and south to Denver. Behind her was her whole life. If only she could see ahead.

CHAPTER TWO

GRACE NAVIGATED through Denver's tidy Bonnie Brae neighborhood, craning her neck to read the street signs. Part of her was calmly aware of how mundane everything seemed in the quiet, middle-class area. Another part of her quivered with nerves in the warm summer evening as the shadows of the trees and houses reached darkly toward her. A dog raced out of the growing dimness and barked, chasing her tires.

"Mommy," Charley said from the back seat, "that's a bad dog. He's going to get in my window. *Mommy!*"

Grace studied the house numbers. This couldn't be the street. It was too...ordinary. In her distress, she must have written down the wrong address.

She shook herself mentally. What did she know about a safe house? She realized she'd been envisioning some foreboding, secret structure set back in trees, all shuttered up, no lights and windows. But she supposed the house could be any sort, even a mansion, for goodness' sakes.

"Mommy, the dog's jumping at my window!"

"Oh, honey, he can't get in the car. There. See? He's leaving, going home to his yard."

"I don't like him."

"Well, he was probably just curious," she said, on motherly autopilot.

She slowed the car to a crawl, squinting at the house numbers. There it was, the house near the corner of Adams and Mississippi. Could this place, this innocuous, square brick home, really be part of the underground railroad?

"Are we there, Mommy? Are we there?"

"Yes, ah, yes, sweetie, it looks like we're here."

Grace parked at the curb, as there was already a car in the narrow drive. She got out, noticed the weak watery feeling in her knees and took a breath. What if this wasn't the place? What if...?

But she wouldn't think about that now. She'd memorized the telephone number. If this really were the wrong address, she'd call the number again. No big deal.

No big deal? her brain cried. But Charley was undoing his seat belt and opening the back door. "I'm hungry, Mommy. You didn't give me dessert. Do they have ice cream?"

"I'm sure they have something, sweetie, but let's make sure this is really my, ah, friend's place first. Okay?"

Charley took her hand. "Okay."

She advanced up the walk, gulping air, trying to come up with an excuse should this be the wrong place. One step, two, three. As she rang the bell, her mind was so full of muddled thoughts she barely realized that someone was standing behind the screen— a young teenage girl.

The girl eyed first Grace, then Charley, then called over her shoulder, "Hey, Mom, your friends are here."

Friends. No names. Just friends. So this *was* the place.

"Come on in," the girl said, pushing open the door, giving Charley a perfunctory smile.

A woman was moving toward Grace, her hand out, a gracious smile on her face. An ordinary-looking woman, with brown curly hair and faded jeans and a tank top. A mother, too, but so different from Grace. So courageous. How many frightened women and children had she sheltered?

Grace took her hand and tried to return the smile.

"Well, let's get you settled," the woman said, and she gently ruffled Charley's silky hair. "And I'll bet you're hungry, young man."

Charley looked up at Grace with soulful eyes.

"Yes," Grace said, "I'm afraid he's always hungry this time of night. I didn't think to..."

"Of course you didn't. Here, your room is just down this hall. It's off the kitchen. There, the light switch is on the left. And there's a small bath just to the right. And, by the way, don't worry, no one can do much rational thinking in this situation. Don't forget, it *is* your first night. Get settled and I'll see you in the kitchen, okay? And you, young man, do you like cookies? Or maybe a Popsicle?"

"A Popsicle."

"What do you say, Charley?"

"Please."

The woman smiled again and closed the door behind her.

"Wow," Grace breathed, sinking onto a queen-size bed.

"What's wrong, Mommy? Can I get my Popsicle now?"

"In a minute. I just need a minute, honey."

"But I'm hungry."

Grace sighed, trying desperately to collect herself. She felt as if she'd stepped onto a train on this so-called railroad, a train with no destination, a train that would never stop. Her heart pounded furiously and suddenly the room was too close. She rose and opened the window that looked out onto a square backyard and an alley behind it. The sound of children playing nearby drifted in, all so normal, so placid in the face of her predicament. She should be home, calling the cats in for the evening, telling Charley to brush his teeth, arguing about his bedtime on this warm summer's night.

After a few more complaints from Charley that he was hungry, she finally took his hand and led him to the kitchen, where the woman was doing dinner dishes.

The situation was so terribly awkward. She and Charley were strangers in a strange place. She felt sick with confusion and unfocused dread.

"Oh, there you are. We'll get your suitcases and you'll be settled in for the night." The woman dried her hands on the dish towel that hung from the refrigerator handle and clucked at Charley. "And I'll bet you want that Popsicle, young man."

"Yes, please." Charley beamed.

She looked at Grace. "Coffee? I have decaf. Or there's iced tea."

"Iced tea would be nice, thank you."

"While I fix the tea, why don't you bring in your bags."

"Will my car be okay? I mean…"

"For tonight it will be fine."

And then what? Grace wondered. Could any of this be happening?

Charley ate his Popsicle while Grace got their bags from the car and sat them in the bedroom. Then it was time to settle Charley down, to insist, despite the newness of his surroundings, that he put on his pajamas and brush his teeth.

"I want to watch TV," he said, and she was afraid he was going to pull one of his "terrible fits," as she called them.

She drew one of his favorite books out of his bag, and he snuggled against her. It was a short simple book called *A Happy Sad Silly Mad Book,* which she found effective with children when they were upset. Not that she did much therapy these days. No time for it since she'd taken on Charley. The book asked children how they felt, described the emotions, told them it was okay to feel them.

The method never failed with Charley.

She turned the last page and bent to kiss her little boy's forehead.

"Good night, Mommy," he said, and he hugged her around the neck.

"Good night, sweetie."

She stood, whispering up a prayer of relief. This was impossibly rough on him. Bad enough for her, but Charley was the innocent one, the victim of an unjust court system. He shouldn't have to suffer. Damn, not this beautiful child.

The ice was practically melted in her tea before Grace finally sat across the kitchen table from her hostess. Down the hall, the door to the bedroom she was to share with Charley was open, and the sound of the TV and the teenage girl talking on the phone came from the living room.

She looked up from her glass and caught the

woman's gaze. "I...I feel so awkward," she began. "It isn't that you haven't been most gracious... It's just that..."

"It's your first night," the woman put in. "And you don't know where any of this is heading and you're scared to death."

"In a nutshell, yes."

"You have to take it one day at a time. If you're strong for your son, you'll succeed. Things work out."

"Do they?"

"Often enough." The woman nodded, an inner strength shining through. The glow made her look beautiful.

Grace tucked a stray strand of mousy hair behind an ear and adjusted her glasses on her nose. Oh, she knew she was a plain Jane and a little timid at that, and she couldn't help wondering, if she'd been more outgoing and assertive in court, would the judge have ruled differently? If, for instance, she had carried herself more like this woman, would she be in this mess?

"I wish I could give you all the answers," the woman was saying. "But that would be impossible. Everyone's situation is so different, you understand."

"Of course."

"There are a few things I can tell you, though, and maybe they'll help."

Grace gave a strained laugh. "That would be nice."

"And a piece of advice here. Don't let yourself become emotionally entangled in other sponsors' lives. In my experience, most people who take you in are pretty closemouthed, but there'll be some who'll virtually dump their troubles on you. You've got enough problems of your own right now. Do you understand what I'm getting at?''

Grace let out a breath. ''Yes, completely.'' She nodded. Oh, God, she thought, it was all too real.

·''As for your car...you'll need to stash it with someone, a good friend, a relative, whoever. Use the bus or train, whatever feels comfortable. And keep moving. I know how awful all this sounds, but you need to lose yourself and, of course, Charley.''

''Is this...forever?'' she ventured, gripping her glass of tea whitely.

''Yes and no. Everyone's situation is so different. I can tell you my own, if it helps.''

''Please.''

''Well, I was on the underground railroad for three years.''

''Three...*years*,'' Grace gasped.

The woman smiled ruefully. ''And my case, unfortunately, is very typical. I've heard of women and their children being on the run for... Oh, never mind, you really don't—''

''Tell me. How long?''

''Ten years, longer. And even now they live under false identities.''

''But...''

''But how? How do they manage? You meet people on the route. People who can help with new Social Security numbers, new names, jobs, everything.''

''I didn't...realize.''

''Why would you? But that aside, you need to stay on the move until it's impossible to trace you. You need to change. Become someone else. And you need to be strong. Above all else, you can never give up. It's your child you're protecting. It will be hard.

Worse than hard. I hope you don't think I'm a doom-sayer. I'm simply being straight. But better to know now just how tough it can be rather than to be shocked later on.''

Grace said nothing.

"Anyway, tomorrow you should leave Denver. Leave Colorado, in fact. And I'll warn you, other than maybe parking your car with them, stay away from family and friends. The authorities will be watching them for a very long time. If you decide to ditch your car with them, do it soon and do it quickly. Just get rid of it and take off. You don't want to put friends or your family in jeopardy. It's bad enough as it is. You'll just have to learn to be alone in this. You and your child.''

Grace bit her lip.

"I know, that's the worst. It's not forever, though. Someday your son will be old enough to take care of himself. And after what he's been through, he'll be strong. You'll never have to worry about that.''

"But I won't ever be my real self again, will I?''

She shook her head. "There will be charges against you. Federal charges. They won't disappear.''

And then Grace had to ask. "But you, your job...? I mean, how did you manage?''

"I was lucky. One of the lucky few. My ex-husband never contacted the authorities when I disappeared with our daughter. Not *him*.'' The woman sneered. "He was very wealthy, you see, and he hired private investigators to trace me. I never stayed two nights in the same spot. For three years we ran. During that period I even had to school my daughter myself. We had no friends, no family we dared to contact.''

"But now…?"

"Well, my very *wealthy* husband finally messed up with the wrong people. He beat up a girlfriend. Badly, I'm afraid. Anyway, her father was a lawyer and made damn good and sure Larry was put behind bars for a very long time. My daughter will be grown and out of college before he sees the light of day again."

"So you were able to resume your life. Your real life."

"Yes. That was years ago now, and I've done okay on my own. If nothing else, living on the run gave me a strength and courage I never knew I possessed. Before that, I was just another abused woman. Frightened, afraid to leave him and afraid to stay."

"Why did you finally leave?"

The woman met Grace's eyes fiercely. "It was one thing when that bastard struck me. It was another when he turned on our child. He broke her arm."

"Oh, God."

"It was horrible, yes, and we'll carry the scars all our lives, but we have a good life now." She nodded toward the living room, where her daughter was still talking a mile a minute on the phone, the TV still on in the background. "Her biggest problem now is what to wear to school. I'm very lucky. We're very lucky."

Grace sat back and stared into the middle distance. She knew, in her heart of hearts, that her own story, that Charley's future, could never be as bright. In four days—closer to three now—the court expected her to carry out the order to surrender Charley to his biological mother. And when Grace failed to turn him over, when the authorities learned she had fled with the child, she would forever be a fugitive. There would be no turning back.

Shortly before midnight, she slipped quietly into bed next to Charley. She could hear the little sounds he made as he slept, and she carefully snuggled up next to him and drew in his scent. She could do this. As awful as it sounded, as frightened as she was, she had to do it. Her hostess on this first night of a long journey had told her to be strong. She could, she *would*, do it.

She shut her eyes and tried to empty her head of all thought. She needed to sleep. Her body was craving precious rest. *Sleep.*

She listened to the night sounds outside the open window and she tried to breathe deeply. All in vain. Rather than slow, her heart drummed against her rib cage and tiny nerves beat sporadically against her skin, causing her to twitch. Once, her heart seemed to do a somersault in her chest and her breath halted in her lungs.

A lifetime of running from the law. Fugitives. Both of them. And how would she support them? What would happen when her classes started in the fall? Where would they end up? What would happen to Charley's psyche?

The digital clock on the dresser blinked 3:00 a.m. and all of Grace's resolve fled. She couldn't handle it. Tomorrow she would return to Boulder, to their lives, and she would turn Charley over to Kerry Pope. Not for long, though. She'd think of some other way to convince the judge he had made a terrible mistake. She'd hire a fleet of lawyers. No matter the cost. Surely a dream team of lawyers could somehow right this ghastly wrong. It might take time, though, and meanwhile, Charley would be in Kerry Pope's care and...

Oh, dear God, what was she going to do?

THE MILES THROUGH the Rocky Mountains crept by. She'd gotten a late start. First, after listening to her hostess and hearing how long she might have to be on the move, she had decided to all but wipe out her checking account, and she'd had to wait for the branch bank in Denver to open. Then the lines had been long and Charley had had to go "Pee-pee, Mommy," and then there'd been heavy traffic along the Interstate 70 corridor crossing the Continental Divide, and then Charley had needed lunch. And they hadn't even reached Vail. Her only good news was that with each passing mile, no matter how slow her progress, she was putting distance between herself and Boulder, herself and the court and Kerry Pope. She was doing the right thing, the only thing possible for the safety of her child, and she clung to that thought as she drove through Glenwood Springs on the Western Slope, toward the high desert of Utah.

Charley was really very good in the car as the afternoon proceeded. She stopped at rest areas and gassed up in Green River, Utah, where she bought Charley an ice cream. *Too much ice cream,* she thought. His teeth would rot out of his head. But it was an easy way to make him happy in this awful fix they were in. A kind of bribe. Though not the best way to handle a child, her psychologist's mind admonished silently.

While Charley busied himself with his treat, she called the number of the next safe house on the underground railroad. She'd been told she could just show up in Salt Lake City, and she'd be given shelter—no questions asked. But what if this person was not home? She supposed she could pay cash for a room that night, but she had no idea how long her fifteen hundred dollars would hold out. Certainly not for years. But, she thought ruefully, like Scarlett O'Hara, she wouldn't think about that until tomorrow.

"Hello," Grace began when a woman answered, "my name is…well, sorry, I was given this number, and I'm on the road with my son in Green River and I was hoping—"

But Grace was cut off. "Get off the interstate. I assume you'll be on Interstate 15?"

"Yes, in a few hours. Going north."

"Okay, then get off at exit 198, take a right…"

Grace memorized the directions, then said, "We'll be awfully late getting in."

"Your room is over the garage. Use the side steps on the left. I may or may not see you in the morning. I've got to work at eight. Will you be here for more than the night?"

"I…probably not."

"Well, then, if I don't see you, best of luck. I'll turn on the light for you and leave another number for you to call. You said you're heading north?"

"No, I'm going to the coast, the San Francisco Bay Area."

"Okay, then, I'll figure around a ten-hour drive from here and leave the number. Is that going to work okay?"

"Yes," Grace said, feeling Charley tug at her shorts with sticky fingers, "and thank you so much."

"It's the least any of us can do."

THE WESTERN UNITED STATES, and particularly the high desert of Utah and Nevada, was suffering an intensely hot dry summer, and as Grace drove away from Salt Lake City the following morning, she knew the day would be a rough one both for her and her son. Last night, just before she'd taken the exit on Interstate 15 to the safe house, her air-conditioning had gone on the fritz.

"Mommy," Charley said from the back seat, where he was playing with his Lego toys, "I'm firsty. It's hot, Mommy."

"Yes," she said, feeling her short-sleeved cotton top glued to the leather seat. "It sure is. We'll stop at the first rest area and cool off, okay?"

"Put on the air conditioner, Mommy," he whined.

"I wish I could," she said, but she'd already calculated the cost of stopping and having the car fixed: the time and expense made that impossible. They'd have to suffer.

By noon, driving along Interstate 80 toward Winnemucca, Nevada, she wondered if they would even survive. Utah at least had mountains and greenery in places, but Nevada... She might as well have been driving the surface of a long-dead, barren planet that broiled unprotected beneath a giant sun.

Charley justifiably complained and wanted to stop often, and she herself felt the summer heat frying her brain cells. Still, despite her discomfort and nagging doubts, a plan was beginning to take hold. She realized there were only two options open to her. Well, three, she decided. But the third—turning around and surrendering Charley to his...to Kerry Pope—was out of the question. So that left two options.

One, she and Charley could stay on the underground railroad until it was safe to stop and take on new identities, even get a job, settle somewhere for the rest of her life—their new lives, that was.

Or, she thought, there was option two. She was not yet a fugitive and at this point she could elicit the advice of her parents, particularly her father, who was a retired policeman. The last thing she wanted was to get her folks involved in this mess, but her dad could at least advise her on what she needed to do to enlighten the court on the inadequacies of Kerry Pope, forcing that court to admit the very real danger to Charley.

In short, as her father, Big Bob Bennett, would say, Grace needed to get the goods on Kerry Pope. And Big Bob had not only been a policeman, but a juvenile officer with the San Francisco PD. Who better to advise her? On the other hand, she hated to lay her troubles at his feet. Really hated the thought. She'd never had to turn to her parents for this sort of support. Thinking about it now, she supposed she'd been a real Goody Two-shoes. Shy, cerebral, nonconfrontational. Heck, the only experimenting she'd done as a teen had been in science class. How was she going to explain her actions?

But who else could she turn to?

They spent their third night on the underground railroad on the outskirts of Sacramento, and from there, using a pay phone at a convenience store, she finally called her parents. As she dropped change into the coin slots her hand trembled, and she had to tell herself over and over that her mother and father loved her as much as she loved Charley. Turning to them for help was the right thing to do.

Amazingly, she realized as the phone rang in her ear, she'd never fully comprehended the true commitment of parenthood. She would ask for their help and they'd unstintingly give it, just as she was going the whole nine yards to protect her child.

The phone continued to ring. Maybe they had already left on their annual summer vacation. Maybe…

"Hello?" Her mother, Sally, whose name Grace also carried.

"Mom?" Grace had to clear her throat. "Mom, it's me."

"Gracie! What a lovely surprise. You never call."

"I do, too. I…"

"Not enough. Is Charley there with you?"

"Yes, Mom, he's standing about two feet away, eating an ice cream cone."

"It must be his bedtime."

"Well, ordinarily it would be, but we're not in Colorado."

"You're…?"

"Mom, we're only a couple of hours away, just east of Sacramento."

"You're where?" Sally gasped, and Grace began the awful tale of the past two days. When she was finished, all Sally Bennett could say was, "I guess I'd better put your father on."

Grace sighed. "Good idea. And Mom, I love you guys. I'm so, so sorry to be dumping this…"

"Oh, for the love of Mike, honey, just can it, will you?" And then Grace heard her call, "Bob! Bob get in here, Gracie needs you."

Telling her father was even tougher. She knew it was because he'd been a policeman his whole life and Grace, in another forty-eight hours, was about to break the law big-time.

He surprised her, though. Rather than tell her to

turn around, drive back to Boulder and obey the court order, he hesitated for a second and then said, "Those damn juvie courts. Sorry, baby, but if this just doesn't top it all. You should have let me come to that hearing. I warned you. Your mother and I were wondering why we hadn't heard from you, but then we figured everything must have gone okay."

"Well, Dad, now you know," Grace said. "And I hope I'm not making things worse. I just couldn't let Kerry Pope have him. It isn't that I'm selfish, Dad, honestly, and I haven't gone crazy. If you could see Kerry's criminal history, Dad. If you could—"

"You think that after almost thirty-five years with juvies I don't realize? Grace, honey, give me some credit."

"Sorry, Dad. It's just that I don't know how to get proof that a girl like Kerry will never be rehabilitated, certainly not to the extent that she could raise a child, and—"

"Look," Bob Bennett cut in, "you get yourself to San Francisco with Charley and call us. Best you don't stay here, okay?"

"Of course, I understand."

"Okay. Then get here and we'll come up with something. You haven't broken the law yet. Maybe... I have to think about this. Talk it over with your mom. Listen, do you need any money? I hope you haven't been using a credit card, honey."

Grace laughed without humor. "No, no credit card, Dad. I'm getting to be a real good fugitive."

Bob groaned.

"Sorry, but that's how I feel."

"Okay. You call us as soon as you get settled in

one of your safe houses, and we'll figure this out together.''

''Dad, I only need advice, really. No way am I getting you and Mom involved.''

''Now, you listen here, Gracie. I may have been a cop, but there's nothing more important on the face of the earth than you and that boy. You let me worry about our involvement.''

''But, Dad...''

''Don't Dad me. Just drive carefully.''

He hung up before she could utter another word of protest. She stood in the growing darkness outside the market and watched the customers coming and going. Ordinary people with ordinary lives. Sure, they had their problems, but not like the ones *she* had. She wished—oh, how she wished—she could be like them, back in her comfortable, safe life in Boulder.

But she couldn't. That life was forfeit now. And she had to learn to live a new one.

CHAPTER THREE

LUKE SARKOV WAS BROODING. He was sitting at his desk in the downtown San Francisco offices of the Metropole Insurance Company, supposedly checking into a client's bank accounts. He knew damn well the client had torched his own restaurant, but he had to prove it; these days, he was an insurance fraud investigator.

But that was only partly why he was brooding.

He stared at the phone, his sandy eyebrows drawn together and his long face taut and angry, the double lines bracketing his mouth cutting his skin harshly.

He wanted to call Judith, his estranged wife, and hear her voice. He wanted her to say their split was all a mistake. He wanted to call his buddies down at the department, get together for a poker game or a few beers, talk cop talk, discuss cases and the latest screw-up perpetrated by the powers-that-be on the heads of the hardworking policemen.

He was forty-one years old, his career down the tubes, wife gone, his life spinning out of control. And here he was, checking into an arson case for an insurance company.

He sneered as he willed himself to pick up the phone, dial the arsonist's bank, get the records, make Metropole Insurance happy.

His finger pressed Judith's number of its own volition, and he waited, hearing the ring, picturing the phone at the other end, the table it sat on, the room the table was in. Judith's new apartment.

God, he wanted her back. He loved her, and despite her protestations, he was sure she still loved him.

The phone rang. It rang again. Then he heard the electronic click, and her answering machine switched on: *This is Judith Bancroft. I am not in at the moment, but if you leave a message I will return your call. If this is in regard to a modeling job, please call the Best Agency at...*

Her voice—slightly husky and sexy as hell. He drank the tone in, even if what he was hearing was only a recording. A lump formed at the base of his throat. Judith Bancroft. She didn't use his name anymore. Damn it, they were not even divorced yet.

He hung up without leaving a message, aware that he was grinding his molars. That he was tense, uptight, not sleeping well, spending too much time alone in the two rooms he was renting. Damn Judith.

Marriage meant loyalty, right? *Till death us do part.* Well, he'd meant it. Apparently, she hadn't.

He shut his eyes for a second, took a breath. Reached for the phone, dialed the bank. He knew the bank officials were going to give him a hassle—they always did. But the bank had been served a subpoena and had to cough up the information.

"U.S. Bank, Haight-Clayton Branch," he heard the receptionist say.

"Regarding Samuel Rae's account. Mr. Dressler, please."

The whole rigmarole would have to be gone through, but Luke could be tough. He'd had plenty of practice being relentlessly tough while on the Vice

Squad. He could spot a lie a mile away, read people without effort, barge through prevarications and misleading statements, dig out the truth. He could handle pimps and pushers and whores and snitches. Hell, this was only a bank president, and the branch bank at that.

A half hour later he had Dressler's promise to send him copies of Rae's accounts for the past three years. And when he got them, he was positive the figures would show a business in trouble, kited checks, overdrafts, stop payment orders, the whole gamut. He'd seen the downslide of businesses before, seen the owner go into the weeds never to see daylight again. And then arson. A desperate act. A dangerously illegal act.

Of course, investigating insurance fraud wasn't like being a cop. He was only chasing the miserable losers who cheated insurance companies.

When he'd been forced to resign from the San Francisco Police Department, he'd convinced himself that he didn't want his old job anyway, that he detested the hypocrisy and addictive violence of big-city law enforcement. But, if he admitted the truth, he'd sucked it up, enjoyed the inside knowledge of man's capacity for evil. What he couldn't abide was the boredom and predictability of the ordinary world. He guessed he'd learned to love the power over the bad guys and the adrenaline high of danger too much.

Well, he sure wasn't making the world better for democracy anymore.

His cell phone rang in the pocket of his sport coat, which hung on the back of his chair. Judith? His heart gave a lurch, as if he were coming alive for the first time that day.

He dug the phone out of his pocket, flipped it open and barked, "Hello."

"Hey, kid."

Not Judith. But a voice nearly as welcome.

"Bob, my man."

"I'm not your man and you know it," came Big Bob Bennett's raspy voice.

"What's up, Bob?"

"How are you doing, kid?"

"Oh, you know, okay."

"Sure. *Okay.*"

"I'm nailing guys right and left. Women, too. You wouldn't believe how people cheat."

"Sure I would." Bob hesitated. "Listen, I have a favor to ask."

"Anything." Luke owed Bob; he owed him big. The man was retired now, but he'd been a Juvenile Division cop back when Luke had met him. Luke had been in college, San Francisco State, when he'd been injured and lost his athletic scholarship. For a while back then he'd felt hopeless and angry, and he'd quit school and gotten into trouble. Luckily, a judge gave him community service instead of hard time, and he was sent to Lieutenant Bob Bennett, to help him coach an inner-city school football team.

Big Bob, as he was known even then, set him straight, got him back into school and then helped him enter the Police Academy. Bob had been his mentor, his father and his family for twenty-two years. Luke had never known his own family; he was an orphan, one foster home after another. Bob understood why Luke had been asked to resign from the force last year. Luke's mentor didn't judge; he accepted. Oh, yeah, Luke owed the man.

"My daughter's in trouble," Bob said flatly.

"Your daughter?"

"Yes, damn it, Grace. You know, my kid."

"Sure, I know her, but, wow, it's been years. I mean…"

"Grace has a little boy named Charley. She got this kid from a junkie. She's his foster mother."

"Oh, right, I remember."

"Anyway, the idiotic judge in Boulder gave custody of Charley back to his biological mother, and Grace took the boy and went underground."

"She did?"

"Oh, yeah, my little angel. And in a couple days she's going to be a federal fugitive. She's in deep, and I'm afraid I'm about to get in just as deep."

"Son of a bitch."

"Exactly."

"You sure it's wise for you to get so involved?"

"Luke, she's my child. I'll go to the ends of the earth to help her."

"Maybe she should turn herself in."

"She's afraid for the boy's safety. She won't do it and I'm not going to advise her to."

"But what…hell, what can I do?"

"You could help get the goods on the biological mother for Grace. She's a sad sack—drugs, jail time for armed robbery. Says the boyfriend forced her to help him. She's no fit mother, that's for damn sure."

"And where is this biological mother?"

"Denver, Colorado."

"Mmm."

"If this wasn't so important, I'd never ask. But, Luke, can you take some time off and help Grace out?"

He couldn't refuse. No matter what. Big Bob had saved his life and his soul, and he'd never once asked for help. Luke didn't hesitate. "Sure I can. Let me get a few things finished up here. I have vacation time coming."

"She's driving in today. I want you to meet her, kid. Sally and I will watch the boy, and she can use our car. I'll take care of hers. I mean, she has to *disappear*. Tell me where she can meet you. She'll be able to give you the whole story."

"Meet her, huh. You want me to come out to your house?"

"No, no. I don't want her here at all. The feebies will talk to our neighbors—the usual drill. Can she come into the city, meet you somewhere, you know, discreet?"

"Sure. Does she know her way around?"

"You forget, kid. She was raised here."

"Okay. How about Lum Lee's, in Chinatown, on Grant Avenue. I'll be there at six. Will that work?"

"Sure. Lum Lee's."

"Does she remember what I look like?"

"I'll update her," Bob said dryly.

"I don't know what I can do, but I'll try."

"Hey, listen, Luke, you're the best investigator the department ever had. You can do it."

"I *was*."

"You're still the best, kid."

"Yeah, sure, my man."

"Six at Lum Lee's. And don't forget, this is my daughter you're helping here."

Luke barely had time to consider what he was getting into before the perfunctory morning meeting at Metropole Insurance was convened. He took up his wrinkled sport coat and slipped it on, gritting his teeth. Every morning, 10:00 a.m. sharp, it was meeting time with the "suits."

This morning, sitting around the giant oval boardroom table, it was the same old litany. Bottom line, bottom line. What the suits meant, was: Who can we screw today to increase the bottom line? Which Luke translated more aptly as, How can we keep Metropole's shareholders happy and increase our personal golden umbrellas?

Metropole's offices took up the entire sixteenth floor of the steel-and-glass skyscraper—earthquake proof, of course—on Powell Street across from Union Square. Next door, an older office building had been razed—imploded, actually—and for the last few months Luke had whiled away his time in the meetings watching the new structure take shape. More specifically, he watched, and marveled at, the steel walkers, the guys who worked fearlessly atop the steel beams as they were hoisted toward the blue heavens.

Luke had a thing about heights. A real thing. He didn't even fly, not if he had anything to say about it. Driving took longer, sure, and the gas and rooms cost, but at least he didn't have to sit on a plane, desperately holding it up in the air through sheer willpower. Yeah. Driving was fine by him.

"Twenty-three cases of suspected arson since January 1 of this year," a voice was saying—one of the suits. "Are you aware, Mr. Sarkov, that Metropole has paid out on nine of those cases? Three of which were assigned to you?"

Luke dragged his thoughts from the swinging steel beam being levered into place and cleared his throat. "Yes, sir, I am fully aware of the numbers." Then he smiled thinly. "The trouble is, sir, those three fires were legit."

"Excuse me?"

"Look, sir—" the *sir* came out a little too heavy "—things just sometimes burn down. There are accidental fires, and a lot of lives are ruined."

"Yes, yes, yes," the suit said impatiently, "but we are not fully satisfied that this structure in San Jose at…let's see, on Marina Boulevard, was accidental."

Luke grinned ferally. "A nursing home, sir? A profitable, family-owned and -operated nursing home? Come on."

"I don't like that tone, Sarkov."

"Look," Luke said, no apology offered, "the report from the fire marshal in San Jose, the nursing home's books—everything came out clean. It was an electrical fire on the new wing. That happens."

The suit made a blustering noise, then moved on to Luke's present case, the fire last week at Sammy Rae's restaurant up near what was known as the Haight. A rough area.

"I'm on it," Luke said, wanting to suppress a yawn right in this jerk's face. He glanced at his wristwatch. "In fact, I'm late for a meeting with the fire chief as it is."

"Well, all right, get going, then. But no matter what the chief says, we all know this is a case of arson. Prove it. Damn it, prove it and let's not get into a long and drawn-out court case. Nothing is more costly, Mr. Sarkov. The restaurant owner knows that and is counting on Metropole to pay off. Do whatever it takes, but dig up enough on this Sammy Rae to force him to acquiesce or face criminal charges."

"Of course," Luke said, rising, escaping. God-damn, he hated this job.

He didn't have to meet the fire chief for an hour, so he checked his voice mail—nothing from Judith—then grabbed a sandwich at the corner deli. Breakfast and lunch rolled into one.

He sat on the bench in Union Square and ate half the Reuben, leaning over and dripping sauerkraut juice on the sparse grass. Idly chatting with the bum resting coiled up behind the bench, he tossed crumbs to the pigeons. "Hell," he said, "insurance compa-nies are no different from carjackers. One is legal. The other is not."

"Hear, hear," the bum grumbled.

Grace Bennett. Gracie, Bob used to call her. Yeah. It was coming back now. She must be in her mid-thirties, because when Luke knew her—or had seen her once or twice—she'd been maybe fourteen or fif-teen years old.

He shook his head disdainfully. She'd been pain-fully skinny when she should have been filling out. Yeah. And long stringy blondish hair—no style to it. Glasses. Right. A real academic nerd. He hated to think about Big Bob's kid that way, but *really*. And he couldn't imagine her any different now. Still, the kid—well, woman—was in trouble. On the run. As far as the law was concerned, she'd shortly be a kid-napper.

Go figure, he thought, splitting the last of the crust with the pigeons, then laying a five-spot on the bum before rising and dusting himself off. Time to go to work.

The fire chief handling the Haight-Ashbury district

met Luke at Sammy Rae's—or what was left of the restaurant—exactly on time.

Luke stood on the still-charred sidewalk in front of the burned husk of building and whistled under his breath. "Well, this one sure went out in a blaze. Any of your men injured?"

Fire Chief Rollins shook his head. "Lucky was all. Whole building went in less than an hour."

"Gotta be arson."

"Oh, yeah, you better believe it. The lab's got at least twenty samples of combustibles from hot spots."

"Good. Where did it start?"

"You mean where was it *started?* Kitchen, of course. Grease trap."

Wearing hard hats, they made their way into the scorched, fallen remains of Sammy Rae's.

"Careful," Rollins kept saying, nodding and pointing, stepping over debris, his big utility flashlight spearing the dimness.

"Phew," Luke said once, "stinks to high heaven."

"Yeah, the whole thing stinks."

The fire chief showed Luke what was left of the grill and the ventilation hood, then pointed out the grease trap on the side of the fire-twisted grill. He showed Luke the so-called hot spots, which had burned too easily and too quickly, at the same temperature and for the same amount of time as the fire source, indicating that the hot spots and grease trap had all gone up in flames together. Of course, modern forensics would no doubt turn up the starter fuel. Nowadays, fires were creating a whole new field of science and a whole new set of problems for the average fire starter, who merely wanted to collect on his insurance.

"Think I can tell the suits over at Metropole they can keep this out of court?"

"Oh, I'm sure. In fact, we'll probably have enough to press charges on old Sammy."

"Well, then, I assume I can have copies of the lab reports when they're done?"

"No problem. I'll sign the requisition."

They made their way back out into the sun, and Luke took off his hard hat and handed it to Rollins, dusting off the sleeves of his jacket. "Thanks for your time, Chief," he said, turning to go.

Then Rollins spoke. "You don't remember me, do you?" he said.

Luke pivoted. "I, ah, no, not really."

"It was ten, twelve, years ago."

Luke shrugged.

"A waterfront fire down on Third Street."

"Sorry, but I..." Then it came back to him. Sure. *Rollins.* He'd been a fireman then, and some real junked-out dudes had been playing chemist at home and blown up their rat hole of an apartment. Luke and his partner had been on a Vice surveillance two buildings down. They'd raced to the scene only seconds after the explosion, and Luke had helped Rollins drag an entire family of illegal immigrants from the blazing second story to safety.

Sure, now he remembered. Back then, Luke had been a hero.

"The fire," Luke said, nodding. "We both got some good press that night."

"Yeah," Rollins said. "Well, anyway, I just

wanted to say I'm sorry about your…job. Your resignation and all that.''

"Mmm," Luke said.

"I saw your name in the papers last year, and well, I felt real bad for you and all the others who, ah, resigned. I just wanted to tell you that."

"I appreciate it," Luke said, and he lifted his hand, gave Rollins a short wave, turned and headed to his car.

No one, he thought, was sorrier than he.

CHAPTER FOUR

GRACE PACED in front of the main entrance to the Avenues Mall in Oakland and gripped Charley's hand. She'd wanted to meet her parents at their house, somewhere familiar and comfortable, for Charley, but, as Bob had told her, it was a bad idea. The feds would be nosing around once she was declared a fugitive, and one of the first things they'd do would be to stake out their house. An ex-cop's home, she thought, cringing, knowing what this action of hers was doing to her father, her law-abiding father.

Charley was being an angel, looking forward to seeing Gramma and Grampa, but he was bound to wear down soon. So much traveling. A new bed every night, new faces, hours and hours stuck in the hot car. It wasn't fair.

She tugged gently on Charley's hand and moved to the curb, where the valets were parking cars. She looked up and down the crowded parking aisles. Where the heck were her parents? Her nerves scratched beneath her skin. It had been Bob's idea to meet at the Oakland mall. One o'clock, he'd said, at the main entrance where the valet stand was located.

She looked at her watch. It was almost 1:05.

Calm down, she told herself.

"Mommy?" Charley kicked at a pebble on the

sidewalk. ''Where are Gramma and Grampa? I'm hungry.''

''I'm sure they're just parking their car, honey. They'll be along.''

''Can we have pizza?''

''I think you've had enough junk food to last a lifetime, young man.''

''Pizza is not junk food, Mommy. Ice cream is junk food. You said so last night.''

''Well, yes, I did. And it's true.''

''Where are Gramma and—'' But before he could finish, Bob Bennett had swooped him up from behind and was giving him a big kiss on the cheek. ''Grampa!'' Charley squealed in delight, and Grace felt tears press against her eyelids.

Big Bob Bennett was a bear of a man, barrel-chested, tall, grizzled hair poking out of the open collar of his shirt. His face was heavy featured and sagging, but it was a good face, strong and kind.

Her mother, Sally, was petite and adorable. A mismatched couple, one would say to look at them, but they'd been married for forty years and were still going great guns.

Sally hugged Grace tightly, then took Charley from Bob. ''Look at this boy, how big you've grown since last Christmas. Oh, stop squirming and let Gramma have all the hugs and kisses she can get.''

''God, I'm so glad to see you both,'' Grace breathed. ''I've got so much to tell you and—''

''I'm hungry,'' Charley announced to his grandparents, the only grandparents he'd known. ''Mommy says pizza is bad for me, but I bet Gramma wants pizza. Are you hungry, Gramma?''

"The boy sure is learning," Bob said, grinning, giving Grace a big hug.

"Oh, pizza, yum yum," Sally said, taking Charley's hand, "that's exactly what Gramma wanted, too. How did you know? Did a little elf tell you?"

Charley shook his head and laughed and held on to Sally's hand, half dragging her into the mall.

Grace and Bob followed a few paces behind, Grace tucking her arm into Bob's, laying her head on his shoulder as they walked. "Oh, Dad," she said, "what have I done?"

"The only thing you could have."

"But you were a policeman. How can you say that? It's wrong. It's just that I…"

"You believed you had no other choice. Do you think you're the first person who's been faced with this kind of decision?"

"No, but…"

"Sure you're having doubts. You're a good moral young woman."

"Not so young anymore."

"Thirty-three is not old."

"*Dad,* I'm thirty-five now."

"You are?"

"Oh, stop teasing. It isn't funny."

"I'm sorry. But I had to see if you could muster up a smile. You know, you're still our baby."

She sighed and squeezed his arm and watched Charley tugging on Sally's hand as they all passed a shoe store and a B. Daltons, his four-year-old nose leading them straight to the food court.

Everything seemed surreal to Grace when they found a table and Sally went to get pizzas and Cokes. The last time Grace and Charley had been here was over the long December break from her classes at CU. The mall had been so crowded, Christmas shoppers everywhere, and Charley had been delighted at the carolers and beautiful displays of decorated trees and huge candy canes and reindeer and elves and snowmen. He'd ridden on the big Wonderland train set up in the middle of the mall, and he'd sat on Santa's lap and been so brave. Bob had taken a whole roll of film, and Sally had sent Grace and Charley copies in January. They'd been so happy.

Grace ate her pizza and looked at Charley and her parents and recalled that Bob and Sally had not always been so pleased about her foray into foster motherhood. Of course they had wanted her to marry and have children of her own. Five years ago, before Charley had even been born, she had dated an associate professor at CU, and Sally had pressed and pressed over the phone.

"Are you two serious? Do you think it's in the realm of possibility that you might marry? He's such a nice man, Grace, an old-fashioned gentleman."

Yes, Grace had thought, he had been very nice. Shy and reserved and terribly proper. And boring. At 10:00 p.m. he watched the news and at 10:20 he always went to sleep. At 6:05 a.m. he got up. At 6:15 he showered. At 6:20...

But that was water under the bridge, and at least she had learned something about herself—she'd never be able to make a life with a man who lived by the clock. Even for plain-Jane Grace, he'd been too dull.

And then Charley had come along. A gift. A miracle. She'd taken him on summer break to meet her very skeptical parents, who'd so much wanted a grandchild of their own flesh and blood. And then they'd seen Charley. Watched him crawl, giggling and drooling around the kitchen and backyard; gotten to know all his baby vocabulary, seen the sun twinkle on his curls, and they'd fallen in love. Just as she had.

And now...

"Gramma likes ice cream, don't you, Gramma?" Charley was saying, pizza smeared on his cheek and chin.

"Actually," Sally said, catching Grace's disapproving eye, "I really *really* like chocolate chip cookies."

"His teeth are going to rot out of his head," Grace admonished. She'd never allowed him so many sweets.

But Charley, clever little Charley, piped up. "I promise I'll brush all my teeth—" he pronounced it *teef* "—extra special tonight. I promise."

Sally bit her lip and got teary.

Bob shook his head sadly. "Goddamn courts," he muttered.

"*Bob.*" Sally collected herself and stood up. "Come on, Charley," she said, taking his tiny hand, "we'll go find those cookies. I can smell them from here. Can you smell them?"

"Oh, yes, Gramma, I sure can."

When they were gone, Grace looking protectively after her baby, Bob covered her hand with his. "I've got a plan," he said in an uncharacteristically quiet voice.

Grace snapped to attention. "Dad, I can't let you get involved. I just need some advice."

"I won't be involved—well, not too involved—and believe me, I'll be covering my tail all the way."

"It's asking too much."

"Look, I've called a friend. He—"

"Who? Who've you called?"

"If you'll just let me finish?"

"I thought you weren't going to get involved. I—"

"I made a call. That's hardly a crime."

"Still…"

"His name is Luke Sarkov. Do you remember him? I helped him out when he got in some trouble. Long time ago."

"I'm not sure."

"Well, you were pretty young, and he didn't come over to the house much. The point is, I got him on the force, and we've kept in touch over the years."

"He's a policeman? But then how can he…?"

"He's not on the force anymore. But he's a top-notch investigator. Best there is. He can help you."

Not on the force anymore, she thought, and she wondered why this man had left the police. Was he old enough to be retired? "Dad, I don't know."

"Trust me on this." Bob leaned closer. "You need to get something on Kerry Pope, right?"

"Yes. That would go a long way toward showing the court that…"

But Bob was shaking his head. "You don't want to just show the court Kerry's past history, which they already damn well know. You want something definitive on her, something horrific."

"But, Dad, what if…? I mean, that's all fine, but as you said, the court knows her history. And maybe she can hold herself together for a time now. And if that's the case…"

"Honey, honey," Bob said, "you're out of your element here, okay? I just want you to put your faith in this man. He was a good, tough cop, as smart and streetwise as they come.''

Was a good cop? ''Is this Luke, ah, Sarkov retired, too?''

''Listen,'' Bob put in, ''none of that matters. What counts is that he's the man for this job.'' He held her gaze. ''Will you please trust me on this?''

''Of course I trust you, Dad. My God, I can't even begin to tell you how much this means to me. I…''

''Sh,'' Bob said. ''We're your parents, Grace. We'll do what it takes to protect you, to ensure your happiness. You should know that.''

Like I'm doing for Charley, she thought once more.

Bob reached into his pocket and pulled out a cell phone. ''This is for you. It can't be traced, okay?''

''Okay.'' She looked it over and nodded. ''Okay. Good idea.''

''And we're going to switch cars this afternoon.''

''But…''

''Will you just listen?''

''Sorry.''

''I've arranged for you to meet Luke in Chinatown at six.''

''Oh,'' she said.

''Your mother and I will take your car and I'll stash it in my garage for the time being. And I think it's best if Charley stays with us, at least till after you've talked to Luke. Okay?''

''I… Yes, sure, Charley will love it. He could really use some downtime, too.''

''We'll take good care of him, honey.''

Grace smiled and squeezed her father's hand. ''Of course you will.''

And then she heard Sally and Charley behind them,

and Bob told her the name of the restaurant in Chinatown, reminded her that the meeting was at six and asked if she was okay with this.

''Fine. Great,'' she breathed as Charley leaped into her lap, a cookie mushed in his fist.

IT HAD BEEN A LONG TIME since Grace had driven around San Francisco. She'd once taken Charley to Fisherman's Wharf for lunch, but she hadn't driven the hilly road to downtown then; she'd just scooted onto the Oakland Bay Bridge and negotiated the streets along the Embarcadero, which ran parallel to San Francisco Bay. No hills there.

But Chinatown was located on the hills right in the heart of town, hills that often terrified drivers new to the city. She had trouble finding a parking space, as this was the summer tourist season, and she was afraid she'd be late for this meeting. But when she finally squeezed her parents' station wagon into a slot on Grant Avenue and glanced at her watch it was only 5:30.

Great. Now she had to sit here and wait, surrounded by hordes of tourists peeking into alleys and sweatshops. Her nerves were pricking at the back of her neck.

Luke Sarkov. She tried to recall him. A cop. *Was* a cop. Maybe he owned a private investigating firm now. Maybe he was... Oh, what did it matter? Her father had said Luke was the man for this job. But what, exactly, did *that* mean?

She studied the passersby, who in turn stared into a tiny grocery store across from her. Ducks hung in the open sliding window and fish gleamed on the bed of ice below. Locals haggled prices with the butcher in mile-a-minute Mandarin. The aroma of fish oils and roast duck and garlic and ginger wafted around her. Familiar. She used to love Chinatown when she'd grown up near the city, the exotic scents and sounds, the early-morning fog furling around the hills. Now, though, everything seemed alien, strange to her senses.

She glanced at her watch. Still fifteen minutes to go.

Lum Lee's was right down the block. Was Luke already inside waiting for her? Should she just go in?

Forty-one years old, her father had said when they'd left the mall earlier. Five-eleven, well built, dark-blond hair, blue eyes. The description had sounded like a police report. But her mother had added, "He's very good-looking, Gracie."

Good-looking, forty-one, used to be a cop. Her father told her she'd met him a couple of times when she was a teenager, but she had no recollection of him. Not a clue.

Five-fifty-five. Okay, enough. She'd walk into Lum Lee's and wait for him. She was a big girl. It was crazy how shy she could be, but she'd always hated going into a bar or restaurant alone. Eating alone was unthinkable. This was different, though. This was for Charley, and Luke Sarkov would show up, and everything would work out.

She opened her door and stepped onto the curb, smoothed her khaki slacks, which were rumpled from sitting so long. She had on a short-sleeved white blouse—wrinkled, also—and she shivered and she felt the breeze off the bay. She'd forgotten how cool San Francisco could be even in the summer.

Lum Lee's was in a narrow building, with the glass

storefront displaying the usual glazed spare ribs and seafood. There was a menu in the window, but Grace didn't read it. She wasn't there for dinner.

Pushing open the door, she walked in, the scent of garlic frying in sesame oil hitting her like a soft blow. Chinese waiters ran around, yelling in their tongue, and most of the customers were Chinese, too. There was a dumbwaiter in one wall, which busboys opened and snatched dishes from and shouted into the shaft to the basement kitchen.

Bedlam.

On the right stood a bar with a few empty stools and a sleepy-looking bartender sporting a Fu Manchu mustache. Grace halted to get her bearings. Would Luke be at a table or…? She saw narrow stairs leading to a second floor. Maybe he was up there.

She wouldn't be embarrassed. She would stand there and collect her wits and take her time looking around.

At that moment it struck her how her entire life had shifted on its axis. Nothing seemed real anymore—especially her meeting a strange man in Chinatown. It was all a nightmare, and her skin crawled with anxiety. This meeting was so furtive, as if she were a criminal.

She *would* be a criminal in another day. According to the law, she would be. Oh, God.

"Dinner, Miss?" a waiter asked, jarring her to awareness.

"Uh, no, I'm meeting someone here."

"Ah, yes, Miss. You look for Mr. Luke?" He was short and round and smiling.

"Luke Sarkov?"

"Yes. He here. Upstairs. He like it better. Quiet up there. You go there."

She made her way up the narrow steps, came out into a dining room. A few Chinese families were eating early dinners, wielding their chopsticks, chattering quietly. Her eyes swept over them.

Why was her heart pounding so hard?

He was sitting in the farthest corner of the room. She spotted him right away, even though he was in the shadows. He was the only Caucasian besides her in the entire room. So much for her worrying about his description.

She took a deep breath and made her feet move. When she got closer, she could see he was looking at her—staring at her, really—his eyes as blue as the empty sky, close under sandy brows. Oh, yes, *now* she remembered those eyes from twenty-odd years ago. All of a sudden, she had an instant of stark terror as he watched her approach, and she didn't know why. He was her father's friend, for God's sake.

He didn't stand when she reached the table. He just looked up at her, his shirt unbuttoned at his throat, tie askew, old tweed sport coat stretched across broad shoulders. A definite whisker shadow on his cheeks and chin.

"Well, well, Grace Bennett," he said.

"And you're Luke Sarkov."

He gestured with a hand. "Sit."

She sat, her mouth abruptly dry.

"You have any trouble finding this place?"

"No. But parking was hard."

"Yeah, it always is." He seemed relaxed while at the same time utterly alert. There was a Tsing Tao beer bottle on the table in front of him, and he lifted it and took a swig before asking, "You want something to drink or eat?"

"Tea, please." She found it hard to get words past the dry tightness in her throat.

He raised his hand and a waiter appeared as if by magic. "*Chai*," Luke said.

The teapot and a cup were set down in front of her. The waiter poured, and the steamy fragrance of jasmine wafted up to her nostrils.

"You must come here often," she began.

"I do. Lum Lee is a friend of mine. I helped his kid brother kick the habit a few years back."

"Drugs?" she asked weakly.

"That's right. Heroin, in this case."

"When you were a policeman, I imagine?"

"Yeah. When I was a Vice Squad detective." A shadow crossed his long face, and grooves suddenly etched themselves from his nose to his mouth. "Big Bob tell you that?"

"Just that you used to be a policeman."

"Enough about me. We're here because of your problem."

"Yes." She took a sip of tea. She knew what she must look like—the dowdy college professor, too ladylike, too timid, playing a role for which she was totally unsuited.

"So, tell me what happened. Bob gave me a short version."

Lord, he made her uncomfortable. He was harsh, direct to the point of deliberate rudeness.

"Well, I..."

"Look, you can trust me. I owe your dad."

"What exactly do you owe him?"

He stared at her for a moment, his blue eyes boring

through her, then they softened. "My life," he said shortly.

"Oh."

"Listen, this isn't the time for old war stories. Tell me about your problem. Your son—your foster son, that is."

"Charley." She took a deep, quavering breath. "I was a volunteer therapist at a women's shelter in Boulder four years ago, and I was counseling a girl named Kerry Pope."

"You're a shrink?"

"I'm actually a licensed *psychologist,* but I rarely practice. I'm a professor at CU, the University of Colorado. I teach psychology."

Those eyes, drilling through her. "Bob didn't tell me that."

"In any case," she said primly, "Kerry was pregnant. Her boyfriend beat her up regularly. She'd been using drugs on and off. She was not in any shape to be a mother. And she knew that. *She knew it.*" Grace took a breath. "So she gave me temporary custody of her son just after he was born. I became his legal foster mother. Then Kerry disappeared. Never wrote or called or asked about him. Then, when I was going through the adoption process, I found out she'd been imprisoned for armed robbery, and…"

"Damn junkies."

"Then…then, she refused to sign the adoption papers and went to court to get custody of Charley."

"Mmm," he said.

Grace told him about the hearing, everything Natalie had said about working on an appeal, about her own decision to disappear. When she finished, Luke leaned back in his chair and took another swallow of the beer; she could see his Adam's apple move in his throat. She sat there, one hand in her lap, the other curving around her teacup, and waited for his reaction.

"Okay," he finally said. "Like Bob told you, we need to get the goods on... What's her name?"

"Kerry. Kerry Pope. P-O-P-E."

"Uh-huh."

"Do you... I mean, do you think you can help me?"

He leveled his gaze on her and his mouth curved in a merciless grin. "You want this Kerry Pope destroyed, nailed to the wall, right?"

Grace recoiled. "Well, I want proof that she's an unfit mother, if that's what you mean."

"That's what I said."

"Can you help?"

He looked down at his beer bottle, then raised his eyes. "Yeah, I can probably do it."

"I can pay you. I'm not rich, but..."

He waved a hand. "Forget that. I owe Big Bob, I told you."

"No, really, I insist."

He reached a hand out and touched her wrist that lay on the table. Her skin burned. "No money, okay?"

"But your time is valuable. I couldn't..."

"Let's talk about it later, when this is over. Right now there are more important things to focus on."

She bent her head and felt heat rise to her cheeks. She withdrew her hand from the teacup and laid it in her lap with the other.

"I'll need the court papers, whatever you've got. And information on this Kerry Pope."

"Of course. I brought everything I have on her."

"And you realize you have to stay out of sight?"
She nodded.

"Do you have a plan—what you're going to do, where you're going to live, anything like that?"

"No, not really. Not yet. I was going to ask my father what he thought." God, she sounded lost and weak and stupid.

"My investigation might take a while."

"I'm… I'm prepared for that. As long as Charley doesn't go to that woman." She tried to meet his eyes steadily. "This is all new to me. I've never broken the law before. It's all so…sordid."

"Hey, that's too bad. You made the choice you live with it," he said bitterly.

Her back straightened, and a wave of anger washed the heat from her cheeks. "I may not be a tough Vice cop, but I am Charley's mother. I have to protect him. Can you understand that, Mr. Sarkov? Do you have any children?"

"No kids."

"Well, then, how can you judge my decision?"

"I'm not judging your decision. Hell's bells, I'm the last person on earth to judge anyone's choices."

"You'll do this, then? Prove Kerry Pope unfit?"

"I can try."

"All right. When will you start? Do you have the time?"

"I asked for my vacation days as soon as I heard from your father. I told you—"

"Yes, you owe him."

Luke studied her face until her skin shrank. "Big Bob said I met you when you were a kid."

"Yes, he mentioned that."

"You don't look the same."

"I really don't remember you, either."

"I wasn't very nice back then. He probably didn't want me around you."

You're not very nice now, she wanted to say. Instead, she asked, "What exactly did he do for you?"

He looked away. "It's a long story."

"Sorry, I didn't mean to pry."

He drank the last of his beer, not replying.

"So, you'll start working on this right away? You'll have to go to Denver, I guess," she said anxiously.

"As soon as you get the files to me, I'll do some preliminary stuff from here. Run a computer check, see if I can find anything new on the Pope woman. Call a few people, ask around. I have contacts."

"But you're not a policeman now."

"No. I'm an insurance fraud investigator these days." His eyes flamed with dark outrage for a split second, then the fire was gone, and his flat blue gaze returned.

She shuddered inadvertently. "But you can do this job?"

"Yeah, I can do it. If there's anything to be found on your kid's mother, I'll find it."

Grace looked away. "It sounds so awful when you say it like that. As if I were trying to frame an innocent person."

"She's not innocent, though, is she?" His voice dripped with sarcasm. "Listen, I know a lot about justice and truth and all that moral crap, and I can tell you there are gray areas. Lots of gray areas. Don't sweat it. I'll nail Kerry Pope for you."

He sounded so positive. She tried to make herself

believe in his assurance, but she didn't know him. He was a stranger, really, and she couldn't comprehend why Bob thought so much of him. But she had to trust her father. She had to.

"Do you want to eat?" Luke was asking. "I can order, if you'd like."

Dinner with this man? "Ah, no, really. I have to get back to Charley. Thanks anyway."

"I guess that's it, then. Bob said he gave you a cell phone."

"Yes."

"Let me have the number. I don't want to be calling Bob's house."

She pulled the phone out of her shoulder bag and read the number off to him. He didn't write it down.

"Um, will you remember...?" she ventured.

"Yeah, sure. I'm good with recall."

"Can I have your number?"

"Bob's got my phone numbers."

"Okay. Should I call you in the morning, you know, to see what you might need?"

"I'll call you." He regarded her for a moment. "Where are you staying?"

"Not at home," she said. "My dad told me I shouldn't be seen there."

"Right. Where will you go, then?"

"Oh, I haven't thought. Another safe house, maybe. I'm not sure."

"Don't use a credit card anywhere."

"Yes." She looked down at her cup of tea, cold now. "I'm aware of that."

"Okay, then." He stood, gazing down at her, and she rose too quickly, her shoulder bag sliding onto the floor. She leaned over to retrieve it, but Luke had already come around the table and picked it up.

"Sorry," she said.

"Here," he said at the same time, handing the bag to her, and their fingers touched for a heartbeat.

He followed her down the steep stairs to the noisy room below. He said something to the waiter who had sent her upstairs, and he smiled as he spoke. The change in his face was shocking; he looked young and carefree and so handsome for a split second that she felt her breath catch.

He turned back to her, his face once again frozen in its implacable lines, and pulled open the door for her. She hadn't noticed when she'd entered, but on the door was a tiny, colorful Chinese birdcage with a wooden carved bird inside, and when the door was opened, the motion set the bird to warbling cheerfully. *So incongruous,* she had time to think, and then the door shut behind her and the sound was cut off.

"Where's your car?" he asked.

She pointed. "Right down the block."

He told her he'd walk her there, and then he pulled out a pair of sunglasses and put them on. The evening sun clicked off the mirrored surfaces. She looked away.

"I'll stay in touch," he was saying as they descended the steep hill, and she felt his hand rest lightly on the small of her back. Her skin shivered.

He took her keys from her when they reached her dad's station wagon, then unlocked the door and held it for her. She couldn't fail to notice from the movement of his head how his gaze behind those mirrored glasses traveled up and down the block. He seemed unaware of his action, as if it were instinctive in him.

Yes. A cop. She slid in behind the wheel and when he handed her the keys their fingers brushed again. She could smell him—beery breath cut with a smoky overlay, as if he'd been sitting around a campfire. "Later," he said.

"Okay. Um, thank you for doing this."

He waved a hand, dismissing her, watched as she turned on the ignition and merged into the heavy traffic. She could feel his eyes on the back of her head, pale-blue icy eyes, until she reached the corner and made a left turn.

Then, taking her totally by surprise, a sob welled up from her chest, shaking her so badly she had to pull over into a gas station and stop. For the first time, she let the tears come, the moan building in her, until her face was wet and her throat hurt and her heart was empty.

CHAPTER FIVE

SPECIAL AGENT RENEE PAYNTER'S career was on the fast track. As the only female African American agent in the Denver FBI office, she got more than her share of attention, and she knew how to use it to advance her career. She didn't feel the least bit guilty about using that advantage, either, because she knew she was extremely good at her job.

She was strikingly beautiful, tall and reed thin, her profile pure Nefertiti, her hair pulled back severely into a bun, which enhanced her exquisite bone structure. She wore Armani suits and Italian pumps and no jewelry but her wedding band.

She was a very ambitious lady, and when Special Agent in Charge Mead Towey handed her the potentially high-profile Grace Bennett kidnapping case, she practically crowed out loud with delight.

She'd read the headlines that morning at breakfast. Her husband, Jay, had been chewing his usual Grape Nuts cereal and reading the sports section of the local paper when she'd called his attention to the article.

CU PSYCH PROFESSOR KIDNAPS FOSTER CHILD the headline screamed. Some stringer in Boulder had picked the story up from the court records and run with the lead. The child's biological mother had been quoted as saying: ''She was supposed to give me back my little boy yesterday, but no one can find her. My heart is breaking.''

The Pope woman's lawyer had stated: ''I am turning this case over to the federal authorities today. Grace Bennett's actions are reprehensible.''

''Jay,'' Renee had said, ''look at this. Kidnapping.'' She'd pushed the paper under his nose.

He'd read carefully and methodically. Jay was a slow-moving, heavyset man, giving some people the idea that he was also mentally slow. But Renee knew better. Her husband was a brilliant, calculating statistician for the FBI. The tortoise to her hare.

She loved her husband. He was her opposite, fitting into her mental and emotional hollows with perfection. He was her rock, and she knew she'd flounder without him. She was aware that people thought them an incongruous couple and that Jay must bore her. But those people didn't know Jay. Nor did they know her.

What seemed to be slowness was careful consideration. He was brilliant, yet still down to earth, and he saw the world perfectly and objectively for what it was. Jay had proposed the move from Washington, D.C., to Denver, insisting that they'd each have more opportunity for promotion, and he'd been right, as usual.

''So this Grace Bennett took the kid and disappeared,'' he had said, watching Renee. ''You have any idea why?''

''Selfishness,'' Renee had replied instantly.

''It says right here she had the boy for four years. Presumably, the biological mother couldn't—or, more likely, wouldn't—take care of her son.''

''You don't know that.''

"Tell me why a college professor, a woman with an excellent career, would give it all up and run away," Jay had said mildly.

"I don't know. But I bet our office gets this case. God, I hope they let me have it." She'd grinned, her teeth white against her café-au-lait skin. "It's got *promotion* written all over it."

Driving with Jay from their home in Englewood to work that morning, Renee talked of inconsequential matters—when Jay's widowed mother was coming to visit, who would do the grocery shopping, a movie Renee wanted to see. But her mind was listing the steps an agent would have to take to find the runaway professor.

Interview the grieving mother; do a computer check on Bennett; talk to friends and neighbors of the woman, relatives. Out-of-state relatives? Boyfriend? Co-workers, yes. Did little Charles Pope attend day care?

All right, so the case wasn't hers, but she still couldn't stop thinking about it.

Jay parked in the usual place near the downtown Denver Federal Building, and they walked to the entrance together. He kissed her on the cheek, as he did every morning, and they parted ways, going to separate offices.

They both loved Denver now, a sprawling western city that was growing by leaps and bounds. True, it was hot in summer, but not with the cloying and oppressive heat of Washington. And always, when she looked to the west, the tall, cool, snow-capped peaks of the Rocky Mountains stood sentinel.

Of course Special Agent in Charge Towey gave the Bennett case to Renee—it would look better to the media if a woman agent located a child for his panicky mother. The top brass obviously figured a woman would have a softer touch, show more sympathy in a child custody suit.

In actuality, Renee had suppressed the female softness in her, and she sure as hell didn't know anything about mother love or kids or what on earth would force a respected professor to commit a crime of this magnitude. After all, the boy wasn't Grace Bennett's son.

The minute Renee looked at Kerry Pope's file, she had her answer to why Professor Bennett had taken little Charles Pope and fled. Kerry Pope had a record: drugs, loitering, petty theft and more drugs. She'd been arrested and tried for armed robbery and served six months in the Colorado Women's Correctional Institute. *Lord.* No wonder the Bennett woman had run.

The first thing Renee did after being assigned the case was to phone the number listed in the file for Kerry Pope. After ten rings a voice, sleepy and irritated, answered. A man's voice.

"May I speak to Kerry Pope, please?" Renee said in her most official tone.

"Who's this?"

"Special Agent Paynter, FBI," she said.

"FBI?"

"Ms. Pope, please."

"This about her kid?"

"Yes, it is. Is Ms. Pope there? I really do need to speak to her."

"Yeah, just a minute."

Renee could hear the man talking in the background, obviously trying to wake Kerry up. What a distasteful couple, asleep at 9:30 in the morning, rude, totally unsavory. But her job was not to judge. Her job was to uphold and enforce the law.

"Hello?" came a young woman's voice, sleep logged.

"Kerry Pope?"

"Uh-huh."

"This is Special Agent Paynter of the FBI. I've been given your case. I'll be locating your son for you, and I need to interview you."

"Oh, sure. Oh, my God, yes. You're going to find Charley for me?"

"That's what I've been charged with. Are you available today?"

"Um, today? Yeah, I guess so."

"I can meet with you at your place, Miss Pope. I have your address here. When would be convenient for you?"

When Renee finally hung up, she inadvertently made a face. Kerry Pope was all that Renee despised—a petty criminal, a junkie, irresponsible, on and off welfare, living with a no doubt brutal boyfriend. But still, genuine longing had tinged the young woman's voice when she spoke of her lost son.

There it was again—mother love. Why didn't Renee feel that instinctive emotion? Was something deeply and profoundly wrong with her? She was thirty-three and had no desire whatsoever for children. Maybe she was influenced too strongly by her career and her need to be successful. The powerful drive of a minority woman to make good. Maybe that vaunted mother love instinct was simply buried under layers of artificial, society-produced values. It was the one subject she was afraid to discuss with Jay.

She drove one of the motor pool cars to Kerry

Pope's address for the 10:30 meeting. The small un-kempt house, unpainted and uncared for, stood on a brown postage-stamp lawn. Everyone knew that you had to water a lawn like crazy to keep the grass green in this arid, high-plains climate. These people hadn't even tried. The neighborhood was shabby, racially mixed, located right behind the old Mile High Sta-dium, a rabbit warren of closed-off streets dead-ending at chain-link fences that overlooked the inter-state.

Renee got out of her air-conditioned car, absorbed the blast of heat, clicked the remote to lock it and strode up the cracked concrete walk to the house.

Kerry opened the door at her first knock, a young girl in her early twenties, as unkempt as the house and the lawn. She might have been pretty, but her skin was pale, her hair hung limply and she was far too thin. She wore shorts and a T-shirt that hung off her bony shoulders.

"Kerry Pope?" Renee asked.

"Yes."

"I'm Special Agent Paynter."

"Yes, sure, I know. Come in."

Cheap furniture, a stale smell, the pungent aroma of marijuana in the hot and stuffy air. But the living room was neat, which Renee bet was not always the case.

"Please sit down," Kerry said. "Would you like a drink? I have Coke."

"No, thanks. Kerry—may I call you that?—let's go over all the information we have here." She took the file from her fine leather briefcase.

"Okay." Kerry sat, nervous, her hands held to-gether between her knobby knees.

"Tell me how you first met Grace Bennett and how your son—"

"Charley."

"Yes, Charley, became her foster son. I'd like to know what your exact arrangements were with Ms. Bennett."

Kerry told the story, how she'd been alone and pregnant and felt she was unable to care for a baby. Grace had befriended her during the group therapy sessions at the women's center in Boulder, and she'd figured her child was better off with someone she knew than with complete strangers.

"But you never intended to leave him with Grace Bennett permanently?" Renee asked.

"Oh, no, absolutely not!"

"Was this documented anywhere legally?"

"I don't know. I just signed papers, you know, temporary custody stuff." Kerry's eyes were wide and blue, but the pupils switched back and forth. Drugs or lies? Renee wondered.

"When was the last time you saw your son, Kerry?"

"Oh, well, I guess…" She pretended to think. "It would have been when I signed those papers."

"You mean when Charley was a baby?" *Good God.*

"Yes." A whisper.

"And that was four years ago. Let's see—" Renee checked the file "—four years last May."

No answer.

"And Charley was three months old at the time," Renee said in a businesslike tone.

"I guess so."

"Have you been in contact with Grace Bennett about your son since then?"

Kerry rolled her shoulders, as if tense, and brought a hand up to hook a strand of hair behind her ear. "Um, well, I don't really remember."

"I see."

"Look, I wasn't ready to have that baby. It was an accident, and I knew he'd be better off with somebody else. But I've changed. I've really changed. I took some classes when I was in...when I was in prison. I read a lot. I'm a better person now."

"That's not for me to judge, Kerry, I'm just trying to get as much background as I can, that's all." Renee gave her a thin smile. "Now tell me everything you know about Grace Bennett."

"Well, like I said, she was running these group therapy sessions for the women in the shelter. I liked her. She was nice. She was real smart, and she told us she taught some classes at CU. She must have been around thirty, I guess. Not very pretty. She wore, oh, sort of old-lady clothes, you know? And glasses and she just kind of stuck her hair up in a clip. It was always falling down, and she'd push it back. But she was, like a friend, you know?"

"Go on."

"She was a volunteer, but she spent a lot of time at the shelter. I was living in Boulder then, and she came twice a week. Kept going off on being responsible and not being self-destructive. She visited me in the hospital when I had Charley, and he was right there next to my bed. She picked him up, and I saw... I could see in her face, and I knew what to do then. She'd take care of Charley for me till I was ready. She'd be real good to him, you know?"

"What made you decide to regain custody?"

"I'm older now. I've paid my debt to society—I'm rehabilitated. I won't make stupid mistakes again. I'm ready to become a mother."

"Do you know anything about Grace Bennett that would help us find her?"

"Oh, wow, I don't think so. I didn't know her except as a therapist. I mean, she never talked about herself."

"Never mentioned a family? Or a man in her life?"

Kerry shook her head. "She didn't have a boyfriend, I don't think. She would say things, you know?"

"Like what?"

"Oh, like, 'Be careful in relationships' and 'Some men tend to be more immature than women' and stuff like that."

"Nothing else about her private life?"

"Not that I remember." Kerry leaned forward. "Will you find Charley for me?"

"Yes, I will. Grace Bennett can't hide forever. I'll go into the FBI database and learn everything there is to know about her, believe me. We'll track her down."

"Then what will happen to her?"

"That's not up to me. But she could be tried for the federal crime of kidnapping. She could go to prison."

"Oh, God, I really don't want her to go to jail. Honestly, I just want Charley back." Kerry looked near tears.

"I'm afraid, Kerry, there's nothing you or I can do to alter Ms. Bennett's fate once we find her."

"But I…"

"That's not my area. I'm an investigator, I solve problems, I track fugitives down. I have nothing to do with the prosecutorial side of cases. And it's not your problem, either, Kerry. Remember that. Grace Bennett broke the law, and she'll have to pay."

"I know, but... I feel bad for her. I mean, I was real mad at first, you know? When I got the adoption papers? I almost fainted. But she doesn't realize how I've changed."

Renee had to listen to some more of Kerry Pope's soul-searching before she left. On the drive back downtown to the Federal Building, she went over Kerry's words in her mind. She was "ready to be a mother." What did that feel like? Renee wondered. How do you know when you were ready? Did Kerry have any inkling of what motherhood meant or was she just mouthing platitudes?

Was an ex-con, uneducated junkie able to comprehend motherhood, when Renee couldn't?

That afternoon she took all the information she had on Grace Bennett and turned it over to Teddy Argent, one of the techies who would do the computer search. By the end of the week, she'd know everything there was to know about Professor Grace Bennett: phone records, car license plate, bank and credit card statements, the works. She'd *own* Grace Bennett.

That night, watching the news in the king-size bed in their luxurious master bedroom, the air-conditioning humming soothingly, Renee looked around and thanked God for her life, for Jay and her big suburban house, for her challenging job, for all the mistakes in life she could have made but hadn't.

"So, what's going on with the Bennett case?" Jay asked during a commercial.

"Oh, the usual. I interviewed the biological mother today."

"What was she like?"

"A loser," Renee said without hesitation.

Jay shook his head, gave a short laugh. "You know, the justice system baffles me sometimes. Now, why in hell would a judge rule that the kid has to be returned to his mother? He's never even seen her, has he?"

"Oh, Jay, you're such a sap. The court ruled—Bennett broke the law. It's that simple."

"*Simple*. What about that little boy? Do you know what statistics show about an abusive parent's effect on a child?"

"You and your statistics. Besides, who said Kerry was abusive?"

"Well, neglectful, then. It's not good for a kid."

"So, you think being raised by a single adoptive parent is any better? Oh, Jay," she said, yawning. "It's my job. It's what I do. You know that."

"I know that, sweetheart, but sometimes I wish you weren't so damn good at it." He rolled over and kissed her cheek, laid a big hand on the silky fabric of her nightgown.

"I love you Jay," she said softly.

"Me, too."

But when the lights were out, she lay there thinking, still feeling the phantom touch of Jay's hand on her stomach. Everything in her life was perfect except *this*. She placed her own hand on her belly. Nothing there yet, nothing showing, but it had been growing in her womb for eight weeks. A tiny human being, hers and Jay's.

Did she feel anything for the baby inside her? The

timing was terrible. Her career. They'd talked about kids, always in the future. But the future had caught up with her.

How could this have happened? She was always organized, prepared, goal oriented. And now, her life, the baby's life—it was all at stake.

She rolled over and readjusted her pillow. She knew she had to tell Jay soon, and she was pretty sure how he'd react.

Or, she thought before squelching the notion, maybe she could take the alternative route and Jay would never have to know at all.

GRACE AWAKENED with a shot of adrenaline to her heart. Where was she? Where was Charley?

She flew to her feet. Oh, God, there he was, on the daybed that her latest underground railroad hostess had set up. She collapsed on the side of her own bed in the strange house, whose address right now eluded her. She put her head in her hands and tried to breathe. This had to end. A new day, a new bedroom—day after day.

It had to stop.

The place was utterly still when she finally tiptoed past her sleeping child and made her way down the hall to the bathroom. She couldn't even remember what the lady of the house had told her about her schedule. Was the home quiet because the occupants were asleep? Were they at work? Grace didn't know. She stood in front of the mirror and saw the haggard look on her face and thought, *I don't know where I am, who I'm staying with, what time it is, what day it is.*

This was not *her*. She'd always been so orderly, to the point of compulsion, for God's sake.

She missed Boulder. She missed her friends and her students and her next-door neighbor. She missed her cats, fat Hazel and tattered-eared Whiskers. She missed her *things*. And Charley, poor little boy, surely he was going to grow tired of this "adventure."

It had to end.

She peeked in on him and then showered in the empty house, recalling, finally, that the woman and her husband had both gone to work. "By seven," they'd said last night. "Make yourself at home."

But no place was ever going to be home again unless it was her own house. She knew that with a spurt of clarity. She absolutely was not cut out for this stressful, nomadic life.

It was going to end.

After getting Charley up, bathed and fed, she took him to a nearby playground and sat in the early morning sun and called her father on the cell phone while Charley swung on the swings and raced up and down the slide, getting positively filthy.

"Any news from Luke?" she asked. "It's been a whole day."

"Honey, this could take a little time," Bob said carefully. "I know you are anxious, but…"

"But nothing, Dad, I'm going crazy."

"Is something wrong? Is it where you're staying? We could get you a hotel or…"

"Dad, all that's fine. The people couldn't be more hospitable. It's me. I woke up this morning, and I knew I'd never last on the move like this."

"Are you thinking about returning Charley to that woman?"

"Good grief, no, never. It's just that I have to do something concrete to protect him. Be careful of that rail over there!"

"Huh?"

"Sorry. I was talking to Charley. We're at a playground."

"Still in the city?"

"Yes. But not for long."

"Grace?"

"I'm going to Denver with Luke."

"You…are? Well, this is the first I've heard about that."

"I just decided. This very minute, in fact."

"Oh, I see. So Luke doesn't know yet?"

"Obviously not."

"Well…"

"I know what you're going to say. It's too dangerous for me to go back to Colorado."

"I was going to tell you that, sure. And don't forget, now the FBI will have been called in."

"I'll lay low, don't worry. It's just that I know Denver and I know Kerry Pope. I need to be helping out on this."

"Now, Grace."

"No, Dad, don't try to talk me out of it. My only problem is Charley. I can't take him along."

She chewed her lower lip and changed the phone to her other ear, her gaze following Charley's rambunctious play. And then the lightbulb went on in her head. "Dad, what if…what if you and Mom took Charley along on your camping trip? You are going to visit the parks again this year, aren't you?"

"That was the plan."

"Anyway, and I'm just thinking out loud, but what

if you didn't know anything about the court order to turn Charley over to Kerry? And what if you'd been planning all along to take him camping with you this summer? I mean, you'll be in the RV, in isolated campgrounds, and—''

"Hold it right there, Gracie,'' Bob broke in sharply. "We do know about the court order. And for that matter, a whole lot more.''

"But—''

"But nothing. I'm a cop...was a cop. If I'm going to break the law, I'm sure not going to lie about it.'' He paused. "Look, your mother and I had a long heart-to-heart when we had Charley the other evening. The most important person here is that boy. Whatever we do, we can't let him go to Kerry Pope. Bottom line.''

"Oh, Dad,'' Grace said gratefully.

"And because of that your mother and I will support you in this one hundred percent.''

"You already have.''

"That was before your time to turn Charley over ran out. Right now, just by talking to you, I'm aiding and abetting.''

"Oh, God.''

"Grace, your mother and I are going to do whatever it takes to protect the two of you. If that means taking Charley on our trip, fine. At least you'll have a couple weeks to... I mean, Luke will have a couple weeks—''

"I have to go to Denver with him,'' she repeated.

"Well now, Gracie, that's not up to me. I'll let you and Luke hash that out. Just remember, we're family, and we're behind you all the way.''

Grace was watching Charley as he chased a pigeon,

Charley flapping his arms and running in circles, and she felt a cry well up in her chest. She couldn't bear to ask her parents to take him, yet what choice did she have? How could she have traveled so far down this road, well past the point of no return, and not foreseen the outcome of her actions? She never should have come to California, never should have—

Her father's raspy voice sounded in her ear. "Grace, I'll get back to you. As for Luke, I think you better brace yourself for a disappointment. He's not going to want to take you along. I just thought I better warn you before you got your hopes up. Okay?"

She stood up from the park bench and began pacing, nudging a pebble with the toe of her sandal. Her dad knew Luke. And maybe—okay, *probably*—her father was right; her plan would be a tough sell, especially to a hard-boiled ex-cop. Okay. But, damn, she thought, it just had to work. She couldn't sit around in a safe house, waiting, all alone, not knowing what was happening.

She paced while the silence stretched out on the cell phone, paced and schemed. A week ago, if someone had told her she'd be a fugitive from the law, a kidnapper, she would have laughed. Now her dad was putting another obstacle in her path.

"You know what?" she finally said. "This whole ordeal has taught me one thing. Don't ever give up. If you want something, do whatever it takes to attain it."

"Is this Sally Grace Bennett I'm talking to?"

"Very funny, Dad. But yes, to answer you, yes, it's the new me."

"Well, I'll be," Bob said.

And she thought, *Yeah, me, too.*

CHAPTER SIX

LUKE ACKNOWLEDGED that it was too early to be calling his wife—she was still his wife, damn it—but he'd been awake since 3:00 a.m., thinking about things, going over and over in his head how they could mend the bridges and give their marriage another try. This was not the first night he'd gone sleepless, not by a long shot. But now that he was leaving town for an indefinite period, well, he figured it was time to lay his cards on the table.

He listened to the ringing in his ear and felt his pulse beating in his temples. If the damn answering machine came on the...

Judith answered. *Be nice,* he reminded himself.

"Hey, it's Luke," he began. "I hope I didn't wake you."

"No. No, I'm up."

He uttered the words cautiously. "Good. Say, when you didn't return my call I got kind of worried, so I just thought I better..."

"Luke, I'm a big girl. I can take care of myself, okay?"

"Well, sure, I didn't mean to..." Goddamn, but just the sound of her voice, that throaty voice, was enough to make his belly coil.

"So," she said, "is that it?"

"Ah, no, not really. I wanted to talk. Have you got a minute?"

She hesitated. In the background he could swear he heard another person rattling around. Anger burned in his chest. It had to be that asshole she'd been seeing. Pain swirled around the anger, hot and molten against his ribs.

"Judith?" His breath was short.

"I'm here. But look, I've got an early shoot today."

"Modeling job?"

"Of course."

"That's nice. You're still the best-looking woman in California, you know." See, he could be charming when needed.

"Thanks, Luke, really. So what do you want to talk about? If it's the divorce, I really don't want to discuss…"

"Give me a sec, okay? It's just that I think you're rushing things. I've given it a lot of thought, babe, and it's only been six months, you know, since you left. That's not much time."

"That depends upon your point of view, I guess."

"Maybe. Anyway, like I said, I've had time to think. What I'm saying is—" he swallowed hard "—well, in these past few months, I've come to realize we belong together. I still care about you, babe. Hell, I feel more in…love and more committed than ever." There, he'd said it. Why was it so hard for him to admit he felt love? Was it because he'd been an orphan and had learned to distrust people too early in life?

"Oh, Luke, please, this is… When you talk like

that it rips me apart. I care about you. Honestly, I do. I always will. But I fell out of love. It just happened.''

''You didn't fall out of love till I got canned, did you?''

''Don't use that tone, Luke. It's ugly.''

''Sorry. But the way I see it, as long as I was a cop you still got your thrills, but as soon as I was an ordinary Joe, you—''

''This is old ground,'' she cut in sharply. ''I don't have time for this, Luke. You're in denial. Long before you lost your job the relationship was over. We haven't been a married couple in years.''

''That's bullshit.''

''Don't swear.''

''Well, it is.''

''Think about it. Face the facts, Luke.''

''You face them.''

There was a stony silence, then, ''Listen. I got the papers in and I need you to sign them.''

''Papers?''

''Don't be coy. It isn't you.''

Now it was his turn for silence.

''Can you stop by this evening and sign them?''

Silence.

''Luke? Let's not make this any harder than it already is. Will you stop by?''

''Maybe.''

''That's not good enough.''

''Well, you know what, Judith?'' he said hotly. ''It'll have to do.'' And he hung up.

The steaming shower followed by a cold stream of water didn't help. He stood in front of the bathroom mirror, half-shaven, towel around his damp torso, and felt betrayed. First by his fellow officers, then by Judith. She'd only waited a month after he'd left the force before she got up one morning and pulled out her suitcases, announcing her intentions. Thirty days after his captain at Vice had come over one night to tell him he'd be very wise to turn in his badge and gun and maybe, just *maybe,* Internal Affairs would let it go at that.

Thirty days was all Judith had waited. Even though he'd started work for Metropole, even though he'd been trying to patch together the tattered pieces of his life, she hadn't cared a good goddamn.

He tipped his head and slid the razor along his cheek and then scraped upward along his neck to his jaw.

Maybe he was nuts. Maybe she was right; the marriage had been over a long time before his disgrace. Hell, he didn't know. He only knew that the separation had given him the time and space to realize how much she really meant to him.

Damn it, he loved Judith. He was only half a person without her. Didn't she see she'd torn his guts out?

Divorce papers. Like hell he'd sign them. And *had* that jerk been with Judith when he'd called?

The knock at his North Beach apartment door startled him and he almost put a new scar on his cheek. Who in hell would be at his door at this hour?

Towel still around his hips, Luke impatiently yanked open the front door. He guessed his jaw must have dropped for a moment before he recovered.

"Grace?" he muttered. "What the…?"

"I'm so sorry, I realize it's early, but I… I have to talk to you, and I was afraid you'd already be gone to work, so I… I got your address from the phone book… I hope that's okay?"

"Uh, sure." Then he looked down. "So, this must be Charley?"

"Yes, yes, this is Charley. Charley, say hi to Mr. Sarkov."

"Hello." A tiny voice. A cute kid, with glossy light-brown hair and blue eyes and a Cupid's-bow mouth. The child stood there, holding Grace's hand, staring unabashedly at Luke, his eyes full of innocent curiosity. It crossed Luke's mind that the little boy could easily have been him as a four-year-old. But he'd been kicked around like an old soccer ball, and this kid, Charley, well, he'd had the same mother practically since birth. Lucky fella.

A spurt of anger shot through Luke—at his own mother, who'd deserted him, at his foster parents, at the system. Damn them all. Then he suppressed the feeling with the ease of long practice.

"How come you're wearing a trowel?" the boy asked.

"A what? Oh, yeah, right, a *towel?* I, uh, just got out of the shower." His eyes lifted to Grace, who was looking anywhere but at him. "Listen," he said, moving aside, pushing the door all the way open, "come on in."

"Are you sure? I mean, we could..."

"I *said* come in."

With a timid smile, she stepped past him and stood in the living room, Charley by her side.

"I'll finish dressing," he said. "Why don't you get a cup of coffee or something. Should be plenty in the pot."

"Thank you, I will."

"And there's juice for Charley. I'll be right out, okay?"

"Yes, sure." She still couldn't look at him.

Luke dressed in jeans and a faded checked shirt. He wasn't going into Metropole today, only finishing up a report at home on the arson case. He was sure Grace had come by to prod him, at least to find out when, exactly, he was leaving for Denver. She could have phoned. Or maybe she had something else to dump on him. Needed to do it in person.

Whatever, he thought, tugging on tennis shoes. He'd be civil. She was, after all, Big Bob's daughter.

When he strode back into the living room, the TV was on quietly in the corner and Charley was sitting cross-legged on the floor, happily watching a cartoon.

"I hope you don't mind." Grace, who was perched on the edge of the couch, coffee mug clasped in her hands, nodded at her son. Her *foster* son. The kid she'd abducted, Luke reminded himself. Amazing.

"No problem," he said.

She sure didn't look the type—a kidnapper. She couldn't have looked more innocent. Yet this woman had given up her whole life for her foster son. He marveled at that, but he couldn't comprehend it. No one had done that for him. No one except Bob Bennett, that is.

He studied her unabashedly. Grace Bennett. She was on the thin side, practically no chest at all under the loose white T-shirt that was tucked haphazardly into a pair of tan slacks—linen, he surmised—which looked as if she'd been in them for days. Maybe she had.

She must have felt the weight of his gaze on her, because she reached up and tucked her taffy-colored hair behind a small ear and tightened the clip holding it at the back of her neck. A nice neck, he grudgingly admitted, long and white and slim, delicate, with loose tendrils of hair lying against the paleness like soft feathers. She could do a lot with that hair.

And she could sure lose the big owlish horn-rimmed glasses. Did she hide behind them? Were they a reflection of a poor self-image?

"So what can I do for you, Grace?" he asked, folding his arms across his chest. "If you're wondering when I'm going to leave for Denver..."

"That's part of it, yes."

Part? he thought. "I'm hoping to be out of here in the next couple of days. I have a few loose ends to tie up. Okay?"

"Yes, of course." She still wouldn't meet his eyes. Instead, she glanced around the room, her gaze coming to rest on one of Judith's photos, one that had made the cover of a national women's magazine. His practiced cop's eye saw color tinge her cheeks.

"You said *part,*" he put in. "Part of why you're here?"

"Oh, yes. Well, it's like this." For the first time she swiveled and met his gaze. "I'm going to Denver with you."

It took him a second. "You are, huh." He laughed sardonically.

She nodded. "Please hear me out."

"Can't wait."

"Well..." She drew a breath, and he could almost see the gears working in her head. "I spoke with Dad, and there's a possibility he and Mom might take Charley along on their camping trip. You know they leave on this trip every year, and..."

"Yeah, sure, go on," he said. He knew all about their trips, the supposed freedom of being on the road in their RV, camping in isolated campgrounds. Sure. Freedom. Try having to apply a year ahead of time for a camping permit in the national parks or making a reservation at campgrounds a year and a half in advance. Some freedom.

"Charley and I have been moving around every night. New faces, new houses, new beds. It's very rough on him."

"Uh-huh." His eyes were riveted on her.

"Anyway, if Dad and Mom can, they'll take Charley and…"

"*And* they'll be accessories to a federal crime."

She lowered her eyes. "Yes," she said, in a whisper. "We…discussed that."

"And?"

"And they want to do whatever they can to help."

"I see." He wasn't so sure, though. Bob Bennett? Breaking the law? Willingly?

"You think I'm awful," she said, cutting into his thoughts. "And I agree. I just pray that we dig up enough on Kerry to force the judge to reverse his decision. We *have* to."

We, he thought, *sure.* Aloud, he pointed out, "You're forgetting one little detail. Even if I, and I mean *I,* get the goods on this Pope woman, that may not erase what you and your parents are doing. It's not the Boulder, Colorado, police we're talking. This is the FBI."

"I know. Oh, God, I know. But maybe…maybe public sentiment or something will help to make them understand we were forced to break the law."

"I wouldn't count on it," he sneered.

But Grace was shaking her head. "I don't know. I just don't know what's right and wrong anymore. I trusted the system, and look what happened. I do know one thing, though—I can't keep moving around like this. I'm going crazy. I need to be actively involved.'' She put the coffee mug down, leaned over her shoulder bag and pulled out a file, which she held up. ''This is everything I've amassed on Kerry. I've got her rap sheet, names of former friends, drug dealers, roommates, addresses, employers... I've got more than enough here to get us started in the right direction.''

''*Us.*'' He shook his head.

''You need me. You need this.'' She waved the file. He reached for it, but she kept it from him.

''I work alone, Grace. I'm trying to be civil here, but I don't have time for this. I'm sorry you're going nuts on the move the way you are. Maybe you could stay right here at my place. You'd have to keep a real low profile, but—''

''No.''

''Well, then, I can't help you.''

''I'm not going to give in on this. You need me and you need this file.''

He just stared at her.

''That's all I stopped by to say. Come on, Charley,'' she said, rising, stuffing the file back into her oversize bag. ''Charley?''

Dutifully, the boy clicked off the TV and stood up.

''Say goodbye to Mr. Sarkov.''

''Goodbye, Mr. Sarkov.''

''And thank you for letting you watch TV.''

''Thank you.''

Luke smiled. ''You're very welcome.''

Grace took the boy's hand and led him to the door. Then she turned back to Luke, who hadn't moved.

"I'll call you and let you know where and when to pick me up."

"Not a chance," he stated flatly.

"I *am* going along," Grace said, and she opened the door, ushered Charley out. Then she pivoted. "I am going," she repeated, and she closed the door and was gone.

He didn't move for a minute. Only stood there, caught between wonder at the surprising strength of her determination and anger that he had to put up with this crap.

Big Bob's daughter. Who would've thought?

He didn't dwell much more on Grace or Bob and their troubles as the day wore on. He was too busy tying up those loose ends. He got his phone messages from Metropole and returned a few calls from home. Then he finished his initial handwritten report on the Sammy Rae arson case and faxed it to the secretary who was assigned to the investigators. She'd type it and file it. And by the time he got back from Denver, the lab reports Fire Chief Rollins had ordered should be ready.

It was boring work. Little real investigation and a lot of paperwork. He basically hated it.

By one, he contacted Bob Bennett, using a pay phone. It was time for care in what he said over the line. For all he knew, the FBI had tapped the man's home telephone by now. If Luke had been in charge of the Charley Pope kidnapping case, that would have been his first move.

"Hey, my man," Luke began, not using names, "thought I'd touch base on that outing we were discussing."

Bob had no trouble taking up the thread. "Right. Now, are we going tomorrow or the following day?"

"Probably the following day, if that works for you. And hey, I understand you're going to have some extra baggage on the outing." Charley. The baggage.

"Oh, yeah, right. You've heard about that?"

"Just this morning. I was surprised."

"I bet you were."

"You real sure about these arrangements?" Luke had to ask.

"Very sure. The wife and I are committed."

"I think we'd better talk about the extra weight you'll be taking along, just how you're going to handle leaving the city with it."

"Good idea. I'll get my new cell phone number to you," Bob said.

"Sounds fine."

"If you don't hear from me today, I'll ring you tomorrow. Before noon, all right?"

"Perfect."

"And let's both put our heads together on how to handle loading the extra baggage. Okay?"

"You got it. Later," Luke said, and he hung up.

Charley. Just how was Bob going to get the boy from Grace without being spotted by the surveillance that was surely stuck to Bob like glue by now?

Paying bills, putting his life in order for the jaunt to Denver, Luke lounged back at the corner desk in his living room and tapped a pen on the top of his knee. His thoughts moved from Grace and her announcement that she was traveling with him, to Bob and Sally and how they were going to get Charley out of the city undetected. That was an immediate problem.

And then he thought about his own troubles—namely, how damn glad he was to be heading off on this trip; at least he was going to be doing some real investigative work. But eventually—a week, two weeks?—he'd be back in San Francisco, back to square one, back to Metropole.

The pathetic truth was that while the four other detectives who'd been forced to resign seemed relieved not to be behind bars, happy to be done with police work, Luke felt just the opposite. He missed the hell out of his former life. He was a cop. That was all he'd ever wanted to be since he'd met Big Bob Bennett. God, but he wished he were still on the job. The irony was that the other dismissed cops had been guilty of their crimes—Luke was the innocent one. The only one who hadn't taken the drug money.

Luke's sin? He hadn't been able to rat out his fellow officers. A sin of omission. That old code of silence on the thin blue line.

Sitting at his desk, tapping the pen on his jeans, a utility bill staring, unpaid, up at him, he knew in his gut he'd never survive away from some kind of police work—and not for an insurance agency and not as a rent-a-cop. Not that. Ever. The problem nonetheless existed: if his former fellow officers came forward and cleared his name they'd dig the old dirt up again and further incriminate themselves. As it was, IA had been satisfied to see them go. Less fuss, less department embarrassment, less public disgrace.

"Swell," he muttered.

There *was* a possibility. He had been mulling it over for a long time. There was one person who could clear him. One person who knew the whole truth.

His name was Manny Morelli. He was the drug dealer who'd paid off the cops.

Yeah, Luke had thought a lot about Morelli these past months. Morelli could clear him without bringing up the names of the other cops again. The only trouble was, Morelli was behind bars already, and Luke couldn't conceive of a single reason Morelli would speak up for him. Not one goddamn reason.

He never quite thought it through that afternoon as he drove north out of the city over the Golden Gate Bridge toward the minimum security prison where Morelli was an inmate. It was a glorious summer day. The fog had lifted; the sun was bright and hot. The bay was choppy in the light breeze, the water dark blue, the graceful curves of the bridge framing the scenery of Sausalito on the opposite shore. He had put the top down on his sporty red Subaru convertible, and the wind gave him a false sense of freedom. But hell, he'd take it. He had few pleasures these days.

He'd guessed this trip had been a long time coming, and he'd guessed he was finally making it because he was leaving for Denver and trying to clear off his desk.

Whatever, he told himself. He only knew that this was something he had to do or he'd spend the rest of his days wondering.

The prison complex was located in San Quentin. Morelli had been given three years less time served at the state-of-the-art prison farm. An easy sentence at a minimum security institution because he'd copped a plea with the D.A., named officers who'd been present for the drug deal payoff—including Luke's name, though Luke had left the ugly scene in disgust long before the payoff. IA and the D.A. had forced the resignations of the officers and Morelli had gotten not much more than a slap on the hand. Why he'd named Luke was no puzzle. He hated cops.

Luke parked at the Visitor Center and went through the security check. He wasn't at all sure Manny Morelli would see him, and he didn't know what he was going to say even if Morelli showed his face. Luke supposed he could get on his hands and knees and beg.

Right. Cold day in hell before that happened.

Still, maybe he could appeal to whatever sense of morality the man possessed. Maybe.

There were no glass partitions or wire screen separators in the visiting room. Luke sat among maybe twenty other visitors and inmates scattered around long tables and he drummed his fingers. Morelli would be given Luke's name. He'd either show or he wouldn't.

He showed.

"Well, well, if it isn't my old pal, Cool Hand Luke. And here I was, folding sheets in the laundry, wondering if my day could get any more exciting."

Luke nodded. "Long time no see. Care if I sit for a minute?"

Morelli shrugged beneath his orange prisoner's shirt and sat across from Luke, folding his hands negligently on the tabletop and cracking his knuckles. "So what gives, Sarkov?"

"I was in the neighborhood."

"Sure you were."

"Hey, Manny, have I ever lied to you?"

Morelli glared at him.

Luke felt his jaw tighten. "So, how much longer do you have to serve?"

"Thirteen months. I can handle it."

"Really."

"Yeah, really. Is that all you came up here to say, Sarkov?" Morelli grinned. "Hey, I almost said Detective Sarkov, you know? But I hear you're with some ritzy insurance company or something. Shame about that, huh?"

A dozen swear words clogged in Luke's throat. "Yeah, Manny, a crying shame. You and I both know I wasn't in on the payoffs. I've always wondered why you let me go down with the others. What did it get you?"

"Satisfaction, pal."

"You know," Luke said, sweat dampening the collar of his checkered shirt, "you could tell the truth. It's never too late."

Morelli stood abruptly. "Sure I could. Question is, why the hell would I? You're a Boy Scout, Sarkov. Always were. Far as I'm concerned, you can take a flying leap." He leaned over, rapped his knuckles on the tabletop, pivoted and walked across the room, so the guard could let him out.

Slowly, Luke rose. He felt a wave of helplessness wash over him. But what the hell had he expected?

Still down in the dumps, he drove back across the Golden Gate Bridge shortly after 6:00 p.m. There was one last thing he needed to deal with—Judith.

He traveled along Marina Boulevard to Van Ness Avenue and threw a left onto California. Judith now lived in a neighborhood directly below Nob Hill, a nice upscale area. She'd rented a house just off California on a steep hill, rented it with an option to buy. Judith made the big bucks modeling. As long as her looks held out, she'd be okay. She was good with money, too, invested wisely. She was smart, well-off, beautiful and had a great sense of humor. But she could be hard.

Goddamn, he still wanted her. What did she see in that banker? A *banker*. Maybe Luke wasn't a cop anymore, but still...

He parked in front of her salmon pink and white Victorian, got out and stood in front of the edifice for a moment, collecting himself. He wasn't about to sign any divorce papers. He also didn't want to piss her off. If only he could get her to step back and take an objective look at what she was throwing away. Maybe she'd see reason.

Much to Luke's chagrin, Fred Lund was there. Luke stood at Judith's door and saw him down the hall in the kitchen, lounging against the center island, a glass of wine in his hand. Like he owned the place.

Luke shifted his gaze back to his wife, who was holding open the door, partially blocking his view. She could have planned to be there alone. Did she feel she needed support from that jackass?

"Oh, Luke," she was saying, looking so damn pretty in a mint-green sleeveless top and cropped white pants, her thick reddish brown hair catching the evening light, "I'm so glad you decided to come by. Would you like a drink?"

"I don't think so," he got out between clenched teeth.

"Well, then," she breathed, smiling, the scent of her expensive perfume filling his senses, lingering. He had the sudden, overpowering urge to grab her and push her up against the wall and ravish her with his mouth, his hands, the way they used to do. Their love-making had always been abrupt and rough—the way she liked it.

Did Fred...? Oh, hell, he couldn't let himself go there.

He swallowed. "I'm out of here for a couple weeks," he said, his voice thick. "I just didn't want to go without—"

But she was already turning, beaming, picking up a manila envelope from the hall table. "You don't know how much this means to me," she interrupted. "I really didn't think you'd...do this, Luke, not without..."

"You have it wrong," he said more sharply than he'd intended. "I'm not here to sign anything. I don't want a divorce, Judith."

Then Fred was there, halfway down the hall, looking belligerent. A big guy, six-three, over two hundred pounds. His dark eyebrows were drawn together in a frown.

"This doesn't concern you," Luke said. "Why don't you make yourself scarce."

"The hell..." the man began.

"Oh, please," Judith said, laying a calming hand on Luke's arm, "this won't get us anywhere. Luke, I'm asking you—no, I'm pleading with you—to sign the papers and not put us through any more pain. Luke?"

He knew he'd lose it if he didn't get the hell out of there. He said nothing, only glared for a moment longer at the banker and shook his head and retreated down the steps to the street.

He managed to unlock his car and was halfway in, when Judith rushed to catch him.

"Don't go like this." Her eyes were moist. Nonetheless, she was holding the manila envelope and a pen. "Just do this for me, please."

Luke looked at the envelope. He looked up at Fred, who was standing in the open doorway, glowering. He looked back at the envelope, then took it from her.

"Oh, thank you..." she began, but he tore it in two. And tore it again and carefully handed the pieces to her.

All he said was, "You don't love that asshole," and he got in his car and drove off.

A half hour later, at a local bar near his apartment on Columbus, he sipped on a beer and realized Judith must have several sets of divorce papers. His act had been childish. Okay. So what? he mused. There was no law that said he had to hand his wife over to some jerk without a fight.

He thoroughly expected to sit there till closing and drown his sorrows, images of Judith bludgeoning his brain.

But it wasn't Judith who came to mind. Instead, he kept picturing Grace Bennett. Grace sitting on the edge of his couch that morning, desperation and determination battling in her expression. Okay, so he had problems. But Grace's troubles far outweighed his own, and he damn well needed to concentrate on helping her. Helping Bob's daughter.

He took a long drink, set his beer bottle on the bar and nodded at the bartender to set him up again.

Grace, with her stringy, mousy hair and those hideous glasses. Yet his practiced cop's eye had seen past her shortcomings, and now he envisioned the fine bone structure of her cheeks and nose and the clear long edge of her jaw. She could be a nice-looking woman. Her figure, though too thin, would be dynamite in the right clothes. Long legs, slim arms, breasts that were small and youthful and firm. Yeah, she'd be okay if she spent some time on her appearance, he supposed.

It didn't matter, though. What counted was her flight from the FBI and the safety of her kid. Cute little boy. Once again Luke thought, *I could have been that boy, little Charley. I could have been, but I had no Grace Bennett to take me in and love me.*

He cleared his head. What he needed to think about was how to protect them from disaster. Because this case sure had had disaster written all over it.

Ah, hell, forget about it, he decided.

He finally pushed thoughts of Bob's daughter aside and tried to concentrate on Judith, but after only moments Grace was there once more, her eyes, the curve of her brows above the glasses. She just wouldn't go away.

CHAPTER SEVEN

THE FILES ON the Bennett case were multiplying like
a rampant virus. Renee now had plenty on Professor
Sally Grace Bennett—known by her peers and asso-
ciates as Grace. Where she lived, how she spent her
money, where she vacationed, who her friends were,
what courses she taught at CU. Even what her super-
vising professor had written for her tenure review.
Renee could say what Grace looked like, where she
bought her clothes, what cavities she had in her teeth
and what prescriptions she'd filled for herself and her
foster son in the past four years.

She knew just about everything there was to know
about Sally Grace Bennett, but she could not comprehend, absolutely could not figure out why the
mousy college professor had pulled such a stupen-
dously stupid stunt as going on the lam with a four-
year-old kid who wasn't hers.

Grace wasn't naive; she certainly wasn't impulsive.
If anything she was too controlled, her life one of
ingrained habit. She rarely went out, had no male
friends except for other college professors, who were
mostly married.

A typical old-maid schoolteacher type. In her pho-
tographs, she appeared plain. Not homely, but she
wore no makeup, and did less than nothing with her
hair.

Renee sat at her desk and pushed aside papers until she found Grace's studio shot for CU's Psych Department newsletter. Fair skin, possibly with pale freckles—it was hard to tell; eyes of indeterminate color in the black-and-white photo. Delicate features, dark-blond hair pulled back. Glasses. Very professional.

The most unlikely federal fugitive in the history of the FBI.

The media were on this case like vultures. The articles had begun in the *Denver Post* and *Rocky Mountain News,* but the wire services had picked up the story and run with it.

Predictably, the public was on Bennett's side. The TV stations were covering the story, and their opinion polls all showed sympathy for Grace and Charley. God, they were practically household names. And Renee surmised that John Q. Public would never snitch on Grace, even if he met her face-to-face.

With the hoopla, the Bennett case took on even more significance than Renee had originally thought. The case still had *promotion* written all over it, but only if she caught Grace Bennett. Failure was unthinkable now.

Why had Grace run? Renee kept thinking that if she could understand her motivation, she'd understand Grace and be able to track her down that much sooner.

Jay insisted it was self-evident. "She doesn't want the biological mother to get her hands on the boy," he said last night. "She's protecting her son. She's the only mother he's known."

But Renee couldn't imagine a woman giving up her hard-won position, her career, for God's sake, over a child who wasn't even hers. Giving up her life, her friends, maybe even her freedom. Did Grace Bennett know she could go to prison for kidnapping Charley?

She had to know that. Grace's father was an ex-policeman in San Francisco. Renee would bet the farm that Grace had already contacted him. Maybe she was staying with him, although retired Lieutenant Robert Bennett probably knew better than to harbor a fugitive. He most likely had stashed her somewhere else.

Renee had already put in a call to the San Francisco FBI office, requesting surveillance on the Bennett residence, which was actually in Oakland, across the bay. The San Francisco office had said they'd handle it. She had also requested a phone tap, but the federal judge in that district was proving recalcitrant. Renee supposed the judge was one of those saps who thought Grace Bennett was some sort of heroine instead of a criminal. She'd kidnapped a little boy, for Pete's sake!

Renee was starving, even though it was only eleven in the morning. She was always hungry these days, had taken to bringing snacks from home, fruit and crackers and candy bars. The morning sickness that was the standing joke of early pregnancy had not afflicted her. She was ravenous, instead. Eating for two. God, what a predicament.

It struck her, as she sat at her desk and stared out her window at Denver's downtown skyline, that she and Grace Bennett had both been put in untenable situations by children.

How very bizarre.

She ate a Snickers bar, licked her fingers and dropped the wrapper in the trash and started in again on the list of Grace's acquaintances she wanted to interview in person.

She'd already spoken to Grace's next-door neighbor, Stacey Carson, who was taking care of the woman's two cats but knew nothing about where her neighbor had gone or when she'd be back. She'd contacted another friend, whose name Stacey had given her, then she'd called Charley's day-care provider, the child's pediatrician and the head of the CU Psychology Department. Some in person, some by phone.

She still had no idea who Sally Grace Bennett *really* was. She had the facts, but they didn't add up to a personality she could read. They all said the same thing: Grace was a good person, a good mother, a good teacher.

By that afternoon she'd tracked down a few more names on the list, been given the runaround by most and secured an appointment with only one, another psych professor. It was, after all, summer break, and most of the students and teachers were long gone.

She drove the thirty miles north to Boulder, beating the rush-hour traffic, and found her way to the Life Sciences Building, where the Psychology Department was housed. Walking down the hall, she passed offices, each with a name bracketed on the door. She was looking for Professor Evan Sandler, but as she scanned the names, she saw Sally G. Bennett on a door, and she stopped short. This was her quarry's lair, and she wanted suddenly, desperately, to enter that office and sift through the suspect's things. She looked around surreptitiously; the corridor was empty. She stepped close and put her hand on the old brass doorknob.

Locked.

Of course it was, and even if the door had been open, she couldn't have gone in without a warrant. But she stood there and tried to feel Grace Bennett, see through her eyes. She turned slowly and impressed on her brain the way the hall looked—the polished wood floor, the heavy dark doors, the bulletin board down a ways, covered with notes. The smell of academia: dust, paper, the hot electronics of computers.

She found Professor Sandler's office past the bulletin board. She knocked, and heard a youthful voice say, "Come in."

There was a flash of surprise in his eyes as he rose from his desk. There always was; Renee was used to it. Not only was she female, she was African American.

"Special Agent Paynter," he said.

"Professor Sandler." She nodded.

"Sit down." He sighed. "I know you're here for the dope on Grace, but I really don't want to cause her any harm."

She sat on a scarred wooden captain's chair. "I understand," she said, "but your colleague has broken the law. You realize that, I'm sure."

"The law," he said. He had a round face and a too-small nose for a man. *Cute,* she supposed. The coeds probably lusted after him. "This particular situation, well, if you knew Grace…she's a good person. She'd never break the law. I mean, not normally. But little Charley was her life. The court had no right giving him back to a woman who hasn't even bothered with him in four years."

"Uh-huh." She had heard all this before. "Now, Professor Sandler…"

''Oh, call me Evan,'' he said. ''Everyone does.''

''Evan, fine. When was the last time you saw Ms. Bennett?''

''Oh, Lord, let's see…''

The interview went like the others: Grace was a terrific person, a great teacher, a wonderful mother. She was quiet, retiring, devoted to her foster son. Blah, blah, blah. No one at the university had run into her since classes had ended in May, because Grace wouldn't take summer assignments so she could be with her son.

Sure, she'd been spotted around Boulder, at the city pool with Charley, shopping at the supermarket, taking Charley to a children's matinee. Usually it was a professor's wife who had seen Grace, because of their children's mutual activities.

''I guess I'm not much help,'' Evan was saying. ''And frankly, I'm glad I don't know her that well.''

''Well, thanks anyway,'' Renee said. Always the polite civil servant. Mindful that this man's tax dollars paid her salary. Mindful, also, that the FBI needed no bad press. Not after J. Edgar Hoover.

She drove back to Denver, the opposing lanes of the Boulder Turnpike jammed with bumper-to-bumper traffic. Thinking, thinking. Was Jay right? Was Grace Bennett's entire motivation based on protecting her child? But her action seemed so…out of character, so out of control. Why? Why?

She got home later than normal that evening, but the summer sun was still hot, the trees along her quiet street drooping and dusty. Jay had already turned on the lawn sprinkler. She found him on the deck behind their split-level house, getting the barbecue ready for the chicken she'd left marinating that morning.

"Hi, honey," she said, giving him a peck on the cheek. "God, I'm starved." She sank onto a cushioned deck chair and kicked her heels off.

"You're late," Jay noted.

"I know. I had to go up to Boulder again."

"Find out anything helpful?"

"No."

"The woman's a cipher. Goddamn, I'm admiring her more and more."

"Oh, Jay, spare me that stuff."

"I know, you're just doing your job."

"Not well enough right now. But I'll bet she's in California, has contacted her father. It's the only place she could go. I'll find her, Jay."

"I'm sure you will, baby. You'll keep this country safe from the likes of Grace Bennett."

"Jay, please."

He left the grill and bent to kiss her cheek. "You're beautiful when you're mad, you know that?"

"Oh, Jay…" She sighed. "I'm tired and I'm hungry and I—" She stopped short, her heart skipping a beat.

"What?"

"Oh, nothing. I'm hot. It's hot out."

She ate half the barbecue chicken, a large helping of coleslaw, then sat in front of the TV eating Cherry Bon Bon ice cream out of the carton.

Jay woke her when she fell asleep on the couch. "Hey, hey, baby doll, time to wake up and get ready to go to sleep."

"Mmm," she mumbled, and she barely remembered brushing her teeth, donning her nightgown and falling into bed.

The next morning Renee had a meeting with Special Agent in Charge Towey and two of the other agents who were doing peripheral work on the Bennett case.

She presented every fact she'd gathered and her theory that the fugitive was in California.

"People go to ground in a place that's familiar," she said. "With someone they trust. That's what she'd do."

"Has the surveillance of the Bennett house come up with anything?" Towey asked.

"No. Not yet."

"Uh-huh," the other agent said. "Well, we can only stretch our resources so far. This surveillance is going to be finite, Renee."

"She's there," Renee insisted.

She left the meeting early because she had an appointment with her doctor. Her OB-GYN, to be exact.

Dr. Bruce Kenton was a good doctor, and Renee liked him, but these days her visits made her shake with nerves.

"You're at nine weeks, Mrs. Paynter," he said, a young, handsome man who looked more like a professional athlete than a doctor. "Time is running out. You're going to have to make a decision here pretty soon."

"I know," she said, but her voice failed her. She cleared her throat and tried again. "I know."

"Have you told your husband yet?"

She couldn't meet his gaze. "Not yet," she whispered, eyes averted.

"Mrs. Paynter... Renee, for an intelligent woman, you're not dealing with this situation very well."

"I realize that. It's...it's very difficult."

"I can't advise you either way, you understand

that, but you must ask yourself if you want this baby. Truthfully. You're young and healthy, and all the tests so far show a perfectly healthy fetus. There's no medical reason—''

''I know,'' she interrupted.

''Here's some advice, Renee. Go home and tell your husband. Talk it over. This is not your baby alone. It's your husband's, too.''

Renee got out of the clinic, sweating, her hands trembling, her stomach growling with hunger. On the way back to the Federal Building she went through the drive-up window of a burger joint and ate in the car, dodging city traffic.

And all the time, every moment of the rest of that long day, her mind spun, trapped in indecision. Her baby, her husband, her career, her *life*. How in God's name was she going to make this decision?

GRACE DROVE her parents' station wagon through North Beach, searching for the park Luke had given her directions to. It was very early, and the fog still hung on the hills of the city like a shroud, softening the edges of the buildings. Charley was in the back seat eating animal crackers, calling out the name of each one before he crunched it in his teeth.

''Lion,'' he said. *Crunch.* ''Horse. Camel.'' *Crunch.*

He'd been cranky when she'd woken him up that morning because it was so early, but he'd mellowed out when bribed by the box of animal crackers. Some psychologist she was.

''Where are we going, Mommy?'' Charley asked.

''I told you. We're going to a park where you can play. Mr. Sarkov will be there, too.''

"Will he play with me?"

Grace smiled at the thought. "Probably not. The reason we're meeting in the park and not his house, sweetie, is for you to have a place to play while we grown-ups talk."

She'd phoned Luke late the night before, a little panicky, afraid he'd blow all her plans and take off for Denver without her. She wouldn't put anything past him. But he said he'd meet her, even given her directions to a park near his apartment that had a playground.

She finally found the place, a tree-lined clearing in a block of typical San Francisco terrace houses. Bare dirt, a swing set, a couple of picnic tables.

She parked, got Charley out of the back seat and walked toward the meeting place. Fog swirled like the breath of ghosts, and she couldn't tell if Luke was there or not. She shivered, pulling her cardigan together in front.

She moved around the perimeter, looking for him, but saw only a few pedestrians hurrying to work. Well, she could go to his apartment if he didn't show up.

Or had he lied, set up this meeting and skipped out on her?

Charley spotted him first. "There's that man," he said, pointing with his fistful of crushed animal crackers.

Grace whirled, her heart hammering.

"'Morning," Lucas said, striding up, almost wraithlike through the tendrils of fog. "Sorry I'm late."

"Oh, well, really, I just got here myself," Grace stammered.

She couldn't help staring at him as he ruffled Charley's hair and pointed to the swing set. He was taller than she'd first thought. And leaner. Of course, she hadn't failed to notice just how well built he was when she'd seen him in nothing but that towel. That had embarrassed the wits out of her, but later when she'd thought about her shyness and confusion, she realized she'd never been alone with a half-naked man who was a complete stranger to her.

Luke was most certainly a man. He was also unlike any male she'd ever known. The strong, silent type, she guessed, his emotions well hidden from the world. He was a bit like a black hole in space—he took in everything but gave back nothing. She couldn't help her professional curiosity where he was concerned. Why did he keep so much to himself? Did he ever let his hair down? What would it take to peel away those layers of self-containment and get to the real Luke Sarkov?

"Mommy—" Charley tugged on her hand "—can I go on the swings?"

"Ah, sure, of course," she said.

Charley didn't like the wet seat of the swing. He wasn't used to a damp climate; Boulder was so arid. She searched in her bag for a tissue or hankie to wipe off the seat, but couldn't find a thing.

"Here," Luke said, taking over. He dried the seat with his rumpled handkerchief and then set Charley on it. "So," he said to Grace, turning back to her, idly pushing the swing for Charley, "what was so vital that it couldn't wait till a civilized hour?"

He did look rough around the edges, a day's growth on his cheeks and upper lip, his blue eyes a little less clear than she recalled. Of course, he'd been out on the town last night. When she'd called to ask if they could get together, he'd slurred his words. Was Luke a party man? Perhaps even an alcoholic? But wouldn't her father have warned her?

"Well?" He kept pushing Charley, but his eyes were fixed on her.

"Oh," she said, switching her gaze to the child, watching as Luke pushed him higher and higher, the chains that held the swing creaking and squealing. "I need to give you Dad's cell phone number. We talked about Charley tagging along on their trip, but how are we going to get them together? I mean, what if Dad's house is being watched now?"

He pushed Charley even higher. "Faster! Faster!" Charley was crowing, absolutely delighted.

"You got me out at this hour to ask me that?"

"Well, yes, I…"

Luke sighed. "I'm working on it."

"That's it? You're working on it?"

"Uh-huh." He went back to entertaining Charley.

God, he was infuriating. He was treating her like the little woman who needed to be coddled. But *she* was the fugitive. *She* was the one who'd put it all on the line.

"I'd like to know what your so-called plan is."

"Didn't say I had a plan."

"I know. You're working on it."

"Uh-huh."

She seethed. She could throttle men like him. And then, as she nervously watched him push Charley far too high, it struck her—Luke Sarkov was the perfect antithesis to her former boyfriend, Mr. Anal Retentive, who worked solely by the clock.

Luke had no schedule whatsoever. She knew he

lived in the moment, existed, as did so many big-city cops, for those incredible highs in life, the moments of fear and danger and thrill all rolled into one life-infusing, bloodcurdling package. The element of danger that smoldered in him, waiting to be reignited, both repelled and drew her, keeping her off balance, tense, waiting for something she couldn't begin to fathom but sensing that something was just around the corner.

"You know," she said, "I need to be with Charley when he's turned over to his grandparents' care. I won't let you—"

"I already factored that in."

"You did?"

"And that's why I'm going to let you go partway to Denver with me. You and Charley."

She felt a flash of triumph, but she said nothing. She knew better than to push her luck.

"Higher!" Charley was yelling.

"That's enough," Grace cut in. "Charley, you're going to fall. *Charley*... Luke, that's high enough."

"He's fine. Are you fine, kiddo?" Luke kept right on pushing the seat.

"I'm having fun! Look at me, Mommy!"

Men, she thought, her heart racing each time his little backside came up off the seat at the crest of the arc. She shook her head and stood there trying not to watch, her arms wrapped protectively around her body, her lips pressed together tightly. And she was profoundly relieved when Charley had enough of the swing.

Luke finally turned to her. "You're cold," he said, frowning.

"Only terrified." Humor was not her strongest point.

"How about we go to my place and I'll make a few calls. Maybe talk about those plans."

His apartment was only a block from the park. They walked, Charley hanging on her hand, skipping and singing to himself.

"He's got lots of energy," Luke observed.

"More than I do."

"All kids like that?"

"Pretty much."

"He's a handful."

"Well, he'll crash after lunch. He's really going to need a nap today."

He unlocked the door of his apartment. Grace went in, tugging Charley's hand.

"Can I watch TV?" the boy asked, then quickly added, "please."

"Sure." He turned on the set and surfed around with the remote controls until he found a Power Rangers cartoon.

"This cool?" he asked.

"Uh-huh," Charley replied.

Luke poured himself a cup of coffee from the pot still warming in the coffeemaker.

"Want some?" He lifted the pot.

"No, thanks." As before, she sat on the edge of his couch, knees together, hands folded in her lap. Luke seemed distracted, his brows drawn, as he pondered something. He stood in his tiny kitchen, leaning back against the counter, cup in hand, a foot crossed over the other ankle. Grace could have been invisible. The only sounds were the canned cartoon noises from the television.

She couldn't help looking at the huge blown-up photograph of a woman that hung on the wall, the same one she'd noticed yesterday. It seemed out of place with the photos of sailboats and mountains. The woman was very beautiful, with long dark-red hair. She was wearing a flowered sarong and sitting on a rock at the seashore. Wind blowing her hair, the sarong plastered wetly to her body. The photograph was a bit grainy because of the size, but very lovely. Who was she?

Not wanting him to catch her staring at the photo, she turned away. Luke was punching numbers into his phone. She didn't wish to appear too interested in the conversation, but she heard every word he said. She heard, but she didn't understand a lot of it.

"So, Stanley, I need a little news," Luke said. *Who was Stanley?* "What's with the feds hanging around the Bennetts' house?" Silence as he listened. "That right? Out of Denver? Are we talking a serious beef here or are they just..." He listened again. "Oh, so that's it. I wondered. You know, just got to keep my hand in." More listening. "What's that name again? Hmm. No, never did, but Denver's a different universe. Okay, Stan, and thanks."

Who *was* Stanley?

"So," Luke said, "your case is in the hands of a hotshot special agent out of the Denver FBI office. She's after you, all right. San Francisco FBI is co-operating."

"Oh," Grace said. She could feel the blood leaving her face. "She?"

"Yeah, name's Renee Paynter. Sounds like a tough cookie."

''Oh, dear Lord.'' She laid her hand on her fore-head.

''They don't know where you are yet, but you need to keep up all the precautions. You have enough cash?''

''For a while.''

''We still have to get—'' he gestured with his head toward Charley ''—him to your folks.''

''It won't be dangerous, will it?''

''No, nothing like that. No gunfights,'' he said dryly.

''But how...?''

''Somewhere outside the city.''

''So you really have a plan?''

''Maybe.''

''Please, don't be so mysterious. You said some-thing about my going along part of the way to Den-ver, so I assume you'll try to lose a tail on my parents and then we can get Charley safely with them. Am I right so far?''

He smiled thinly. God, but he annoyed her.

''Why won't you confide in me?'' she demanded.

''I haven't worked it all out. When I do...'' He trailed off.

''You'll tell me. If it were just me, but we're deal-ing with a little boy. I don't want him traumatized.''

''I'm taking that into consideration.''

''Good.'' She glanced down at her lap, then up again, her gaze drawn once more to the photograph of the beautiful woman who dominated Luke's apart-ment. She looked away quickly.

''I'll get in touch with your father today. I figure tomorrow we'll go for it.''

She let out a breath. ''Tomorrow.''

"Uh-huh. And by Reno, Nevada, the switch should be a done deal. You can fly back from there."

"I'm going all the way to Denver."

"I don't think so." He shook his head.

"I'll change my appearance. I'll…"

"No."

"But I know Kerry Pope. I know Denver. I can help."

"Is there something wrong with your hearing?"

"You need me."

"Need an untrained woman? A professor? That's a laugh."

"Don't you patronize me," she said, trying to keep her voice down so Charley wouldn't hear. "I wouldn't hinder you. You just don't want to admit that I could help…" She stopped short, near tears, her voice catching. Then abruptly she got up and walked to a window and stood looking out, not seeing, her eyes blurred.

"Look, Grace…"

She pivoted to face him. "You think I could bear to stay here, changing safe houses every night, while Charley's with my parents somewhere and you're in Denver? And I'm just marking time, alone, not knowing what's going on?" She shook her head. "No way. I won't do that. You're not going to do that to me."

He didn't say anything for several moments, just scowled at her, his blue eyes flinty. She was afraid, but she suppressed the fear and met his gaze. She simply would not be left behind.

There was an infinitesimal shift in his stance and she knew, just *knew,* she had made headway.

In a barely controlled voice, she pressed on. "I'm... Luke, do I have to beg you?"

"Good God," he muttered.

"I will. I'll beg if I have to, I'll do anything."

She saw his eyes flash, but he tempered whatever was going on inside him, and then he said in barely a whisper, "Okay."

"What?" The word burst from her.

"I said *okay*." Frustrated, he ran a hand through his hair. "But I'm warning you. Damn it, Grace, if you interfere in any way, if you screw me up, if you do something dumb, you're history. And before we're anywhere near Denver, you're going to get a makeover. I mean a whole new look. Do you understand?"

She drew herself up and stared him down. "I'm not a child, you know. Your success is far more important to me than it is to you."

He quirked a lip, exasperated, but she didn't care. Her spirits soared. She was going with him!

"Is there anything else I should know about?" she asked. "Something I need to do?"

"Just be ready to leave tomorrow."

"I'll be ready, don't worry." She wanted to ease the tension between them somehow; they'd be spending so much time together from now on, and she couldn't face that with an enemy. She was such a coward.

She stood and went over to Charley. "Come on, sweetie, let's go."

Charley complained. "But it isn't over. The good guys have to beat out the bad guys. *Mommy*."

"We have to go. Mr. Sarkov is busy. He has a lot of things to do."

"Hey, Charley," Luke said, surprising her, "you know the good guys are going to win in the end, don't you?" He patted Charley on the head. "They always do, kiddo."

CHAPTER EIGHT

THE MOUNTAINS JUTTED UP on the horizon. Luke drove along Interstate 80 through Gold Run, Baxter and Emigrant Gap, up into the Sierra Nevada, staying a good quarter mile behind the FBI sedan that was tailing Big Bob's RV.

Ahead lay the California-Nevada border and Route 89, the road that twisted through the Tahoe National Forest, where Bob planned on getting lost.

But first, Luke knew, they had to shake the feds.

He'd had no trouble spotting them. They'd tailed Bob and Sally Bennett's RV from a block away from their Oakland home. Two broad-shouldered, clean-shaven young agents in dark suits, their eyes hidden behind sunglasses.

When Luke had been a cop, occasionally dealing with the FBI, it had never ceased to amaze him how they stuck out like sore thumbs. And they didn't care. They seemed to wear their dark suits and the ubiquitous sunglasses as a badge of pride. Well, today that had worked in Luke's favor.

He glanced at the mileage signs. Fifteen miles and he'd call the sheriff's department in Soda Springs and implement the plan. There was no doubt in Luke's mind that it would work.

"Jackson, Mississippi," Charley said from the back seat. He pronounced it *Missippi.*

"Right, sweetie," Grace said. "Now, how about the big big state where the cowboys live?"

"Wyoming?"

"No. Bigger."

"Oh! I know. Montana."

"Uh-huh. You remember the pretty lady who lives in the cowboy state?"

"Uh-huh. Helen."

"Helena."

"Hel-en-uh."

"That's it."

Grace and Charley had been playing the state capital game for an hour, and Luke couldn't believe how quick the kid was. Well, to be precise, how cleverly Grace had put together the game. Each state had a nickname that appealed to a boy. Like the cowboys and Montana. Then Grace had made up associations for the capitals, such as the pretty Helena whom all the cowboys liked. Obviously, Charley had learned the capitals with no trouble, and Luke would bet the boy would retain the information for life.

"How about the state with the big rocks and the ocean and the seals?" Grace asked.

"Oregon. Sail 'em up to the rocks and see all the seals."

Luke frowned. "Salem? I don't think that's right."

But she only smiled and said, "Want to make a bet?"

He thought about that, then shook his head. "I'll pass."

Despite his annoyance, feeling as if he were a baby-sitter to these two, he had to admit that so far the trip was nothing like he'd envisioned. Not once had Charley whined or wiggled or asked the inevitable: "When are we going to get there?" Luke had always figured car trips with kids had to be the low point of parenting. Not that he'd ever had the experience. Foster parents didn't take their charges on road trips, nor did they play clever mind games with them. Well, *most* foster parents didn't. All they did was collect the state compensation checks.

He glanced at Grace, feeling enormous respect for her. She was a devoted mother, gentle and loving. Now he knew she was smart, too—a teacher who was able to put theory to practical use. The boy was well adjusted. He clearly felt secure and knew his boundaries. Lucky, lucky boy.

They were on North Dakota when he had to interrupt. "Sorry, Grace," he said, catching the mileage sign, "but I need you to dial that number for me now."

"Okay. Yes, sure," she said, taking up the cell phone, which had been plugged into the cigarette lighter, charging. "Charley," she said, pivoting for a moment, "you play with your computer game for a few minutes, all right? Mommy has to make a call."

She dialed the number of the sheriff's department in Soda Springs and handed the cell phone to Luke. He took it, noted that the FBI sedan was some six vehicles ahead of him, and then he gave Grace a nod. He noticed she was clasping her hands whitely. He mouthed, "Take it easy."

He got the sheriff in person. It was, after all, a very small town. And then he identified himself as Officer Pacheco of the San Francisco PD, gave a phony badge number and told the sheriff he was on a code 603— apprehension of a stolen vehicle.

"I could use some backup, Sheriff," Luke said.

"I've been trying to catch up with these carjackers for sixty miles and I've got them spotted. They're about six miles west of Soda Springs right now, dark-blue Buick sedan, two men, both in suits and sunglasses, and get this, the car is FBI, government plates, stolen this morning."

The sheriff couldn't have been more enthusiastic. "You bet, we'll nab those SOBs for you." No doubt he saw a commendation plaque on his office wall. "Take me just a couple minutes to intercept," the sheriff said, and he was apparently off and running. Luke could just see the scene, siren blasting, lights flashing all the way to the entrance to the interstate. He'd probably bring in the whole fleet of patrol cars, too.

"Okay," Luke said, "call your dad's cell phone now, Grace. Tell him we'll be at the truck stop in fifteen minutes. And tell him don't forget the screwdriver and license plates. We've got to make this quick."

"Got it," she said, taking the phone from Luke, dutifully punching in Bob's number.

Now it was just a matter of waiting.

They didn't have to wait long. Less than an eighth of a mile past the eastbound Soda Springs entrance to the interstate, the sheriff was pulling the sedan over, sirens and lights going full bore. Luke drove by slowly, saw the FBI agents turned toward each other, one gesturing wildly, obviously mad as a hornet at being stopped. Wait till the sheriff put them through the stolen-car routine, Luke thought, unable to stifle a grin.

Grace was turned in her seat, also watching the scene. He saw the excited rise and fall of her chest and could hear the quick intake of her breath. It struck him how thrilling all this must seem to the staid professor, thrilling and frightening at the same time. For a moment, he was curiously glad she was along to see the bait and switch. As she'd said in San Francisco, she wouldn't have been able to stay in the shadows, wondering, worrying, doing nothing. Then he caught himself. Glad she was along? Was he nuts? He resented the hell out of her presence. He'd been sort of looking forward to the trip, getting away from Metropole, doing a bit of real investigating. Him versus the bad guys. Bad *woman,* that was.

Anyway, he thought, if he'd known about Grace insisting on making this trip when Bob had first called, he would have said no way. Sorry, no can do.

How had he gotten into this predicament? Was he getting soft? Losing his edge now that he'd been away from the streets for months?

Damn.

But then there was Charley, who so desperately needed Grace. He had to do this for the boy. No matter how much time he had to spend with Grace, the boy was worth it.

"Oh, wow," he heard her say as she spotted the exit ahead and the towering truck-stop sign. And then he had a flash—he'd been here a few times before, in this same car, but with Judith. They'd always gassed up here both coming and going from ski trips to the Tahoe resorts. A spurt of regret shot through him before he forced it aside.

He exited and gave Grace a surreptitious glance. So very different from Judith. Different in every way. Including physical appearance.

"Are we going to see Gramma and Grampa now?"

Charley pressed his nose to the window, struggling excitedly against his seat belt.

"In just a minute," Grace said, letting out another ragged breath.

"It'll be fine," Luke told her. "You just hold up your end. Got that?"

"But what if that FBI car is already back on the road? I mean…"

"They aren't," he assured her. "But we can't dawdle, okay? Bob and I will switch plates on the RV, and you take care of Charley." He turned into the truck stop, pulling around to the parking area behind the gas pumps. "There they are."

"Okay," Grace breathed, "okay."

The switch went quickly. Parked behind some trees, the RV shielding them, Luke and Bob put a set of designer California plates on the RV, while Sally and Grace hugged and threw Charley's belongings into the side door of the camper. Charley was jumping with excitement, crying, "We're going fishing, huh, Gramma?" But Grace was looking stressed, her face white, her teeth worrying her lower lip.

When Bob said, "Okay, guys, in the RV now. We're outta here," both Grace and Sally clutched hands. Then Grace gave Charley a hug that must have cracked his little ribs. She started to cry.

"Grace," Luke urged, "Bob's got to get going before the feds check out this exit. *Grace?*" *Goddamn.*

"I know, I know," she said, her voice breaking. She put Charley down and then squatted in front of him. "Sweetie, you have fun fishing and camping and Mommy will call every day. Okay?"

"Okay, Mommy. Let's go, Grampa!"

"I love you, Charley." Grace wept, and at that

point Luke had to haul her to her feet and drag her to his car.

"It will be fine," Sally called out.

Bob stepped into the driver's seat, giving a thumbs-up.

"I love you, Charley," Grace kept saying as Luke gently but firmly pushed her down into the passenger seat. Thirty seconds later they were pulling back onto the interstate, while Bob and Sally and Charley took off driving north on Route 89. Luke gave a last glance at the RV as it lumbered up the twisting road along with at least four other RVs, all heading toward the national forest. No way was the FBI going to find them. Charley was safe for now.

"Oh, God." Grace was still crying. "I'm sorry, but I didn't realize... I mean, Charley..."

He clenched his jaw. What could he say? It had to be done. So the kid was safe. That was what was important. Then the thought snuck into his head: had anyone cried like that over him?

"I already miss him. Will he be okay? What if the FBI...?"

"They won't find them. If the campgrounds that Bob plans to visit are like the ones I've seen in the summers, they can stay lost for weeks in the crowds."

"Are you sure?"

"Yes, I'm sure."

She sniffed and took off her glasses, wiping at her tears, embarrassed, shooting him an apologetic smile. "I trust you. I really do trust you and Dad. It's just...oh, hell," she said, swearing uncharacteristically, "I'm being a bigger baby than Charley, aren't I?"

Luke glanced over. "Nah. I'd say it's a mother

thing.'' But she didn't exactly look like a mom right now. Her glasses lying in her lap, her cheeks and nose pink—and why hadn't he noticed that bridge of freckles on her nose before?—her hair cascading from its clip... Grace, Professor Grace Bennett, looked soft and vulnerable and not too bad.

Whoa, he told himself suddenly. He wasn't that hard up. He put his eyes back on the road and kept them there.

RENO SAT on the high-desert floor only a few miles past the California-Nevada border. He couldn't believe the urban sprawl outside of the city, a city that had sprung up like a mushroom after a spring rain; except in this arid, hot climate, Luke doubted a mushroom could grow.

While Las Vegas was glitz and glamour, Reno still retained its western atmosphere. The only real changes Luke noted were the number of subdivisions skirting the city and, of course, a few new casinos.

At the second exit, he turned to Grace, who had been quiet for miles, merely staring out the passenger window, her thoughts locked tightly inside.

"We should stop here for the night," he said, trying to be civil.

"Mmm," she said.

"Is that okay? Get a fresh start in the morning?"

She turned and gave him a weak smile. "That's fine. Anywhere you like."

"I'll try downtown, then. One of the older motels. We can get dinner...."

"I'm really not hungry. But thanks, anyway."

"Fine," he said, "whatever."

Well, *he* at least was hungry. And he was trying to

be reasonable. He was trying to understand her distance right now. She'd just suffered the separation from her child, the child she'd given up everything for. Okay. Still, they had to eat and they had to sleep and he sure as hell wasn't going to drive all night while she sulked.

"This place on the left look okay?" he asked, Mr. Friendly.

"Sure. I'm sure it's fine." Then she sat up straight. "Oh, here, let me give you some cash. How much do you think the rooms are?"

Luke parked in front of the office, opened his door and was smote by the inferno outside. "Not much. And I'll take care of the rooms."

"Oh, no, I won't let you…"

"Let's not argue. We'll even it up later." He got out and closed the door, effectively shutting off her protests.

He paid for two rooms next to each other, parked, got out again and handed her the key to her room. "It's right over there, first level." He nodded. "I'll get your stuff. Go on in."

"Oh, here, I can carry—"

"Damn it, Grace," he snapped. Then he ran a hand through his hair. "Sorry, but for once will you just follow directions without an argument?"

She looked down at her sandals. "Sorry. You bring the bags, while, I, ah, open up the rooms…my room, that is."

"Do that," he said, the late-day sun beating down on his shoulders.

He spent the next half hour in his room, trying to get the air-conditioning to work. He was hungry, hot and tired and in a foul mood. The air in the rooms never got above stuffy, and he couldn't stop smelling the cheap disinfectant they used in the bathrooms. He lay on the bed, TV on, hands behind his head, and glanced around—cream-colored stucco walls done over cinder blocks. The seams showed through. Green-and-pink-and-yellow patterned curtains and bedspread, green patterned carpet ruined by cigarette burns and a few large circular stains. Of course, you weren't supposed to come to Reno and hang out in a motel room. The whole place, like Las Vegas, was geared to lure you into the casinos.

Not a bad idea, he mused.

But first some food. Idly, he wondered if Grace had changed her mind.

He got up, opened his door and rapped on hers. She answered his knock at once.

"Oh, hi, I got hold of Mom and Dad, and I talked to Charley." She was beaming, breathing as if she'd run a race. "They're all fine. In a campground. They wouldn't say where, of course, but Charley went on and on about helping Dad buy worms and how they were going fishing first thing in the morning. I'm so relieved. Well, you know."

"I'm glad they're okay," Luke said. Then, "Listen, I'm going to get a bite to eat now. I just thought I'd check in again, see if you were hungry yet." He shrugged.

But she wasn't. She wanted to shower and lie down and close her eyes. "I feel as if I just climbed Mount Everest," she said. "Crazy, huh?"

"You've been through a lot," he allowed. "Well, see you in the morning, then. Early. Right?"

"Oh, yes, no problem, I always get up early, anyway."

"Good. Well, later, huh?"

"Yes, sure. 'Night.' "

"Yeah," he said, and she closed her door.

He ate at the casino adjoining the motel and wandered into the gaming arena. Bells and whistles and coins clanking into trays met his senses not unpleasantly. When a cocktail waitress dressed as a cowgirl stopped and asked if he wanted a drink he said sure.

"Are you gambling?" she inquired.

"Why not," he said, knowing the drink was then on the house.

He bought fifty dollars' worth of chips, figuring when they were gone so was he—back to his room and to bed. The cocktail waitress found him eyeing a craps table, getting a sense for the crowd and the play. He felt curiously at home here, though he was not really a gambler. Because of the people, he supposed, as he glanced around. Over there was a guy Luke would swear was a vacationing cop. And there, a hooker, hanging on the arm of either a bookie or a drug dealer. Luke felt he should recognize which.

Must be slipping, he thought.

And then, as he was tossing a couple of chips onto the Come Line, getting a feel for the action at the craps table, he spotted someone who could have been Manny Morelli's twin brother.

His mood deflated a notch. That son of a bitch Morelli. Luke's best chance at redemption and Morelli was no chance at all.

Morelli... Judith and her banker friend and those damn divorce papers that would still be waiting for him when he got back to San Francisco—he guessed he could run, but he couldn't hide.

He won the bet, then moved his winnings to a hard

eight—two fours. An older woman in a big Stetson was on the dice and having a gay old time, her eyes glassy, her makeup worn off probably eight hours ago.

She let out a cowgirl yelp and threw the dice. Two fours. Luke had won again. He moved his winnings back to the Come Line. This lady was hot.

Judith, he thought anew, holding his empty cocktail glass up for the waitress to see. Could Judith be right? Had their marriage been over for years and he was too stupid to know it?

"The point is eight, a two and a six. The lady in the hat wins again," the croupier called out, paying the winners with deft fingers.

"Oh, whee, I'm on a roll!" the lady cried, and everyone cheered her on.

And Luke mused, yeah, he was on a roll, too.

CHAPTER NINE

GRACE AWOKE in a strange room, the drapes pulled shut, the room dark, the unfamiliar thump of a door closing somewhere. She sat up with a start, her heart banging, and tried to fight through the fog of sleep. For a moment her mind screamed at her, *Where am I?*

Then recollection flooded back like a wave of cold water. A motel. A motel in Reno. Of course. No one knew where she was but Luke. Charley was safe with his doting grandparents, and no one knew exactly where they were, either. Grace herself had no idea, nor did Luke.

Okay, she thought. *Okay.* Everything was all right, under control. She was on her way back to Denver with Luke, who was going to dig up hard evidence to take Kerry Pope out of the running for Mother of the Year.

The first thing she did was pick up her cell phone, which she'd dutifully set on the recharger for the night, and dialed her parents' cell phone number.

"Good morning," came her dad's distinctive voice.

"It's me, Dad."

"Well, it was either you or Luke. You're the only ones with the number."

"I won't ask where you are. But everything's okay?"

"Just fine. Your mother is spoiling that boy of yours. He may never recover."

"She's entitled. Is Charley around?"

"Since this place isn't exactly the Taj Majal, I guess I can find him. Charles, my boy, it's your mom."

"Mommy," Charley said, and Grace felt herself relax, her whole body reacting to his familiar piping voice.

"Hi, sweetie. You been a good boy?"

"Um, well, I, um, spilled my orange juice, Mommy."

"That's not being bad. That's an accident, angel."

"Oh."

"Are you having fun?"

"Boy, oh boy, this RB is way cool, Mommy."

"RB?"

"The big car, you know, that we're living in."

"Oh, the RV."

"That's what I said, Mommy."

Eventually, she hung up, relieved. Everything was going according to plan. Charley was in good hands. That was what really mattered. He'd told her that Grampa was taking him fishing. She knew that they were in the mountains somewhere, in a campground, but that was all. If the FBI caught her and questioned her, she couldn't give away their location, not even if she wanted to.

Visions popped into her mind of a medieval torture chamber, hot irons held to her feet, the rack stretching her joints. She still wouldn't give away Charley's location. And then she told herself she was being ridiculous. Psychologically, she was girding her loins, so to speak, for something that could never happen. She was inventing fantasy situations, not facing reality. Classic denial.

The question she needed to address was quite different from physical torture—it was mental torture, though. Oh, God, yes. What if she was caught, Charley was caught and she had to give him up to that woman?

That woman. Now she was evincing avoidance behavior. *His biological mother, Kerry Pope.*

She took a shower and dressed in one of the few tired items of clothing she'd brought along. A beige vee-neck T-shirt and a pair of brown linen-look slacks. Not that she was a fashion plate, but she was getting very tired of the clothes she'd packed. And she was justifiably hesitant to spend any of her cash to buy new clothing.

Thank goodness Luke could use his credit card to pay for their rooms and meals. *He* wasn't a federal fugitive.

Then, as she stepped into her sandals, she remembered Luke telling her that she would have to change her appearance before arriving in Denver. He was right, of course. But change her appearance how? And where was this transformation going to take place? When?

She supposed she'd better ask him. And wasn't it time they got back on the road?

She punched in his room number on the in-house telephone. Maybe they'd have breakfast together and then get going. The phone rang in his room. It rang over and over. He could be in the shower. Or downstairs eating breakfast. She'd wait awhile.

She turned on the TV and watched a news program, but the attractive morning-show host and hostess seemed utterly alien to her own life. The weather in the Sierras was warm, with the possibility of afternoon thunderstorms. The temperature on Donner Summit was only fifty-one degrees.

She phoned Luke's room again. No answer. A slight, gnawing worry assailed her. And impatience. If he'd gone out for breakfast, why hadn't he let her know?

Because he'd rather forgo her company, she thought. He was stuck with her for days—weeks, maybe. And she could tell he had small patience with her kind of female. The gorgeous woman in the photograph in his apartment was more Luke Sarkov's type.

She ran a brush through her hair, pulled it back and stuck a clip in. A few strands fell. Damn her fine, slippery hair. She stuck the loose ends behind her ears, grabbed her purse and room key and let herself out into the fresh air of morning.

The restaurant adjoining the office and casino was dim and smelled of cigarette smoke and coffee. It advertised a free breakfast for anyone producing a motel room key. Grace walked into the place and peered about, hoping to spot Luke. A few people sat at tables, drinking coffee, eating plates piled high with eggs and bacon and waffles. They all looked gray and exhausted, as if they'd been up all night.

They probably had—gambling.

Luke was not in the restaurant.

She used a house phone in the lobby to call his room again. No answer.

Panic assailed her. Had he left? Had he snuck out

and ditched her? No, no, he wouldn't. He... She strode out into the bright morning sun, straight to the parking lot. Oh, my God, what if he...?

The car was there, his shiny red convertible. He hadn't abandoned her. Where was he, then?

The bastard, she dared to think. She had never, ever thought of a man in that light, but Luke Sarkov was verging on fitting the description.

Where was he?

She went back inside the motel and tried one more call to his room. Damn, no answer.

She checked the restaurant again, then made her way into the casino. It was not at all like casinos you saw in the movies. No potted plants, neon lights, soft carpeting, huge expenses, men in tuxedos, women in gowns. No elegantly attired croupiers flipping cards expertly on green baize tables.

As far as casinos went, this one was small. Mostly it consisted of rows of slot and video poker machines. In daylight the place looked used up and tawdry, and the air reeked of booze and cigar and cigarette smoke. A few people were playing the video machines. Card games took up a corner of the large room.

She walked around the perimeter, searching for Luke. Up and down the aisles of slot machines, where grandmothers pressed buttons, oblivious to the world; where a young couple in black, with pierced noses and lips and eyebrows, stuck quarters into a poker machine; where a man in overalls and hard hat—obviously a construction worker—played some sort of a game with dinosaurs and lost-world explorers and pots of gold. No Luke.

The men at the card tables were slack-faced, wan

from fatigue, cheeks shadowed with whiskers. The odor of stale sweat emanated from them.

She finally found Luke at an empty table in a far corner, head down on his arms, passed out. He smelled, too, of liquor and smoke.

Distastefully, she shook him. Nothing. She shook his shoulder harder. "Luke," she said. "Wake up."

"Unh," he groaned.

"Wake *up*."

He raised his head, bleary-eyed. "What?"

"Luke, we have to get going. What are you doing here? Have you been...?"

"Sh," he rasped. "God, keep it down. My head."

His appearance was ghastly.

"Remember me? Grace Bennett? Remember the job we're doing? We have to get to Denver."

"Denver, yeah."

"You're drunk. You've been drinking."

"Right on, sister."

"I am not your sister." She was near tears she was so angry. She'd placed her life and Charley's into this man's hands, and he was completely undependable.

"Let's go," she said sharply.

"Sit down for a sec. Take it easy."

"I won't sit down. We have to get out of here and on the road. Are you capable of standing up?"

"Capable? Maybe."

"Can we go now?"

He didn't answer; he thrust his hand into his pants pocket and pulled out a wad of twenty-dollar bills, which he let drop on the beer-stained table. "Won for a change."

"Fantastic. Wonderful. Now, let's get going.

Please, Mr. Sarkov.'' She gave him a disgusted look.
''I'll drive.''

''Okey-dokey. I'll sleep. I feel like hell warmed
over.''

She tugged at his arm, got him on his feet. He
swayed while she scooped up his winnings. ''Down
to your room. I'll have coffee sent in. Take a
shower.''

''Yes, Mommy.''

She shot him a look. ''Just hurry. I can't believe
you'd do this. It's so...so irresponsible. My father
told me—''

''Don't you say a goddamn word about this to Big
Bob,'' he said harshly, abruptly sober.

''All right, but please, let's go.''

She was, frankly, afraid to leave him alone in his
room, figuring he'd just fall into bed and pass out, so
she stayed there with him. He was slow and cranky
and uncooperative, but she finally got him to take a
shower. She was angry and upset. How could he have
pulled this stunt?

Room service delivered a pot of coffee. She had
the waiter set the tray on the dresser, then grabbed
one of Luke's twenty-dollar bills, which she'd gathered up from the table, and handed it to the waiter,
not even noticing the man's eyes light up.

Luke was in the shower so long she began to get
anxious. Would she have to go to the bathroom and
drag him out of there?

But finally he emerged, towel around his waist, the
way he'd been attired when she had first visited his
apartment. This time he was pale and still unshaven
and his eyes were bloodshot.

''Coffee?'' she offered.

"Is that a question?" he asked.

"No."

"I didn't think so. Lots of sugar, please."

"Do you want me to order you breakfast?"

He groaned. "God, no."

He drank two cups of coffee and took clean clothes into the bathroom to dress.

She felt terribly uncomfortable in his room. Never in a million years would she ever have expected to be in this kind of situation, and she wasn't sure how to handle it. The forced intimacy with a stranger, the awkward silences, his obvious impatience with her—were all so different from her normal life, as if she'd landed on an alien planet. She didn't understand the people she had to deal with, and they didn't understand her.

Luke emerged from the bathroom dressed in a polo shirt and khakis. He still looked ill.

"Can we go now?" she asked.

"Yeah, just a minute."

"We could get to Denver tonight, but it would be an awfully long drive for one day."

"Let's see how it goes," he replied.

"The car keys?" she said, holding her hand out.

He stared at her for several seconds, evidently weighing the merits of letting her drive his car.

"I have a valid license," she said coolly. "I drove all the way here from Boulder without having an accident, you know."

Wordlessly, he reached in his pants pocket and gave her his keys. "It's a hard clutch," he said. "Can you drive stick shift?"

"Yes."

"All right. I'll check us out."

"Can you handle that chore, Mr. Sarkov?"

"Look, Grace, give me a little slack here."

"My child's life is at stake. I can't give you any slack. I can't give myself any, either."

His eyes got that flinty look. "Don't worry, *Professor*. I'll get the job done."

The silence between them was fraught with tension as Grace steered his car onto the interstate. Luke didn't say a word; neither did she. For a time he watched as she drove his small, peppy convertible; then, satisfied that she was competent, he closed his eyes, and soon he was asleep, his head lolling.

Turning off the interstate onto the two-lane highway that shortened the route between Reno and Denver, she drove down out of the Sierras, onto the barren high plains that stretched across the Great Basin all the way to the Rockies in Colorado. It got hotter as she descended, and she switched on the air-conditioning. At least it worked in his car.

Charley would have loved the sporty convertible, she thought, and tears burned in her eyes for a moment. She could have put the top down for him, and he would have had so much fun.

As she drove she almost enjoyed the powerful feel of Luke's car. He slept on, and although she was grateful she didn't have to deal with him awake, she found herself taking her eyes from the road quite often to glance at his profile.

A real man's man. Hard, flat cheek and jawlines; a good-size nose; short sandy-colored hair. His eyes— they were closed, but she recalled their hard blue stare. He was tough. But there was something behind that tough-guy facade that interested her. As a psychologist, of course.

So many questions. Who was the gorgeous woman whose photograph hung in his apartment? He obviously didn't live with her. Why was he no longer with the police force? Why had he dropped everything to help her? What exactly did he owe her father?

An enigmatic, difficult man. And his fall into utter irresponsibility last night—clinically speaking, she would have to say he was crying out for help with that kind of a lapse.

She knew so very well that everyone had problems, but this man, this Luke Sarkov with the faintly Slavic cheekbones and narrow eyes, a certain magnetic power yet a vast vulnerability, he was…well, he was intriguing.

She drove through the sere, vacant high desert for hours, until she saw signs announcing Eureka, Nevada. Yes, she recalled the tiny town. Downshifting, she slowed at the turnoff and pulled into the nearest gas station.

Luke jerked awake when the car stopped. He straightened and glanced around. "Where are we?"

"Eureka," she replied.

He rolled his neck as if it had gotten stiff. It probably hurt like hell, she thought with a certain satisfaction.

"You feeling any better?" she asked.

"I must be. I'm still alive." He opened his door and got out to fill the gas tank.

"I'm going to the ladies' room," Grace said. "Be right back."

They ate lunch at the only restaurant in town, a café that served burgers and steak and baked beans with iceberg lettuce salad and poison-pink dressing. At least Luke got some food in his stomach.

"You want me to drive now?" he asked as they walked out into the hot midday sun and they both put on their sunglasses.

She eyed him up and down from behind dark lenses, marveling at her newfound courage. "You still look shaky to me. Impaired, I'd say. I'll drive."

He didn't argue. His silence spoke eloquently for him as the miles rolled under the car's tires.

"Okay," she finally said, "we have to spend a lot of time together. I don't think it's healthy for us to be so antagonistic."

"Antagonistic. Wow. I just thought I was hungover," he said.

"You don't like me. You resent having to do this job. You certainly resent my company."

"Hey, hold on there, Grace. I don't dislike you. It's nothing personal. I'm glad your father asked me to do this. I like to pay my debts. And Charley deserves our help."

"If that is all true, then why did you go on a binge last night? Certainly you must have considered that it would jeopardize your...*our* enterprise."

He put his hand over his mouth. "God, you talk like a college professor."

"Answer my question, please."

"Why did I drink and gamble?" He was silent for a long while, staring out his window.

She waited, realizing the value of quietness. A useful tool a therapist employs.

"Why did I?" he finally said, then paused. "Hell, I don't know. It seemed like a good idea at the time. I've...had some problems lately... I suppose you could call it stress."

Grace drove on, the barren brown plains sliding

past endlessly, the sun making her squint even through sunglasses. She was aware she had to be very careful in how she handled Luke. He was prickly and defensive and undeniably chauvinistic.

"Do you want to talk about it?" she finally ventured. "I'm a good listener."

He gave a short laugh, then hunched down in his seat, seemingly asleep again.

But he wasn't asleep.

"My wife wants a divorce," he said very suddenly, his voice rough with discomfort. "Judith. She's even using her maiden name now. As though she never married me. Ten years we were man and wife, and she wants a divorce."

"I'm sorry," Grace said softly.

"Yeah, great, that's so much help."

She said nothing. Misdirected anger required no reply.

"She handed me the papers, the final divorce papers, and wanted me to sign them. You know what I did?" He turned toward her. "Mature Luke, that's me, I tore them up. As if that would stop it from happening."

"It's an understandable reaction." Grace waited a beat, then asked, "Is that your wife in the photograph in your apartment?"

"Yeah, that's Judith."

"She's very beautiful."

His mouth twisted. "Isn't she, though? Goddamn it, I was an idiot to think it could work. She was already a successful model when we met. We fell in lust, I guess you'd say. I've had a lot of time to think, too damn much time, and I figured it out. She got off on the dangerous side of my life, my job. A big bad

Vice cop. She liked my...shit, this is nasty stuff, Grace, and I'm sorry I'm dumping it on you.''

''No, no, please, go on.'' She tried a very small smile. ''It's better than antagonism.''

His voice became very quiet. ''She liked my gun.''

''A symbol of power. Authority.''

''The bitch.''

''You loved her. You say you still do. So you truly don't think she's a bitch.''

''Look, I'm angry, I admit it. I'm angry at her. She liked me as a cop, and when my job was over, so was our marriage.''

''That sounds like a superficial relationship. Was it, do you think?''

''No, of course I didn't think that. I loved her. I still do. And I think she still loves me, but she's too damn stubborn to admit it.''

''Yet you believe the reason she loved you no longer exists.''

''Yeah. No. Damn it, I don't know.''

''Tell me why you left the police force. Well, that is, if you feel comfortable doing so.''

''Hell, why not? What else is there to do?''

''It makes the time pass, at least. And you know all about my problems. Your turn.''

''Big Bob knows about it. Judith knows a little. Otherwise, nobody knows the real story. Nobody.'' He stopped, rubbed his jaw in a way she was finding familiar.

''I was a good cop,'' he said bitterly. ''I headed a team on the Vice Squad—drugs, prostitution, child pornography. I really felt I was doing something beneficial for society. Well, I was dumb. Naive, I guess. Idealistic. The guys on my team were pulling a scam, accepting drug money. Letting the dealers off. Hey, it's not new. Cops have been on the take…well, you read the papers. To make a long story short, I walked in on a deal going down. Right in front of me. My men, who I trusted with my life. I'll tell you—'' he let his head fall forward and shook it ''—it was like my world came apart.''

''What an awful thing.''

''So, they begged me. God, I promised. I owed them, like I said. I owed them my life. Jack saved me from a bullet once. Tom pulled me from a car a crackhead had rammed. I owed them. They needed money. They weren't bad men. It didn't hurt anyone, they said. Well, it did. Sure it did. But they were my guys. And there's that code of silence thing.''

''What did you do?'' she asked, her voice soft, nonjudgmental.

''I kept my mouth shut. But when one of the dealers who was paying them got arrested, he told Internal Affairs all about it. Received a light sentence instead of hard time. There was an investigation. It hit the papers. No proof, so nobody actually went to trial, but me and my guys were out on our asses. To put it politely, we were advised to resign. Case closed.''

''But you were innocent.''

''I couldn't tell IA that. First of all, they would have called bullshit on me. But more important, to prove myself innocent, I would have had to supply names and dates and amounts. I would have had to provide IA with proof to indict my team. I couldn't do it. I couldn't rat them out.''

''I see.''

''You couldn't possibly see. How in hell could you

begin to understand? The code is what we live by.''
He folded his arms tightly across his chest.

Grace held her tongue. No wonder, she thought, no
wonder. She understood now, his bitterness, his loss.
His world collapsing. And Judith. The loving wife.
Maybe he was right. Maybe Judith was indeed a
bitch.

He took his glasses off and squinted, rubbing a
hand across his face, then replaced them. He stared
straight ahead, the harsh lines around his mouth deepening.

''I probably can't understand exactly how you feel,
not emotionally. But believe me, I can understand
your decision on an objective basis.''

''Oh, good,'' he snapped.

''I'm not trying to be patronizing. In your line of
work, you needed a moral code to survive mentally,
emotionally. Even physically.'' She thought and
spoke very carefully. ''It was as necessary to you as
your weapon. It was your protection. And in view of
that, you did the right thing. No, wait, let's hypoth-
esize. What if you had ratted out your friends? They'd
be in prison now, and you'd still be with the police.
You think any of your co-workers would trust you? I
imagine you'd have been transferred to some other
position, something administrative. You'd be ostra-
cized.''

''Yeah.''

''Would that have been a better outcome?''

''Hell, no.''

''So, you made the only possible choice.''

He growled something.

''Can you live with your choice?''

"I *am* living with it, Professor. I have a new *career*," he sneered, "and here I am, right?"

"You might want to work a bit on acceptance."

"You're a real card, you know that?"

"Mmm," she said. "Can we stop up there for something cold to drink?"

They bought drinks and gas at a truck stop; Luke insisted on driving after that. He had to, she figured, for him to regain some of his authority and pride. Now, why did she analyze everyone and everything like that?

"Tell me," she said, as they crossed the dry, jagged mountains in central Utah, "what about the drug dealer who got easy time for giving your men up?"

"What about him?"

"Presumably he knows you weren't guilty of taking money."

"He knows." A scowl.

"Well, why didn't he tell them that? Those men in IA?"

"Oh, sure, a drug dealer do a cop a favor? He'd see me in hell first."

"This man...where is he?"

"In a minimum security prison in the San Quentin complex. Two years."

"You know him?"

"I know him."

"Could he be persuaded to help you out?"

That short bark of a laugh again. "Last time I saw him he told me to take a flying leap."

"Mmm."

"I'm the enemy. He hates my guts." He switched his gaze to her for a second, his dark lenses reflecting prisms of light. "You're out of your league here, Grace."

"He's a human being. Maybe he can be persuaded..."

"Manny Morelli a human being? That's a laugh." His eyes were back on the road, his profile sharp, his hands strong and competent on the steering wheel. "Drop the subject, Professor. You don't have a clue what you're talking about."

Wisely, she kept her mouth shut. But the new revelations about Luke crowded her brain. And then she realized she hadn't thought about Charley for a whole half an hour.

Charley. She wondered if he missed her. Was her mother spoiling him too much? Was Sally letting him eat too many sweets? What if he got one of his stomach upsets? He was prone to them—periodically he'd be awake all night throwing up. A childhood thing, her pediatrician had told her. He'd outgrow it. But her mother didn't know about the spells. Or had she told Sally?

Dusk was falling by the time they crossed the Colorado state line.

"It's too far to make it to Denver tonight," she said. "We can stop in Grand Junction. It's only a few miles ahead."

"Then how long is it to Denver?"

"Oh, three and a half—maybe four—hours. We'll be there by lunchtime tomorrow." She hesitated. "Are you tired? Do you want me to drive? It's getting dark."

"I'm fine," he said harshly.

"You don't have to speak to me like that."

He said nothing; his mouth tightened. The sun set

behind them as they followed Interstate 70 along the Colorado River. The Rockies lay ahead, but you couldn't see them yet. Strangely, she was glad to be back in Colorado. Despite the danger, despite what she had to face, she was happy to be home.

Luke hadn't spoken a word in ages, and she felt the need for some kind of communication between them. A woman would never have such a ridiculous reaction. They were, after all, stuck together for as long as it took to prove Kerry an unfit mother.

"That man," she began, "that man you called, what was it? Manny something."

"Morelli. Manny Morelli."

"Is there any way you could influence how long he stays in jail? I mean, could you talk to the parole board or something?"

"Grace, drop it."

"No, I don't think I will." She felt stubbornness harden in her. "What if you could trade something with him? Offer him time off for a word from him to your police department?"

"They won't hire me back."

"But your name would be cleared. Is that important to you, Luke?"

"Not at the expense of my men."

"No, certainly not. You said there was no proof against them in any case. All right, but what if this Manny person just said to them that you were not in on the deal?"

"I told you..."

"Yes, he wanted you to take a flying leap. But, and I'm assuming this, I bet you approached him in an authoritative way."

"*Authoritative,*" he mocked.

"Antagonistic."

"There you go again."

"Well, did you approach him like that?"

"How the hell do I know?"

"As a policeman, I'm sure you were trained to approach the criminal element that way." She paused, but he didn't answer. "There are other ways to deal with people. Productive ways. I could help you..."

"I don't need your goddamn help."

"But you're helping me. We could help each other. Just keep it in mind as a possibility."

A large green sign announcing the first Grand Junction exit loomed up out of the dusk, then flashed by.

"Is this place really *grand?*" Luke asked.

"No, but it's a nice small city. Friendly."

"I've never been to Colorado before," he admitted.

"Really?"

"I've been to the Northwest, the East Coast, the South. Never Colorado."

"It's a beautiful state. A wonderful place to live."

"Yeah, real wonderful. They took your kid away."

"That was an aberration. It could have happened anywhere."

There was silence for a while, then, "So, just out of curiosity, how would you approach Manny Morelli?"

"Oh, goodness, I'd have to ask you a million questions about him. Then I'd have to think about it. But you would need to treat him as an equal, show him respect. People respond to respect."

"*Respect.*" His tone dripped with disgust. "He's a criminal, and when he gets out of jail he'll go back to dealing drugs. Hell, maybe he's even doing it from his prison cell."

"You'd have to put your feelings about him aside, but it could work. I'd be glad to help you with the—"

"I was just curious," he said quickly but he shot her a sidelong glance, and he didn't sound angry for a change. Good, maybe she'd gotten through his defenses for a moment. He was a difficult man, but perhaps he'd never been treated well. Judith had wounded him. He had reason to be defensive.

His prickly side had softened and she thought it was safe to push a bit. At least he'd confided in her. But some pieces to the puzzle still didn't fit, or were entirely missing, and she needed them to understand him. The business about his owing her father his life. What had he meant by that?

"So," she began cautiously, "why were you willing to drop everything and help me out?"

"Big Bob asked me to."

"I know, but...well, it seems like an awful lot to ask."

"I owe him."

"You said that." She let the silence build.

"Curious, aren't you?"

"Yes. It comes with my profession."

He drove on, staring straight ahead. Outside the car, the arid flat landscape slid by in the deepening hues of a desert evening. Finally he spoke. "Not many people know about me. Your father does, though."

She said nothing.

"Look—" his voice turned harsh "—I was an orphan. My mother disappeared somewhere. I never knew my father. I lived in foster homes. Lots of them. Bob helped me out in a real bad time in my life. Okay, are you satisfied?"

No wonder, she thought, and all the pieces of the puzzle slipped into place.

"You seem to have compensated extraordinarily well." She tried to keep a neutral tone. Her heart beat fast, though. Sympathy overwhelmed her.

He gave a short laugh. "Sure, I'm a real golden boy, aren't I? Screwed up big-time."

"You did what you had to do. That counts for a lot."

"Yeah, a job at Metropole Insurance," he said acidly.

"But you're good at your job."

"Uh-huh."

"Dad said you're an excellent investigator."

"So what?"

"So, you're the one he asked to help me. That shows his confidence in you." She was trying to bolster Luke's self-esteem, but oh, it was hard going.

"Yeah, Bob has confidence in me. He's about the only one."

"*I* have confidence in you," she said softly.

He turned his head for a second, met her eyes, then turned back to the road.

"I feel for your boy," he said after a long time. "I guess you'd say I identify with him."

"Mmm." It was terribly hard for him to admit this, she knew.

"I'll get him back for you. Every kid deserves a mother, a stable home. Hell, I'm the best example of what happens when you don't have those things."

"You've done just fine," she said. "Don't denigrate yourself."

"*Denigrate,*" he mocked. "Hey, I love it when you talk dirty."

And he didn't say another word until the road sign announced Grand Junction, Horizon Drive.

"We can get off here," she said. "This is where all the motels are."

"Whatever you say, Professor."

His voice was lighter than normal. Excellent. Perhaps their working relationship was improving. And that was important. She needed Luke's cooperation, and he needed hers. They had to be a team, not two bickering strangers.

A team. So they could save Charley. That was all that mattered, after all. She had to focus on that and not on the unfamiliar way her stomach rolled over whenever he called her Professor.

She had to concentrate on Charley.

CHAPTER TEN

THE MORNING SUN outside the window of the Grand Junction motel was ferociously bright. This was the desert, Luke had to remind himself, and not the mild, sea-influenced coast he was used to.

He felt so much better this morning he almost laughed out loud. God, what a fool he'd made of himself yesterday. Up all night, then hungover, falling asleep in the car. Missed most of Nevada and half of Utah while Grace drove. He cringed mentally. No one had ever driven his car before—never.

And then she'd pulled that "I'm a good listener" crap, that psychological mumbo jumbo, and he'd blabbed like a total wimp.

Damn, he was embarrassed. He had poured his guts out to that woman. He'd never let anyone see that deep inside. Not his wife, not even his cop buddies. Ever.

He got into the shower, remembering yesterday morning in Reno, how Grace had stayed in his room while he'd showered, how horrible he'd felt. What a mess he'd made of this situation so far. He was a jerk.

And Grace. He realized he had no idea anymore what to make of her. Sure, there was still that shy, bookish side to her, which was utterly alien to his experience. But there was another Grace Bennett he hadn't allowed himself to recognize. A strong Grace, a woman abounding with insight and compassion.

She was filled to overflowing with goodness and courage and sacrifice. The enormity of what she'd given up for her foster child amazed Luke.

She'd been really annoyed with him yesterday, and he didn't blame her, yet still she'd listened, not making fun of him, not even venturing one word in judgment. Was that her psychology training or *her?*

It was her, he decided. He'd seen the way she was with Charley; he knew what Big Bob thought of her. Grace was purely and simply a worthy human being.

Unlike Judith. Unlike *him.*

It occurred to Luke as he shaved that it must be hellishly difficult for Grace to spend all this time with him, to be stuck—trapped, really—with a man so different from what she was used to—college professors. Gentle, intellectual, tweedy types.

His brain was spinning as he confronted emotions he'd never touched on before. Seeing the world, himself, from another person's point of view. And he felt a dart of misgiving stir inside him somewhere, because he admired Grace, he respected her.

Goddamn, he had even grown to like her. Never in a million years would he have figured he'd be attracted to her type.

Grace? With that scraped-back hair and those glasses and her innate shyness and timidity? *Impossible.*

Ouch. He'd nicked his chin. He stanched the blood, stuck some tissue on the cut and finished shaving.

Professor Grace Bennett. Crazy.

He decided right then that the only way to handle this situation was to clam up and reestablish the distance between them. Yeah, he'd slip back into his old comfortable shell. He convinced himself he'd be doing her a favor.

Nevertheless, there was tomorrow and a whole lot of tomorrows ahead. With her. He had to right their relationship, though he wasn't stupid—he knew it could never go back to the way it had been.

How could he have confessed to her like that?

He dressed and took a deep breath. Okay. Yesterday was history. Today the worm had turned. He was in control of this situation once more, and he'd remain like that. Speaking of which, he thought, no way were they going to Denver, only a few miles from Boulder, until Grace radically changed her appearance.

During breakfast at Denny's next door to the motel, he put both hands on top of the table and looked her in the eye. "Today," he stated flatly, "before we leave here, you get that makeover."

She stared at her plate.

He made an impatient gesture with one hand. "I don't know what you call it…a makeover. You know, part of the deal before we left San Francisco. You change your hair, lose those glasses, maybe get new clothes, too. And no argument," he added. "Either you alter your appearance entirely or I swear I'll put you on a plane back to San Francisco today. It's too dangerous for you in Denver. San Francisco was one thing—your face hasn't been plastered all over the place—but we both know Denver is close to Boulder…"

"Okay," she said, shrugging, "I agreed to do that. By noon you won't recognize me."

They went to the Mesa Mall. While Luke tagged along, she made an appointment at a one-hour optical shop, then walked over to a beauty salon and did the same. Then she said she was going to do some clothes shopping.

"Give me till one o'clock, all right?"

"That long?"

"Luke," she said, standing in the middle of the mall, "these things take time. Just meet me in front of the optical shop at, say, one. Will that work?"

"I guess," he said. Then he turned to leave. "Oh, you need a credit card. Use mine."

But she assured him she still had enough cash. He had absolutely no idea how much a makeover could cost, though he supposed she would know.

"One o'clock then," he said.

She smiled reassuringly. "I promise, you won't even know me."

"Uh-huh," he said, and he made off toward a sporting goods store. Three hours to kill. *Swell.*

LUKE SAT ON A BENCH in the center of the mall across from the optical shop, checking his watch. One p.m....1:05...1:10. No Grace.

Knees splayed, an arm outstretched on the back of the bench, he impatiently tapped his fingers on the wood. He'd never been good in malls. Where the hell was she?

Idly marking time, he people-watched. The air-conditioned mall was crowded on this blistering summer's day on the high desert of western Colorado. Damn. Despite his trained cop's eye, he must have missed her. Had to have been the crowds. He was momentarily distracted by a cute redhead with long legs, who was hurrying past a gaggle of teenagers, toting an oversize shopping bag.

Real cute. Short, spiked reddish-brown hair, big green eyes, skin the color of milk. She was wearing a black spandex top, no sleeves, three inches of bare skin showing between her black stretch capri pants and the scanty top. Not much bosom, but enough. And certainly no bra.

His eyes followed as she neared. Past the bookstore, past the jewelers. On the thin side, but she was shapely thin, like a lot of tall women. Of course, she was wearing two-inch wedged sandals, so maybe she wasn't all that tall.

In a hurry, yes, staring quickly into the optical shop before pivoting, the heavy bag swinging—

"Luke. Oh, gosh, I'm so sorry. I was…"

It took him a sec. "Grace?" he stammered.

Her lips, deep glossy rose-colored lips outlined in an even deeper shade, split into a white smile. "I was saying, I got hung up at the cosmetic's counter over at Penney's, and…Luke? What…? Oh, I guess I must look awfully different. I'll tell you, I certainly feel weird." She stood over him and blushed. "I told you you wouldn't know me."

"I, ah, yeah."

She put down the bag and ran her fingers through the stiff red spikes of her hair. "I don't know. I could have gone blond. Or black. But the girl said…well, never mind, what do *you* think? Am I recognizable?"

"Ah, no." He swallowed.

"Good. That was the idea. Oh, and I went with green contact lenses."

"I can see that."

"But I really never have too much success with contacts, especially in Colorado, where it's so dry. So I bought another pair of glasses." After rummaging, she produced them from the bag and put them on. Small oval frames that perched on her nose. "Punk, aren't they? I look like one of my students," she said.

"Yeah, I mean yes, I imagine you do."

"I guess we better get going." She shrugged, then started to pick up the bag, but somehow he found his feet and stood, taking the sack from her.

"Thanks," she said. "Car still in the same place?"

"Ah, sure, I hung out in here."

"Okay, then, let's go. We can be in Denver by six." She led the way, and he couldn't take his eyes off her, the thin shapely legs, the firm round bottom, the milky-white skin, that hair... Something in his belly seemed to give way, like a dam cracking, and he felt a hot rush of need saturate his insides. *Whoa,* he told himself. He'd pictured a lot of different scenarios about this trip. He'd figured he had them all factored in. But this he hadn't counted on.

As he followed her out into the sizzling afternoon and across the shimmering asphalt in the parking lot he broke into a sweat. "Goddamn," he muttered.

IT WAS GRACE'S IDEA to rent the two-bedroom apartment on the south side of Denver near the complex known as the Tech Center. He and Grace had checked out weekly rates at several motels, but because it was the height of the tourist and convention season, the rates had been sky-high.

Then Grace had remembered a short-term rental complex that was frequently used by visiting professors, and before Luke knew it, they were settled into the two-bedroom apartment.

He did not like the arrangement. Not only was he used to working alone, but this transformed Grace—

her appearance and even a more confident, carefree demeanor—was muddying the waters. Better, he thought, that they had taken two one-bedroom units. Except there hadn't been two available.

Grace surveyed the living room and adjoining kitchen unit, then stood near the couch, hands on her hips. He tried to see the place through her eyes: white walls; the absolute minimum of furniture, all of it upholstered in brown tweed synthetic fabric; beige industrial carpet; on the walls, cheap prints of snow-capped mountains. A small kitchen, a hallway leading to the bedrooms. Impersonal, adequate. Ugly.

She met his gaze squarely. "So where do we start?" she said. "You'll want to review the files on Kerry, of course, and then—"

He put up a hand. "I want to get some things straight right now," he began. "You're here for one reason and one reason only—because you couldn't stand to stay in California and do nothing. I accepted that. I gave in. But now you're going to have to fade into the walls and let me do my thing."

She appeared to be taken aback. Started to say something, but then thought better of it.

"Okay," he went on, "we got that settled. Now—" he checked his watch "—it's after nine, and I'm going to take the file and study it and I'll see you in the morning."

"All right," she said, her voice losing some of its determination. "But would you like me to walk down the road? I saw a market. I could get, I don't know, a frozen pizza or whatever and—"

"And," he cut in, "that's another issue. Yes, you'd be difficult to recognize, but that doesn't give you a license to paint the town red."

"I never said…I was just thinking about dinner. And maybe coffee in the morning. Luke, I can't sit here all day and all night and…"

"The hell you can't," he snapped. "We had a deal. Live with it."

She folded her arms defensively then and looked away. "But we have to get some food sometime. I'm hungry. Maybe you aren't, but I…"

He swore and glared at her. "All right," he ground out, "make a list and I'll get whatever you need."

"I don't see why you have to run these kind of errands," she said. "I mean, this isn't Boulder. Denver is a city of millions of people, and I don't even recognize myself in the mirror. Wouldn't it just be easier if I—"

"Make the damn list," he grumbled.

In the end he did the shopping. He agreed with Grace that the way she looked now she could have blended into the crowd in the supermarket and never been spotted. But he knew if he gave in this once, it was the thin edge of the wedge. She'd think she could come and go around Denver at will. Royally screw up his investigation. He wasn't about to risk it. He also wasn't about to let her get even a toe into the door of his authority.

The following morning he was up before her and made the coffee that he'd purchased last night, and he sat with the local news on the TV in the background and flipped through Kerry Pope's file one more time, his plan jelling in his head.

Grace appeared in pink-and-white flowered pajamas at eight. She ignored him and poured herself a cup of coffee. He ignored her, too, as best he could. This living arrangement sucked, he thought again, flipping through the file, trying real hard to discount the new Grace, this redhead he didn't know at all.

Finally, she cleared her throat. "I didn't sleep a wink last night."

"Sorry," he mumbled, face still buried in the manila folder.

"I'd like to know why you turned so nasty all of a sudden."

He shut his eyes for a moment in exasperation, then looked up at her. "I'm trying to concentrate on the case. Don't take it personally."

"But it is personal."

"It's not. This is strictly business."

"I don't think so."

His jaw locked. "And I think you're trying to analyze a situation that doesn't exist. Don't play the shrink right now, okay?"

"See? There you go again. Biting my head off."

"You're tired. You said so yourself. I suggest you get some rest today and let me do my work."

"It's the way I look, isn't it? I thought about it all night, and I decided you don't know how to deal with me."

He gave a harsh laugh.

"See? You can't even be civil anymore. You've barely spoken to me in twenty-four hours. When I was *Professor* Bennett, you were at least—"

He came to his feet abruptly. "Don't flatter yourself," he said, positive she'd retreat in the face of his stinging insult.

But she only nodded and smiled knowingly. "Guess I was right," she said.

"Whatever," he got out. Then he strode into his bedroom, picked up his keys and loose change and dropped them into his khaki pants pocket. Ready, he reappeared. "I'm out of here," he said, trying to keep his tone even. "I don't know when I'll be back."

"I don't suppose I could go along? Sit in the car?"

"Not a chance."

"You won't even tell me what your plans are?"

He shook his head. "Let's just say I have a plan. You want me to bring Kerry Pope down. That's my plan. I'll see you when I see you. And don't go out. There's plenty to eat here now, and I'll stop and get some takeout on my way home."

"Yes, sir," she said, and she gave him a facetious salute, marched into her bedroom and closed the door.

Holy God Almighty, he thought, he was never going to live through this.

He was still thinking about Grace and the unsettling truth of her accusations as he was driving down Federal Boulevard, a map of Denver open on the seat next to him while he hunted for Kerry Pope's street. It was somewhere near the old Mile High Stadium. The road she lived on backed up to the interstate that skirted the downtown area.

He'd been a real prick this morning. He knew it. He'd done it on purpose, trying to keep his focus, trying to reaffirm the original status of their arrangement. He was the hired investigator; she was the fugitive in need. He was sure she had not forgotten that the FBI wanted her. Her concern for Charley never left her. But somehow—he had to admit she'd hit the nail on the head—*somehow* the astounding transformation of her physical appearance *had* thrown a wrench into their relationship. She was suddenly more confident. She'd changed from a sincere, intelligent, caring individual to desirable woman.

And he had no idea how to deal with the butterfly that Grace had become.

He almost missed Kerry's street and had to jam on his brakes and make a sudden turn. See? he thought. She'd totally distracted him. He'd known this was going to happen. *Damn it.*

The block was a short one. Luke parked, then got out and surveyed the neighborhood. Pretty shoddy. Paint peeling on the clapboard houses, bricks missing from chimneys, trash caught on chain-link fences, yellow weedy lawns and cracked sidewalks. It figured. From what Grace had told him and from the info he'd gleaned on Kerry, this was exactly what he had expected.

He reached back in the car, grabbed the notebook he'd purchased down the road and found the house number. If she wasn't home, he'd wait.

Kerry was home.

"Hi," Luke said brightly at her door, the screen between them, "my name is Lucas Sarkov. I'm with *Weekly People*—you know, the…"

"Yeah," she said, eyeing him, "I know, the magazine. I see it at the stores."

"Good, then. Good." He gave her his nicest smile. "I was hoping I'd find you here."

"Oh, yeah? Listen, Mr., Mr.…"

"Sarkov. S-A-R-K-O-V."

"Yeah, whatever. But I don't give interviews anymore."

"Oh," Luke said, "hey, I'm sorry, I didn't make myself clear. I'm here for an interview, sure, aren't we all?" He laughed. "But I'm also authorized to pay for your story."

"Pay?"

"You bet."

"How much?"

"Well, now, see, that's really negotiable."

"I don't get it. You said…"

"Why don't I come in and explain. And Miss Pope, but hey, can I call you Kerry?"

She hesitated, then nodded shyly.

"What I was going to say, Kerry, is I could sure use a glass of water. It's hot as the dickens out here, and then I could explain how the magazine pays."

"Well, I…"

"It will just take a minute. And my magazine really understands your position—you know, you being the biological mother of Charles and all that."

"You…do?"

"Absolutely, Kerry. We feel a lot of the media are giving you a bum rap, if you get what I mean."

"Boy, are they ever. You'd think Grace Bennett was a saint."

Not if you could see her now, Luke thought. Halfway in the door, he said, "You bet, I really hear that."

It took a little commiseration and some fast thinking about how much his magazine was going to pay, but five minutes later he was sitting on her couch, glass of water in front of him, notebook open on his knee.

She wasn't a bad person. He was aware of that immediately. She was a victim of her circumstances, a lifestyle that she had apparently fallen into as far back as junior high school. Booze, drugs and the wrong men. He'd seen young women like Kerry before. Hundreds of them, when he'd worked Vice. They could have been clones.

Kerry was talkative as long as she believed Luke and his magazine were sympathetic to her cause. And she sure had one thing straight: the vast majority of the media had taken Grace's side.

"Not that Grace isn't perfectly fine," Kerry said, hands between her bony knees. "It's just that Charley is mine. He's all I got."

"I understand." The hell he did. This woman had dumped her baby as if he were an unwanted puppy, the way Luke had been dumped. Had *his* mother been a sad sack like Kerry Pope? He didn't know, couldn't remember more than a vague image of a face and arms and a voice. The difference between him and Charley, though, was that he'd never had a foster mother like Grace. But he kept the sincere expression on his face, listening with half an ear.

Kerry talked a lot about how she'd messed up her life but was now on the straight and narrow. She truly believed she was going to make a good mother. Luke looked at her, the stringy hair, the mottled skin and glazed eyes of a habitual druggie, and he felt sickened by her lack of a grasp on reality.

She kept talking; he kept scribbling and mentally assessing her living conditions. How could this young woman delude herself into believing she could care for a child?

How could the judge have failed so badly in his duty to protect little Charley Pope?

But Luke had to shake off his thoughts. Okay. Grace was absolutely right—this woman couldn't even fend for herself, much less her boy. In his mind there was no longer any question about that. His entire focus now was to prove her inadequacies. Looking at her, looking around this excuse for a home, he knew he'd bring her down.

He was still writing in his notebook, more like doodling, when abruptly the front screen door flew open and banged shut behind one very tough dude. Luke sized him up in a flash: drug dealer or pimp, most likely both.

"Who the hell is this?" The unshaven, T-shirt-clad man demanded to know, and Luke had to quickly shift gears.

"Whoa," Luke said, dropping his shoulders submissively, "I'm a reporter is all. Miss Pope here..."

The man just about blew a gasket. He ignored Luke for the time being and strode over to Kerry, then grabbed her skinny bare arm and squeezed till she yelped. In any other situation, Luke would have dropped the bastard on the spot, but he swallowed his rage, choked it down because this was about Charley, about Grace and Charley and the boy's entire future.

"He's on our side," Kerry was whimpering. "Honest, Eddie, he's doing this story for *us*. Let go of me. That really hurts, Eddie."

Then Luke tried. "Hey, really, Eddie, I'm here for Kerry. My publication is sympathetic to—"

Eddie whirled on him. He thrust out a finger and jabbed at the air an inch from Luke's face. He swore. Then swore some more. Not until Kerry explained that she would get paid did Eddie suddenly cool off.

"Money?" He was spitting. "What kind of money you talking here?"

Luke knew this guy wasn't half the fool Kerry was, and it took a minute, but finally he convinced him that if the story came out well—"And I'm sure it will''—then they were talking five, ten grand at the least.

Eddie eyed Luke. ''You don't look like a reporter to me. We had plenty of them nosing around, and you sure don't fit the ticket, man.''

Luke smiled apologetically. ''I'm from California.''

''So? What the hell does that mean?''

''Geez, I'm not sure. I dress different?'' But Luke knew it wasn't his clothes. It was in his eyes—too many years on the street busting characters a whole lot meaner than this pussycat.

Eddie stared at him some more and Luke forced his own gaze away.

Don't lose it now, he told himself, aware that through Eddie he'd get the goods on Kerry and her so-called reformation. Oh, yeah, Eddie was going to be Grace's salvation.

Finally, after prompting and cajoling from Kerry, Eddie backed off and went to get a beer out of the fridge.

''Well,'' Luke said, turning to the young woman, ''I guess this will have to do for now.'' He flipped the notebook closed and stuck his pen in his shirt pocket.

As he stood up he smiled sheepishly. ''You realize,'' he said, ''there may be one or two details I need to clarify before I hand this in. I wonder if I could come around again. I mean, only if there's something…''

But Eddie was back. Eyeing Luke suspiciously again. ''You can do it on the phone, man.''

''Oh, right, the phone. And the number's under…?''

"Edward Daniels," Kerry said before Eddie shot her a look.

She walked Luke out. Standing on the cracked sidewalk that was lifting from the upward thrust of cottonwood roots, she told him, "You should talk to this lady, this FBI lady named Renee Paynter. She's real nice and she's going to get Charley back for me."

"Is that right?" Luke said.

"Oh, yes, she's very smart. If I, well, you know, if I hadn't had Charley and all and been at the correctional institute, I would have done something like that."

He raised a brow. "Like what, Kerry?"

"I'd have been an FBI agent like Renee."

"Well," he said for lack of anything else to say, "well, that's very nice. I'll, ah, be in touch."

He walked down the sidewalk, turned, saw Kerry smile a little and wave, and he thought he'd remember her like that always, remember that sad sinking feeling in his gut when he realized the odds were she'd never see thirty.

On his way to his car, about halfway between Kerry's place and his Subaru convertible, he noticed a spanking new black Toyota 4Runner that hadn't been there when he'd passed by earlier.

He slowed, cognizant that Eddie might well be watching, but he nevertheless couldn't resist leaning against the front bumper, lifting his leg as if to tie his shoe, and just as he expected, the engine was still warm and ticking. Eddie's new car. Luke would have bet a bundle on where the money to buy it had come from. Oh, yeah, it would bear watching Eddie Daniels.

He got back to the Tech Center late after stopping

to get takeout at a local deli, and parked near the apartment. As he turned the engine off the air conditioner spewed some hot moist air for a moment before it, too, hissed off. He didn't get out immediately, just sat with one hand draped over the steering wheel. A part of him anticipated seeing Grace. Another part recoiled from the thought. Again he acknowledged that she really had called it this morning—since her metamorphosis he didn't know how to deal with her. How very superficial, he knew, getting turned on— and that was what it was—by her outward appearance, when the best part of Grace was a radiance from within.

Well, he couldn't change his reaction to how she looked. And he wasn't going to deny his interest. He could, however, try to deal with it in a more mature manner than he had this morning. Her appearance might have changed, but inside she was still suffering, aching from her ordeal, missing the child she'd raised for four years. He'd bet she'd called her folks and Charley the moment he'd left this morning. Called them and been hurting all day from the loneliness. Even if everything worked out here in Denver, she might still have to face whatever charges the FBI brought against her. She had to know that. And the judge, despite everything, would have to address the stunt she had pulled when she'd taken off with Charley. It could be a helluva mess.

He suddenly wished he could help her on that end, but all he could do in his capacity was to amass hard evidence that Kerry was still a habitual user. Beyond that, Grace might be wise to find a damn good lawyer. And even then...

Luke opened the car door. No point, he thought, dwelling on something that hadn't happened yet.

Carrying the white take-out sack under one arm, he unlocked the apartment door and pushed it open with the other. He hadn't even passed the threshold, when Grace was there, relieving him of the sack, bursting with questions.

"You saw Kerry today, didn't you? Did you see that man she's with? Where they live? Did you...?"

"Slow down," Luke said, peeling off the summer sport coat he'd forced himself to wear, then haphazardly tossing it over the back of a chair.

"Well, did you see Kerry?"

He turned around to face her and noticed two hectic spots of red on her cheeks, red that matched her spiky hair. He noted, somewhere in his brain, that she'd put on her makeup again today. Even though she wasn't going out, she'd assumed her new identity.

"Luke, please, I'm going out of my mind."

A corner of his mouth lifted in the semblance of a smile. "Yes, Grace, I saw Kerry Pope."

She sucked in a huge breath. "And?"

"And she's everything you said."

"So you...you believe me? You believe the danger Charley would be in if Kerry got hold of him?"

"I never doubted it," he said, his eyes fixed on Grace.

God, she looked pretty, all soft and young and vulnerable, biting at her lower lip, her eyes moist with pent-up emotion.

"Yes," he finally said, "she's basically a wreck. Not a bad young woman, just too many miles on her, and from what I could tell, she's still using."

The tears Grace had been holding in check spilled

from her eyes and ran down her pink-stained cheeks. She bit her lip harder. "Can you...do you think you can get proof she's still on drugs?"

"It's what I've always done best. Yeah, I'll get the goods on Miss Kerry Pope."

"Oh, Lord," Grace sobbed, her relief pouring out. She appeared so forlorn, so lovely, so emotionally destroyed, that without thinking, he moved to her and gently brought her against his chest, where she laid her head, and he could feel the hot tears wetting his shirt.

It seemed innocent and natural to brush her bangs from her brow, to stroke her neck and move a finger along her jawline, stopping at her chin, bringing her head up so that he could look at her.

"It's all right," he whispered.

She took a deep quavering breath and her lips parted slightly. He felt the shift in her muscles that mirrored his own, the tensing, the building of heat that flowed suddenly between them.

He didn't think. His eyes held hers and his hand tipped her chin up farther and his head descended without any conscious thought.

And he tasted her lips, tasted the lipstick and tasted Grace. Gently at first, feeling the ripple of her flesh against him, the shudder of desire.

He parted her lips with his and she responded, her arms going around his back, hands clutching at his shirt. He moved his arms around her, and pressed her to his chest while the kiss deepened. He lifted her slightly, tightening his embrace, wanting more of her, feeling that tautness of her breasts against him. He was on fire. In a minute, in a second, he was going to—

Reality crashed back into his brain. His arms relaxed, he began to break off the kiss, slowly, reluctantly, but knowing one of them had to take control.

For a time, when their lips parted, Luke held her to his chest and felt that tension ease from her muscles. What had he been thinking? Damn it. And yet he still tasted her, wanted her, his groin aching.

"Hey," he finally said, his mouth brushing the crown of her head, "you okay?"

"I...I don't know," she whispered against his shirt. "Luke, do you... I mean, what just happened?"

He closed his eyes, silently pleading with her not to analyze things, to just let them go. "Nothing happened."

"But..."

"It doesn't mean anything," he said, easing her away, meeting her eyes, praying, hoping against all hope she couldn't read the lie in his gaze.

CHAPTER ELEVEN

RENEE PAYNTER WAS TORN, confused down to the very core of who she was. Her doctor had told her she needed to make a decision about her pregnancy and make that decision quickly.

But she couldn't. She simply couldn't bring herself to the point of a definitive yes or no.

And she hadn't even told Jay yet. *My God,* she thought as she drove into work, what had happened to her nerve?

She tried to weigh the results of either decision. She envisioned her career going up in smoke. A pregnant FBI special agent did not pack a punch or command respect. She would never be allowed to place herself in jeopardy. And without that ability, she'd be assigned to a desk job, her career irrevocably stalled.

On the other hand, her child was growing inside her. Hers and Jay's. Their *child.*

She had barely arrived at work, when the hunger pangs began. She ate two doughnuts from a box sitting on the receptionist's desk and then hurried into a 10:00 a.m. meeting in the conference room, the Bennett case file tucked under her arm as she brushed powdered sugar from the lapels of her blazer. *My God,* she thought again.

Teddy Argent, the resident computer guru, was already in the room, along with Mead Towey. She brought them up to speed on the case, cringing inwardly as she related the story of the San Francisco agents getting waylaid by the Soda Springs sheriff.

"We know someone called in the false stolen-car report. The sheriff didn't even check out the call, just jumped on his trusty steed and rode out to the rescue, six-guns blazing," Renee explained.

"Which was why whoever made that call picked a small-town sheriff. It was done very deliberately," Towey suggested.

"Yes," Renee admitted.

"So your San Francisco agents lost the Bennetts' camper, and no one's picked it up since," Towey said.

"We're working on that," Teddy put in, "but we figure they must have changed license plates, because I haven't had one sighting. And I got the word out."

"Hmm." Towey drummed his fingers on the polished table.

"Whoever made that stolen-car report is a cop or an ex-cop, somebody like that," Renee said. "He knew the drill, even used the correct code number, according to the sheriff."

"Robert Bennett was a cop," Towey reminded her.

"He wouldn't have dared make the call. But you can bet it was one of his pals." Renee leaned forward, resting her forearms on the table. Was there still powdered sugar on her blazer? "If I can find that man, he'll lead me to Grace Bennett."

"Okay, fine. Where's the boy, though?"

"We think he's with his grandparents," she said. "That's what the whole thing was about. Switch the boy, change the plates, *poof,* disappearing act."

"This is beginning to be embarrassing," Towey

said. "The whole damn country thinks we're the bad guys for trying to find Charley Pope and return him to his mother. I want this handled quickly and discreetly."

"I'm working on a lead right now," she lied. "I'll know who called in that phony report within a couple days."

"Okay, take care of it," Towey said, rising.

I've been trying to decide how to do just that, Renee thought. And then, crazily, the words nearly burst from her: *Oh, Special Agent in Charge Towey, did I mention that I'm pregnant?*

When she got back to her desk there was a message awaiting her. A reporter from the magazine *Weekly People* wanted to interview her. Some guy named Luke Sarkov. About the Bennett case. What else?

Renee sighed. She shied from this part of her job, but she understood the value of good press relations. And it didn't hurt her profile in the Bureau to be quoted in the press. She knew what to say; they'd all been prepped carefully. And, damn it, she'd actually like the chance to give the FBI's side of the story. So far Grace Bennett had had all the good press.

She called the reporter's number, and he answered immediately.

"Thank you for replying so promptly, Agent Paynter. Can we meet as soon as possible? I'd like your take on this case."

"I can talk to you, certainly, Mr.—" she glanced at the message "—Sarkov, but I insist that you keep an open mind."

"That's my job," he said. His voice was deep, very masculine. She tried to picture what he'd look like.

"How about lunch today? Get it done, and I can go about my business of upholding the law."

"Lunch? Perfect."

"Can you make it by, say, 12:30?"

"Sure. Where?"

"The Wynkoop Brewery in LoDo. You know where it is?"

"I'll find it."

"Okay, 12:30. Ask the hostess at the door. She knows me."

"I'm looking forward to meeting you, Agent Paynter."

"That's *Special* Agent Paynter."

When Renee walked into the Brewery, the hostess told her that Luke Sarkov was already there at the table in the rear corner by the big copper brewing vat.

He stood when she approached, and as usual, she saw the slight widening of the eyes, the surprise that was cloaked instantly.

"Mr. Sarkov." She held out her hand.

"Special Agent Paynter."

He was good-looking. Around forty, she'd guess. Military-short light-brown hair, piercing blue eyes, lean jaw. Yes, he fit the deep voice on the phone.

She sat down and picked up the menu. She was starved. They ordered sandwiches, a draft beer for him, iced tea for her. He pulled out a pad, laid it on the table by his plate and leveled his gaze at her. "Tell me about the Bennett case," he said, "from *your* point of view."

He took notes as she talked, pausing to bite into a thick sandwich. She gave him the background quickly; he most likely knew it all anyway.

"And this Professor Grace Bennett," he asked, "can you describe what she's like?"

"All I can tell you is what her friends and colleagues have told me." Renee stopped to chew her sandwich, dabbing at her lips.

"Which is?" he pressed.

"She's a wonderful person, a great mother, a fine teacher. Everybody seems to think she's terrific."

He eyed her, not saying anything—a hard blue stare. His pen was poised above his notebook.

"But, you know, I have a difficult time believing anyone could be so perfect. Don't quote me on that," she warned. "For a woman to kidnap a child like that, well, there's got to be something wrong with her."

"It's been said she's protecting the child."

"I can't comment on an obviously prejudicial statement like that. Professor Bennett may *think* she's protecting the boy, but no one—I repeat, no one—has made any allegations that Kerry Pope is a danger to her son."

"Have you met Kerry Pope?"

"Yes, I have. I interviewed her at length."

"What was your assessment of her?"

"I wasn't there to make an assessment," Renee said carefully. "I was there to find out all I could from her in case something she knew would help us apprehend Grace Bennett."

"Did she help?"

"Not much."

"Is it true, Special Agent Paynter, that Kerry Pope relinquished custody of her son to Grace Bennett when he was three months old?"

"Yes, that's true, and I know what you're going to say. Don't bother. People change. Kerry Pope is four years older. She's been approved by the court. Presumably, Child Protective Services checked up on her.''

"Presumably," he agreed, but mockery laced his tone.

"Mr. Sarkov, you said you had an open mind."

"Do *you*, Special Agent Paynter?''

"Look, I'm a federal employee. I took an oath to serve my country, to obey and uphold its laws. I am— all of us in the Denver office are—doing the job you pay us for. No one can afford to allow anyone who feels like it to break the law. That's anarchy. That's an unstable society. That's crime taking over.''

"Yes, certainly, but sometimes the law makes mistakes. And it can take a long time for the law to admit that. Many people believe Charley Pope belongs with the woman who raised him for four years.''

"I'm not here to argue the issue. I thought you weren't, either.''

He gave her a taut smile. "Sorry, sometimes us press types just can't help needling. We get good quotes that way.''

"All right, but let's keep this evenhanded. Now, I can tell you that there's going to be a break in this case soon.''

His eyes lifted to hers, keen and icy blue. "Break?''

"Of course, I can't divulge what it is, but it will bring us much closer to locating Charley Pope.''

"And Professor Bennett?''

"I'm not at liberty to say. Our job, first and foremost, is to find Charley and return him to his biological mother, the woman who carried him for nine months and gave birth to him.'' *What a hypocrite I am,* she suddenly realized.

''You're sure you can't give me a hint about the break? A scoop, you know.'' His lips drew into a smile, but there was no humor in his eyes.

''I'm sorry, Mr. Sarkov.''

''Well, thank you for all the information. I appreciate your time.''

''I don't suppose I could look at your article before it's printed, check the facts and so on?''

''I'm afraid not. The magazine's policy won't allow that.'' He upended his glass and finished his beer, then signaled the waitress for the bill. He smiled that glacial smile again. ''My treat.''

''Thank you, Mr. Sarkov.''

''No, thank *you,* Special Agent Paynter.''

GRACE DROVE Luke's car south along the Front Range of the Rockies, her nerves leaping under her skin. What she was doing was utter insanity. And when Luke found out he would go ballistic, no doubt about it. Yet she could no more turn back from this mission than she could hand Charley over to his biological mother. And if she was successful today, this could be the break she and Luke needed. She had to do this.

She'd gotten the idea that morning when she was reading Kerry Pope's file. She'd studied it over and over, searching for a bit of information, anything that would lead to proof that Kerry was an unfit mother. Her idea frightened her at first; she didn't dare pull such a crazy stunt. But as she read over Kerry's prison record, a plan solidified in her mind. The information she needed was all there: sentence, time served, parole board report, cell mate.

Cell mate. Who else would know Kerry Pope's secrets? Who else would Kerry confide in?

Her destination, the Colorado Women's Correctional Institute, was still an hour away. In a moment of uncertainty, Grace realized she hadn't reached the point of no return. Then the moment passed. She'd succeed. She'd make this work. No one on earth would recognize her, she told herself a dozen times. And the last place an FBI fugitive would show up was a prison.

"You can do this," she told herself aloud, her heart thudding against her rib cage. Heck, she knew the drill. She'd conducted interviews at the prison complex years ago, when she'd been working on her Ph.D. All she had to do was clear the security check, which was a search of her purse and a careful screening with a metal detector. She'd sign in as *Sally* Bennett, interview Kerry's former cell mate and get out of there. If she played her cards right, she'd have more fresh information on Kerry—enough, she prayed, to take to court.

If Luke didn't kill her for this stunt first, she thought abruptly.

The dry brown prairies of eastern Colorado stretched away to her left as she drove through the foothill country. She was getting more and more nervous. But she'd do it; she had to. Her brilliant plan had crystallized, complete in all details, the minute Luke had offered her the car.

"I can take a cab into downtown," he'd told her after Renee Paynter had returned his call. "I know you're going nuts stuck here," Luke had said, "but that doesn't mean you can show your face all over the city. Go to the grocery store and then straight back here."

"I'm sure I won't be recognized," Grace had said eagerly. "And I'll wear the contact lenses, too. No one will spot me. For that matter, I doubt Mom and Dad would. And Charley," she'd said wistfully. "I wonder what he'd think. God, I wonder when I'm even going to see him again. A week—" she'd thought aloud "—surely we'll have enough to take to the judge in a week."

But Luke had reminded her of an unsettling fact. "Grace," he'd said carefully, "it's the FBI we're going to have to worry about."

"Oh, right," she'd replied, a shot of adrenaline spurting into her heart. "The FBI."

"We'll cross that bridge when we come to it, though. No point getting ahead of the game. First we deal—that is, I deal with Kerry. Then we'll see. All right?"

"Yes, of course," she'd said, giving him a shaky smile, and she'd recognized the concern in his eyes. Concern and something else, something she was afraid to put a name to.

The miles clicked by, billowing cumulous clouds amassing in the high country to the west, a glorious summer day. Despite her trepidation, she felt curiously alive, her mind never resting. She tried concentrating on Charley and her parents and wondered every ten seconds exactly where they were now. Idaho? On their way to Yellowstone National Park?

She knew they visited Yellowstone every summer, had their reservation in at their favorite campground a year ahead of time, and there was no reason they would have changed plans now.

Was Charley still enjoying himself? She talked to him once a day—had talked to him this morning, in fact—and he said he'd caught a rainbow trout and, "Grampa made me let it go. Mommy, it was too small, Grampa said."

Was her mother spoiling him rotten, letting him stay up every night past his bedtime, feeding him chips and cake and candy and ice cream? He tended to get hyper if he had too much sugar.

God, how she missed him. His bright eyes and impish smile, the crooked front tooth, the special smell of him, little-boy dirt and sweat and something sweet and all his own. She longed to hug him till he squealed; she ached for her child. *Her* child.

She ached, too, in a place inside she had denied for so long now she'd assumed the spot was dead. Deep in her stomach she felt jittery and achy at the thought of Luke. She sometimes felt faint with yearning in his presence, hot and dizzy and so hungry and so in need of being fulfilled her head spun.

He had kissed her. Oh, how he had held her to him and pressed his mouth to hers and parted her lips...

She had wanted him with a fierceness she'd never known. The heat in her belly had become a firestorm of desire. She hadn't cared that he was a troubled man, shamed and humiliated, forced to leave a job that was *him,* through and through. He was a lost soul. She didn't need his problems. My God, she had enough troubles of her own to last several lifetimes.

And he was married. Worse, he was still in love with his gorgeous wife. *Judith.*

"I don't need this," she said. "It was just a stupid kiss."

But as soon as she'd spoken, she knew her words were a lie. She wanted Luke Sarkov, wanted that wounded body and soul even if he never loved her. At any cost, shamelessly, she wanted him.

He must have felt something for her, she told herself. He'd kissed her, hadn't he?

She arrived at the prison complex east of Canon City shortly after one, and parked in the visitors' check-in center.

Gaining entry was going to be the worst part. She was fairly sure Kerry Pope's former cell mate would agree to see her, but first she had to get through security. She was fairly certain no one in a million years would recognize her. And only a maniac would visit a prison if the law wanted her. She couldn't recall having shown the guards an ID card, and even if they asked her to produce one, she'd pull out whatever she still had that read Sally G. Bennett, anything without a photo.

Nevertheless, when she went through the routine at the check-in, her hands trembled as she fiddled with her purse, showing the guard the contacts. The stupid smile pasted on her lips was as false as her hair color.

How could she have forgotten that so many guards were on duty? All of them big and well-muscled men who would no more show emotion than they would open the gates and let the inmates free.

"And your purpose here, Miss Bennett?" she was asked at least three times during the procedure.

"I'm here to interview Jackie Whelan. I'm putting together a syllabus for a criminal psych class. I'm a student, you know."

It took half an hour to clear check-in before she was allowed to board the prison bus that would take her to the minimum security facility. The guards had called ahead, of course, and hopefully Jackie Whelan would be waiting for her.

Grace sat on the bus with the other visitors and tried to catch her breath as they passed the various buildings in the huge complex: the men's correctional institute, Super Max, where the worst of the worst were kept locked up twenty-three hours a day, and the low-security farm. The entire complex spread for miles on a rolling plateau between the town of Florence and Canon City—miles of open grassy prairies broken by occasional prison buildings surrounded by endless coils of barbed wire. Everything about this place was spooky. She suddenly wished Luke were with her; he would have been in his element. She allowed herself to believe he would have covered her hand with his and nodded reassuringly, giving her that half-crooked smile that sent shivers along her spine.

But he wasn't here and she was alone and she had to focus on her plan. *Focus, Grace.*

Jackie Whelan was waiting for her in the visiting area, a small cinder block room with several tables and white plastic hard-backed chairs. Only a lone female guard monitored the room from a wire-fenced office. Grace showed the guard her ID, was checked off a list in front of the guard, who then pointed. "Jackie's over there, last table by the window."

The Whelan woman, like so many other females behind bars, was in for making bad choices when it came to men. In Jackie's instance, she'd participated in a carjacking with a boyfriend in Denver and gone right down with him when he'd been apprehended.

Grace shook her hand, judging her to be in her thirties. She was an ordinary-looking woman, round face, brown eyes, long curly brown hair, blunt-cut bangs. Nice skin. She was, like all the inmates, wearing a green vee-neck short-sleeved top and matching pants. Grace could see the Prisoner lettering on the back of everyone's shirt and assumed it was on Jackie's, too, though the inmate remained seated, facing Grace.

"So you're a shrink from CU?" Jackie asked, looking Grace over.

"A psychology professor, actually," Grace said.

"Bennett, huh. Sally Bennett?"

"That's right, and please call me Sally."

"Sure, why not. You're teaching a course on criminals?"

Kerry Pope's former cell mate was extremely inquisitive, Grace discovered shortly, but that could work in her favor—Jackie liked to talk.

They spent a few minutes getting to know each other, Jackie even saying she loved "Sally's" hair and had been thinking of going short and red herself.

They conversed some more, and Grace made sure to interject a few professorial questions here and there to keep the interview legit. She was ready to ask Jackie about her cell mates over the five years Jackie had been incarcerated, when Jackie grinned like a cat.

Grace cocked her head.

"Why don't you get to the point?" Jackie said.

"The point? But this whole interview is the point," Grace said.

Then Jackie unfolded her clasped hands and leaned forward. "You want to talk about Kerry."

"I…" Grace's heart began to pound. How could she know that?

"Hey, it took me a while, and you might have fooled the guards, but I'm a little more savvy than that, *Sally*."

Grace felt the blood drain from her face. My God, she was busted. Busted right here…

"Hey, don't sweat it," Jackie said in a low whisper. "I'm not about to turn you in. If you really want to know, half the women here who knew Kerry are rooting for you. That girl is on a fast track to nowhere. A junkie, you know? Then we heard about her plans for her kid—what's his name?"

"Charley," Grace got out past the lump in her throat.

"Yeah, Charley, and how the dumb judge gave him back to her. We were going crazy. I mean, she didn't once send him a Christmas card or a birthday card or anything the whole time she was locked up. I should know, I had to listen to her bull for eighteen months in the same cell. All she ever yapped about was this guy and how he was waiting for her to get paroled. Never a word about her kid. I mean, she was obsessed with this man, you know?"

Grace nodded, still in shock.

"Anyway, if it helps, the guy's name is Daniels, Eddie Daniels, and he's messed up with the Mile Highs…that motorcycle gang? He's some sort of a honcho, according to Kerry. The main man." Jackie looked at Grace in earnest. "You know, *drugs*."

Grace licked dry lips. "Why…why are you telling me this? It isn't that I'm not grateful, but—"

Jackie cut her off with a wave of the hand. "I'll tell you why. Because I don't like that chick. How could anyone as screwed up as Kerry Pope bring a kid into the world? What I can't figure is why she all of a sudden got out of prison and decided she could be the world's greatest mom. Maybe she's stupider than I thought. Anyhow, we're all rooting for you. But I'll tell you, *Sally*, you better go to ground till you can get the hard goods on Kerry. You got help in this?''

"Yes," Grace breathed, "I do. And this information you've given me is great. I mean, my friend who's helping me…well, it might have taken him weeks to dig this up.''

"Glad to have been of service," Jackie said, giving Grace another catlike smile. "Now, go get her."

GRACE WAS JUMPING with excitement the whole way north to Denver. A couple times she found she was speeding and had to slow down. That was all she needed—flashing lights in her rearview mirror. Still, she couldn't wait to tell Luke the news about this Eddie Daniels and the gang—the Mile Highs. Surely Luke, with his experience in Vice, could amass hard evidence on this man in no time, hard evidence to bring in the Denver PD and present to the judge.

For a moment her sparkling mood flickered and was nearly extinguished. Just by association with Daniels, Kerry was breaking her parole. She could wind up right back in prison. And once there the two-time loser would have the key thrown away on her. But Kerry wasn't a bad person; she was simply messed up. She needed help, not prison.

Then Grace caught herself. This was for Charley. For his very life. *Kerry* was making these choices. Kerry had had ample time in prison to learn and grow, yet, according to Jackie, all Kerry had done was obsess over this Daniels character. And God knows, Kerry sure had wiped Charley from her mind. Grace wondered about that a lot. Why had Kerry sued for custody of her child? Had a spark of motherly instinct ignited in her? Or was she doing it just as a lark?

Grace was still high on her news when she pulled into the parking lot at the Tech Center apartment complex. High as a kite.

Wait till Luke hears, she thought, hurrying along the sidewalk to their unit, her stomach doing somersaults at the prospect of her seeing him in a matter of moments. Would he kiss her again? Run his hands through her short spiky red hair and smile at her?

Oh, she was learning plenty about obsession herself. Who would have thought?

She unlocked the door, breathless, a winning smile on her face.

"Luke? Luke? Are you here? I've got the most unbelievable news..."

He was there. He appeared before her, and the instant she saw his eyes, she stopped short.

Before she could say a word, he was demanding to know where she had been all day. "I can't believe it," he said between clenched teeth. "What the hell have you been up to?"

As intimidated as she was, she held her ground. "I was getting information on Kerry and Eddie Daniels. Just wait till you hear."

He was practically in her face now. "I don't give a rat's ass what you learned. You got that? I gave you an order this morning and you ignored it. Do you know what you risk gallivanting around Denver?"

She took a hesitant step backward until she came up against the kitchen wall. "I...I wasn't in Denver."

He just glared at her.

She nodded. "I talked to Kerry's former cell mate. It was okay, Luke, really, because she's on my side and—"

He went crazy. He pinned her against the wall, holding her chin hurtfully with his hand. "You stupid... You're telling me you went to Canon City! Are you nuts? Are *you?*"

"No, I... With my hair and my contacts, I was sure I'd be okay. Luke, you're hurting me. Let me go. Luke?"

"I'd like to goddamn hurt you, woman," he growled. "I'm so goddamn mad I..."

He let her go, then pivoted and sucked in a deep breath.

She began to reach out toward him, but thought better of it. "I learned something today," she said defiantly to his back. "I found out that Daniels is a member of this gang, and..."

Luke laughed harshly. "*And* he's the lead dealer and the gang's called the Mile Highs."

"But, but how did you know?"

"Good God, Grace," he said, as if weary to the bone. "What do you think I've been doing for the past two days?"

Her brow furrowed and she bit her lower lip, her bubble burst. Her mood sank into an abyss. He already knew! She'd risked arrest, and he *knew*.

"You...you should have told me," she whispered. "If you just would have told me, Luke, I..."

"How many times, how many *times*," he repeated, "do I have to say this—I work alone. You're here only because I got soft. Okay? Because I got soft and you're Big Bob's daughter. I made a mistake. Boy, did I ever screw up.''

Tears formed behind her eyes, hot and stinging. ''I'm sorry. I'm sorry you got soft and I'm sorry I went to Canon City and I'm sorry I'm such a...burden. Okay. *I'm sorry.* What more do you want?'' She put her face in her hands and hid her tears. Didn't he know he'd torn her apart, taken the fragile world she'd just discovered and shattered it?

''Grace,'' he said after long minutes, ''hey, come on. It's done. All right, I'm still mad—you could have gotten yourself in deep today—but it's done. I only hope you won't think about pulling another stunt like that. Consider this...'' She heard him take a deep breath. ''Right now you can tell the FBI that you had a breakdown and lost touch with reality, and that's why you took off with Charley. I know that's bull, but at least the law would have to consider it. But if the feds get wind that you were out trying to destroy Kerry Pope's credibility, you can kiss the nervous breakdown story goodbye. They'll throw the book at you. Do you hear what I'm saying? For the time being you're the innocent victim in the public's view. You don't want to fall from...grace,'' he said, ''if you'll forgive the pun.''

''That isn't funny,'' she said with a catch in her voice.

''Sorry. But you better have heard what I just said.''

''I did. I get it. I don't know what I was thinking. If you'd told me, confided in me, then I wouldn't have gone off half-cocked.''

''Hey,'' he said, ''that's not my style.''

"No fooling."

He frowned. "I can't take it when a woman cries."

"I'm not crying."

Then he stood there in front of her, hesitant, uncertain. "It's okay. You tried to help. I overreacted. Come on, Grace."

She let him enfold her in his arms, and she felt the warmth of his breath in her hair. Suddenly, nothing mattered. There was only Luke and pure raw sensation flowing through her veins. She tried to focus on the hurt he'd caused her, on how close they were to their goal. Charley, soon, soon, Charley would be safely back with her.

But at the moment there was only Luke and her hopeless, spiraling need.

CHAPTER TWELVE

"If I show you this," Jay said to his wife, Renee, "promise you'll cook dinner for the next month?"

Renee looked up from her desk. "What?" she asked, seeing Jay and Terry Argent, the computer whiz at FBI headquarters, both standing there grinning like Cheshire cats. Jay was holding a piece of paper.

"I want the promise first."

"Okay, okay, dinner for a month. But this better be good. What have you got there?"

Jay was obviously enjoying the moment and wanted to drag it out. "Shall I tell you how I came up with this?"

"Oh, come on, let me see what you have." Renee reached for the paper.

"It was like this. I kept thinking about the professor's parents taking off with the kid in their camper."

"So?"

"Anyway, it's the height of the summer tourist season, right? And I thought, where the heck are they going to spend the nights? Can't just pull off the road any old place, not like you could years ago. Right?"

"Yes, yes, sure. Go on."

"So, not only can you not park an RV on the road, but to get into a KOA or a national park campground, you have to think months—in some cases years—

ahead and apply for a permit or make a reservation. Right?''

Renee sat up straight. ''Oh, my God, of *course*,'' she breathed. ''The Bennetts had to have made reservations at campgrounds. *Of course*. And they have to check in, register. Oh, my God, why didn't I think of that?''

''Because I'm the thinker in our family is why.'' Jay winked at her.

''You…you and Teddy *found* them?''

''Uh-huh. I went to Teddy as soon as I thought of it. Took a while. There have to be a hundred campgrounds between where the San Francisco agents lost them and—''

But Renee wasn't listening. She snatched the printout from Jay and did an impromptu little jig behind her desk. ''Oh, I love you guys,'' she sang, pressing the paper to her breast. ''Where are they?'' she asked, even as she scanned the printout.

''I almost hate to tell you, feeling the way I do about this case.''

''Come on, Jay.''

''But I am an employee of the FBI, and I—''

''Jay!''

''Yellowstone National Park,'' he said.

''Yellowstone,'' she whispered. ''Wyoming, here I come.''

RENEE WAITED anxiously all day for a return call from head ranger Remy Whitsett at Park Service Headquarters in Yellowstone. At 4:30 she finally heard from him.

''Special Agent Paynter,'' he said, ''I have in cus-

tody Mr. and Mrs. Robert Bennett and a boy named
Charles Pope, whom they say is their grandson.''

''*Excellent,*'' Renee said.

''What do you want me to do with them?''

She had considered this point carefully and dis-
cussed it with Mead Towey. ''I'm going to fly up
tomorrow and take the child into custody. Can you
keep them safe until then?''

''Sure. You want me to move them to the Teton
County Jail?''

''No, no, I don't think that would be good for the
little boy. This is a high-profile case, Ranger Whitsett.
I don't want any harm, physical or psychological, to
come to any of them.''

''Well, Mr. Bennett is pretty damn mad.''

''That's not your problem. Can you, well, *contain*
them until I get there?''

''I can leave a couple of rangers with them.''

''Yes, that sounds like a good plan. Just don't let
them get away. They're pretty smart.''

''Don't worry, I've got the keys to Bennett's RV
right here. He's not going anywhere.''

Then Renee had to make her arrangements—the
Bureau's leased plane ready early in the morning,
Field Agent Jim Marshall to accompany her.

She'd considered having Charley escorted to Denver, but she wanted this collar herself. Too bad Grace
hadn't been with them, but that would have been too
easy.

Grace. Where exactly was she? Well, she was going to find out Charley was in the hands of the FBI
damn soon, and when she did, she'd show herself.
There was no way this woman was going to stay in
hiding and watch her foster son returned to his bio-

logical mother. Grace would be flushed out like the criminal she was.

The next morning Renee kissed her husband good-bye and drove to Centennial Airport, where the leased jet was waiting. The flight plan was filed for arrival at a small airport near the west entrance of Yellowstone. Renee and Towey had decided it was a better choice than the main airport in Jackson; somebody there might recognize Charley when she returned with him. This task had to be completed with the utmost discretion.

Ranger Whitsett met Renee and Jim Marshall at the airport and drove them the nearly sixty miles to the campground where the Bennetts were being detained.

Renee hardly saw the majestic mountains and lakes, the wilderness, the rustic settlements that catered to tourists, the world-famous West Thumb Geyser Basin. Her mind was consumed with the fact that she was going to have her hands on Charley Pope. And, after that, she was going to have to face down a very angry Bob Bennett.

She'd worn the wrong clothes. Not thinking, she'd dressed in her official capacity, which meant suit and low-heeled pumps. Jim had on a suit, too. They stuck out like sore thumbs in the campground, where formal dress was shorts and T-shirts.

Renee knocked and climbed into the RV, Jim following. The inside was small but luxurious—couches, kitchen, bedroom, bathroom, everything built in with total efficiency.

Charley was at the kitchen table, coloring. Sally Bennett was fixing lunch, and Bob Bennett sat in a chair, his huge arms folded across his barrel chest.

"Mr. Bennett," Renee said, her voice calm, her heart bursting with triumph. "Mrs. Bennett."

"You'll never get away with this," Bob Bennett growled.

"I'm not *getting away* with anything, Mr. Bennett. I'm doing my job, upholding the law."

"Don't give me that crap. I was a law officer for thirty-five years. You feds don't know right from wrong."

"Regardless of your opinion, Field Agent Marshall and I are here to return Charles Pope to the lawful custody of his biological mother."

Bob muttered something, and in the kitchen Sally, a petite woman, began to cry softly.

"What's the matter, Gramma?" Renee heard the little boy ask.

"Nothing, sweetheart," Sally said, going to Charley and hugging him. He squirmed, a darling four-year-old in shorts and a brand-new T-shirt that had a snarling grizzly on the front and read Yellowstone National Park. There was a purple splotch on the shirt. Jam, Renee guessed.

"Sally, maybe Charley would like to go outside and play." Bob met his wife's eyes meaningfully.

Sally dabbed at her tears with a tissue. "All right. Come on, Charley. Let's go dig up worms."

"This is wrong," Bob said. He stood up, his head nearly touching the ceiling. Renee forced herself to hold her ground. "You know it and I know it. You're endangering this child's life."

"Stop being so dramatic, Mr. Bennett. And may I remind you, I'd be well within my rights to arrest you on the spot for conspiracy to kidnap a minor."

"Crap!"

"No, sir, it's the law." Renee paused. "By the way, where is your daughter, Grace?"

"I haven't got a clue." He thrust his jaw forward and glared at her.

"We'll find her," Jim Mitchell interjected.

"Fine, go for it." Bob said. "Incompetents."

"We found you," she reminded him. "Frankly, I'm surprised you checked into the campground under your own name."

Bob Bennett shrugged. "And *frankly,* I'm surprised you thought to check. Pretty fancy footwork for the FBI."

Renee let his wisecrack go. She didn't tell him that she wasn't the one who'd thought to check. Instead, she smiled thinly and reiterated, "You're lucky I'm not arresting you and hauling you back to Denver with me."

Oh, she'd considered it, all right, and talked to Special Agent Towey about just that. The trouble was the media. The entire nation would accuse the FBI of bully tactics. All Bennett had to say was he and his wife were on the road camping with the kid, out of touch, and they knew nothing about any court order.

No, arresting them would get her nowhere. And Bennett realized it.

She stared at the big man for a moment longer and then said, "We'll be taking charge of the boy now. Do you have his belongings packed?"

He was a bright, engaging child. Curious. "What's a special agent? Where are we going now? Will I see my mommy? Gramma, are you coming?"

Sally knelt down and held him. "You're going with this lady on a trip in an airplane. No, sweetie, we're not coming. We have to drive down in the camper. But you get to fly. Be a good boy, Charley.''

"We were going fishing," Charley said.

"We'll have to do that another time," Bob said, his voice tight with anger and pain.

"But we will, won't we, Grampa?"

"Yes, Charley, I promise."

He insisted on carrying his own bunny-shaped backpack, containing his blanket and some toys and a couple of books. Jim Mitchell took his bag of clothes.

Bob and Sally hugged the boy. Sally wept. Renee took Charley's hand and led him to the Park Service vehicle, where Ranger Whitsett waited to drive them back to the plane.

"We're going on an adventure," Renee told Charley. "It'll be fun."

"Is it a *big* airplane?" he asked, spreading his arms wide.

"You know what? It's a small plane, but it's very fast."

"Where are we going?"

"Denver."

"Denber," he said. "Denber is the capital of Colorado. I live in Colorado," he said proudly.

Wow, Renee thought. *This is some smart kid.* Would hers be as smart, as cute, as curious? Would hers be a boy or a girl? Would her child even be born?

He was very good on the flight back. The pilot let him visit the cockpit, where he stared wide-eyed at the array of instruments. He looked out the window when they took off, then he played with the puzzles Sally had given Renee to keep him occupied.

"Will my mommy be in Denber?" he asked several times.

"Yes, Charley, your mommy will be there to pick you up." Renee knew she was lying to the child, and she was squirming in her belly because it was wrong. But how could a four-year-old understand what was happening?

"I can't wait to see Mommy," he said once, and Renee cringed.

She was shocked at her emotional response to Charley. She kept seeing inside her head images of Kerry Pope, of that house, the boyfriend, the pale unhealthy sheen of Kerry's skin.

She thought of the child growing in her womb. What if she had this baby? Could she give it away to someone as Kerry had done?

No, her mind screamed, surprising her with the vehemence of her reaction.

Okay, she thought. Tonight she'd tell Jay. Tonight. Together they'd make the right decision.

SOMEONE IN THE FBI office, or Kerry Pope herself, had leaked the information that Charley was back in Denver. Renee turned the boy over to Children's Services late that afternoon while arrangements were made for his reunion with his biological mother, and when she returned to the Federal Building, the place was besieged by the media.

Special Agent in Charge Towey held a press conference and gave an update to the press just in time for the evening news. He had Renee say a few words, cameras flashing at her, videocams grinding, reporters shouting questions. It was hot that late afternoon on the curving steps of the Federal Building, and Renee perspired, feeling weak with hunger, her stomach growling and empty.

Afterward media scattered to reorganize at the building that housed Children's Services, where Kerry Pope was scheduled to pick up her son at 7:00 p.m.

Renee had to be there, of course. The Bureau needed the credit, and the coup reflected well on her. *Career advancement,* she thought. *Fast track.* But she was tired and feeling wilted from the long day, the tension, and the heat. And from the disturbing knowledge that Charley would be under Kerry's care from now on.

That sweet, trusting, smart little boy, who thought he was going to see his mommy.

The whole world watched that evening as Kerry Pope arrived in the shiny black 4Runner, chauffeured by Eddie Daniels.

Renee was surprised that Kerry was decently dressed—blouse and skirt and sandals, her hair pulled back by barrettes on either side. She looked young and scared, expectant and thrilled. Just right for the cameras.

Her lawyer met her in front of Children's Services, then they disappeared inside. Sometime later they re-emerged, Kerry leading Charley by the hand.

Renee's superiors directed her to say a word or two to Kerry, to answer questions, to put forth a united front to the cameras. And she wanted to be there, because at least her face was slightly familiar to Charley, when everyone else surrounding him was a complete stranger.

Poor child.

He was very confused, a trace of dried tears on his round cheeks. Kerry stopped and smiled uncertainly at the crowd; her lawyer began to speak, but Renee didn't hear. She leaned down and said, "Hi, Charley."

He stood there, his bunny-shaped pack on his back, the grape jam smudges still on his new T-shirt, his blue eyes welling with tears and overflowing. His nose was running.

"You promised I was going to see Mommy," he said to Renee, his lower lip quivering. "I want Mommy."

Oh, God, she thought, her smile stiff on her lips, her heart breaking.

Then Kerry leaned down to put her arms around her son, but Charley pushed at her. "I want my mommy," he wailed.

And the media recorded every detail for the voracious public to feed on.

GRACE'S MOOD HAD SWUNG wildly between hysteria and terror all day. Ever since her father had phoned to tell her about Charley, she'd been going out of her mind.

All she could do was survey the circus on television—the grave-faced anchors; the frenzied questions; the scenes of the Federal Building, of Kerry Pope, of Children's Services and her son, Charley, her little boy, with his backpack and tear-stained face.

"I can't...I can't bear it," she whispered.

"Don't watch. I told you not to watch," Luke said.

"I have to!" she cried.

"Grace..."

"No, no, you don't understand. He isn't your son. You have no idea... I have to do something."

Luke came to where she was sitting on the couch

in the rented apartment, staring at the TV, her eyes sunken, tears near the surface, not caring what she looked like, not caring what Luke thought. Only suffering.

"Grace," he said awkwardly, taking one of her hands, "it's not the end of the world. It's a glitch. I'll get Charley back for you."

She turned her face toward him. "When? How long will it take? *She's* got Charley now. What's she going to do? She can't take care of him!" Then she drew her fingers from his and put her face in her hands, bending over, forehead to knees, sobs torn from her. She never felt him stroking her back, trying to calm her.

She rose suddenly, her body taut. "I have to go," she said. "I have to get him. Give me the car keys."

"Grace, no, think about it," he began.

"No! I won't think about it. He's my son, my baby. I have to go get him. I'll talk to her." She began pacing frenetically. "I'll offer her money. That'll work."

"Grace, stop it. You can't go to her. That's crazy. We have some stuff on her already. It'll just take time."

"I can't leave Charley with her!"

"Sit down." His voice permeated her hysteria, and her knees collapsed under her. He caught her and helped lower her to the couch.

"Now, stop and think. A little patience. I thought we'd have more time, but now we have to adjust."

"Look," Grace said, pointing at the TV.

Renee Paynter's face filled the screen. A beautiful African-American woman in a tailored suit. Her expression was somber, and she appeared tired.

"Special Agent Paynter," a reporter was asking, "can you tell us what developments there are regarding the search for the boy's foster mother, Grace Bennett?"

A photo of Grace flashed on the screen as Renee continued. "We do not know Grace Bennett's location at the moment, but we are expecting a break in the case very soon."

"Since you have Charley back, will the FBI be pursuing the kidnapping charges against Professor Bennett?"

Grace moaned, unaware of the sound coming from her throat.

"Yes, of course. Grace Bennett broke the law. She is guilty of kidnapping. We will not drop the charges at this time."

"Shit," Luke muttered.

"Thank you, Special Agent Paynter," the reporter was saying.

"Thank *you*," Renee replied.

"And now we switch back to coverage of Kerry Pope's reunion with her newly found son, Charley. Kevin, are you there?"

Luke clicked the TV off, and the room buzzed with silence.

"You can't go to see her," Luke finally said. "If you flaunt yourself, stick yourself right under their noses, they'd have no choice but to arrest you. Grace, do you hear me?"

"Yes," she breathed.

"All right. You need to sleep."

"Sleep?"

"What good will it do you or Charley to stay up all night?"

"I can't operate from your kind of logic," she said dully.

He sat next to her on the couch. "Listen to me. You hired me to do a job. We had a setback here, but they still don't know where you are, and they don't even know I exist. I'll do the job. You'll get your son back."

"Do you understand what he's going through right now? In a stranger's house? And that boyfriend? I can't stand to think about it."

"Then shut it out."

"You don't realize what you're asking."

"Look, Charley's going to be fine. He's certainly better than you are."

"Please."

"Okay, okay." He ran a hand through his short hair.

She turned her tear-stained face to him. "And what if you prove Kerry unfit but the FBI have already arrested me? Where will Charley go then?"

"Stop worrying about the FBI. They're bluffing. They can't make the charges stick. They know public opinion is with you. They're only posturing to cover their butts. If you just keep out of their sight until this blows over, you'll be fine."

"I wish I could believe you."

"Believe me."

She pulled in a deep breath. "So that was the agent you interviewed?"

"Yeah. Smart lady. Tough as nails."

"I wonder..." She thought a minute. "I wonder if she has children. Then she'd understand."

"I don't know." Luke put a hand out and drew her face around to his. "Take it easy. All that stuff on

TV—that was just hype. It doesn't mean anything.''
He ran a finger down her cheek and along her jaw.

She shivered.

"Now, you have to pull yourself together. I'm going to need your help.''

She laid her head against him, giving up for the moment, giving in. She wasn't alone in this. He'd help her. He'd sworn he'd get her son back, and she had to hang on to that, to believe it.

"Better?'' he asked. An unfamiliar gentle tone.

"Yes,'' she said. "Yes.'' Then she straightened and brushed back her short red bangs, set her shoulders. He was right. She'd have to be strong for Charley. But, oh how hard it was going to be.

CHAPTER THIRTEEN

LUKE STOOD AT THE WINDOW inside the apartment and held the curtain aside, staring across the parking lot of the Tech Center complex. A new building was being erected in the distance, and he idly marveled at the huge towering crane that sat silent at this evening hour. He was reminded of the project going up next to Metropole Insurance in San Francisco.

Did he wish he were sitting in the conference room there, wish he'd never met Grace and gotten so involved in her life?

Yes and no, he thought. Right now he was completely useless. Grace sat behind him on the couch, devastated, and he couldn't do a good goddamn thing to help.

That mattered to him a whole lot more than it should. He felt frustration and anger bordering on rage. The system stank.

He recalled Charley's gleeful cries on the swing in the park such a short time ago, and now the boy was in the custody of a drug addict. Even if he hadn't met Grace or Charley, he would still feel for that little boy, who could have been in the same predicament he'd been in at that age, handed from one uncaring home to another. No way should Kerry Pope have custody of the child. Not for a night. Hell, not even for an hour.

He let the curtain drop, pivoted and gazed at Grace. She was verging on hysteria again and no words of comfort would help. He'd be mumbling platitudes and she'd know it.

So he watched her suffer in his own silence. Grace, so fragile and small on the oversize couch, too quiet, her head bowed. Her nape was slim and white against her red hair. He wanted badly to go to her and just touch the fine skin of her neck, feel the silky strands of her hair.

"You haven't eaten all day," he said finally.

"I'm not hungry," she murmured.

"You need to eat."

"Leave me alone," she said wearily.

"Grace…"

"What?"

"Nothing." He felt foolish. He could imagine Judith watching him, laughing and mocking his ineptitude. Judith, a woman who could be no more different from Grace.

Grace rose. "I think I'll go to bed," she said.

"All right." He leaned back against the wall and eyed her.

"I can't…I can't do anything now. I…" Then she just stood there.

His feet moved of their own volition, until he was close to her, too close. Her eyes were red from weeping, her nose shiny, her skin blotched. But he saw the beauty of her, glowing through.

"Grace," he said, hardly recognizing his own voice.

She only stared at him, her eyes slightly unfocused without her glasses or her contacts.

"I promise I'll get Charley back for you." He put

a hand out to touch her cheek, felt the warm smoothness. She didn't move away, just kept her eyes locked to his.

"Tell me what I can do to help," he said, his palm still on her cheek. Dimly, he realized he should lead her to her room, allow her to lie down, sleep, conserve her energy.

"I don't think I want to be alone right now," she said in a voice that was barely audible, and something inside him shifted.

An instant later, in one of those defining moments of time, a current leaping between them jolted him. Suddenly, a pulse beat heavily in his groin. She was so lovely, with the kind of beauty that grew on you, a fragile, exquisite beauty that was part and parcel of who she was. Eyes, lips, nose, ears, skin. All Grace. Not like Judith, whose beauty was a startling thing separate from who she was.

He felt her move her head, pressing against the hand on her cheek, leaning into it, her eyes closing. Drawing her near, he bent his head to touch her lips.

No pulling back this time. No excuses, no lies, no saying it didn't mean anything.

It meant everything.

She tasted of salty tears and sadness. And he couldn't stop. He tasted her, licking her lips, his hands on her back, pulling her nearer. And she answered, opening to him, her mouth, her softness, her hands on his shoulders.

They both paused simultaneously, eased back, sought each other's gazes.

"Is this...?" she began.

"Yes," he said.

"This isn't...wasn't supposed to happen, Luke."

"Shut up, Grace." And he bent to her upturned face again, not caring whether he was acting out of the already intense emotions that crowded around both of them, or out of the enforced proximity, or if it was both those things and more, so much more.

She was passionate, surprising him, although he shouldn't have been surprised. Her hands were all over him, her breath fast, her body strong in its insistence.

The dowdy college professor.

She said his name a dozen times, ran her fingers through his hair, down his neck. Their mouths plundered each other. He ran his hands up under her new tank top, feeling her ribs, her backbone. She was as taut and slim as a Thoroughbred.

Judith, he thought once, shocked at how little he cared about her, how insipid she seemed now.

He kissed Grace's ear, sucking in its sweet pink shell; kissed her neck, her shoulder, her collarbone. Sweet and salt and a foreign spice that was Grace.

"Please," she said, and he wasn't sure what she meant, but he didn't ask. He swept her up and held her, feeling powerful, and she hid her face in the hollow of his shoulder.

He took her into his bedroom, laid her on the bed, with its ugly spread of blue-and-brown flowers.

She pulled her top off and reached for his shirt; unfastened it too slowly, her eyes meeting his, the light from the living room scalding one side of her face.

She had on a plain white cotton bra, nothing like the bright lacy ones Judith wore. He unbuttoned the waistband of her capri pants, slowly unzipped them. She pushed them down herself.

He kissed her belly, her thighs, the arches of her feet. She unzipped his pants and felt him. It was as if hot electricity scored him there.

They were naked then, and he lay on top of her, one arm curled around her head, his hand stroking her hair.

"Now?" he asked, bending to kiss a nipple, then to suck, then to kiss again.

"Yes, yes," she said, then, "I'm afraid."

"Of what?"

"I won't...I won't be good for you."

He didn't answer; he rose above her and entered her, and he felt her around him, holding him. Perfectly still at first, then moving, drawing him deeper. He gasped and went with her. The heat rose in him, the almost pain, the unbearable waiting, the beautiful waiting.

She cried out a second before he did, and he felt her undulate, all hot red movement, then felt the sweet release of tension, the emptiness and oblivion of delight. Grace's hands on his sweaty back, her words in his ear, her body under his.

"Oh," he heard, a breathless entreaty.

"Grace?"

"Yes...yes?"

"It was good for me, okay?"

He awoke sometime in the night, hearing her smothered sobs. He held her close and whispered, "It'll be all right."

"I'm so scared." Her face was against his chest, and he could feel the heat of her tears.

"Sh, it's okay. Charley's okay. We'll get him back."

"We have to," she said. "We have to. Oh, Luke."

"Go to sleep." He stroked her shoulder, silky, warm and smooth, with fine bones underneath. And then he thought she breathed the words "I love you," but he must have dreamed that.

In the light of day everything looked different. She was up and dressed and making coffee when he awoke. Tense, sober, focused, as if she'd come to a momentous decision in the night while he'd slept.

"It was a mistake," she said carefully. "People in tense situations do…do that. It's a way of compensating. Of coping."

His heart turned to stone in his chest. "Do what, Grace?"

She couldn't meet his eyes. "Have sex."

"Is that what we did—have sex?"

"Yes," she whispered.

"I thought…shit, for a minute there I thought we *liked* each other, but I guess I was wrong."

"Don't…please, don't do that. This is a difficult enough situation. You've got a wife you're in love with, and I…my whole life is a mess. I have to concentrate on Charley."

Luke wore a pair of jeans, no shirt. He was cold all of a sudden, as if the air-conditioning were on too high. "Sure, you're right," he said offhandedly. "Dumb trick, huh?"

"Yes." Her eyes were wide, apprehensive.

"Okay, we forget about it. It didn't happen. We have work to do."

"Yes."

He poured himself a cup of coffee and raised it to his lips. It was hot, and he blew on the liquid. He met her gaze across the cup. "Don't worry, Grace, you're in no danger from me."

"Let's be objective," she said.

"Of course," he agreed, then he drank his coffee, finishing half the cup before he realized he hadn't put any sugar in it. God, he hated black coffee. Bitter as gall. But this morning, somehow it suited his sentiments.

RENEE PAYNTER MADE an excuse and took a long lunch break that day. She could have told Mead Towey the truth about where she was going, but she felt uncomfortable doing so. She drove the short distance to the house Kerry Pope lived in, thinking about what she was going to say when she arrived. What she was really doing, she admitted to herself, was checking on Charley and trying to assuage her own sense of guilt.

The conditions were as bad as she'd expected.

Charley was dressed in the same clothes he'd worn the day before, the same purple-stained T-shirt. He was sitting on the dirty plaid couch, watching television, when Eddie Daniels let her in.

"Checking on us?" he asked sourly.

"I'd like to see Kerry, please," Renee said.

"She's taking a nap."

"Who's watching Charley, then?"

He thumped a thumb on his chest. "Me, that's who. Something wrong?"

"Could you please tell Kerry I'm here," she said patiently.

"Geez, I didn't think you'd be this goddamn nosy." Daniels grinned nastily.

"Please get Kerry." Renee drew herself up to her full height and used her official voice.

"Okay, okay."

While he was gone she sat down next to the boy. "Remember me, Charley?"

"You said you were taking me to see my mommy." His young voice held such accusation she quivered inside.

"This *is* your mommy, Charley."

"No, she's only a baby-sitter until my mommy comes to get me."

Renee sighed. Words out of the mouths of babes. "Did you have lunch yet?"

"Uh-huh."

"What did you have?"

"Peanut better and jelly."

"Do you have your own room, Charley?"

"Uh-huh, but my room at home is better. I want my toys."

"Maybe we can get them for you. That'd be good, wouldn't it?"

He sat with his back against the couch, his legs stuck out straight in front of. him, his chin on his chest, his lower lip pouting. "I want to go home. I want Mommy. I don't like it here."

God Almighty, Renee thought, *what have I done?*

Kerry entered the living room then, her eyes puffy from sleep, her hair tangled, her clothes wrinkled and stained.

"Hello, Kerry," Renee said.

"Hi." She put a smile on her face. "How's Charley? How's my boy?" she asked with false animation.

He pouted. "I want to go home."

Kerry's eyes slid away from Renee. "This is your home now, Charley. Remember, I told you."

"It is *not.*"

Apologetically, Kerry turned to Renee. "It'll take him a while, I guess."

"Yes, I suppose so." She hesitated. "Kerry, I really do think it would be better if you didn't leave Charley in your boyfriend's care."

"Why? Eddie's great with kids."

"Charley is *your* responsibility, not Eddie's."

"But...well, I was just taking a nap. I was up so late last night, you know, all those reporters and stuff."

"As a mother, Kerry, you have a huge responsibility. That little boy's life is in your hands."

"I don't need any lectures from you." Kerry put her head on one side and studied her. "You have any kids?"

"No." A pang struck Renee, a blow to her insides.

"Then what do you know?" Kerry laid a hand on Charley's head possessively. He reached grubby fingers up and pushed it away.

"Kerry, I'm trying to be helpful."

"Yeah, right. You're spying on me. Well, Special Agent Paynter, you did your job. Now, leave me alone."

Renee had trouble concentrating the rest of the afternoon. Should she call Boulder's Child Protective Services and report Kerry Pope as unfit? Should she call the judge who had handed the boy over to her? She could do it anonymously, then no one in the office would know. Neither would the ravenous media. But then, neither Child Protective Services nor the judge would take her seriously. An anonymous caller was invariably a crank, an irate neighbor, a jealous relative. They'd give the complaint no credence whatsoever.

What should she do? Maybe Kerry would come around, turn into a good mother. Maybe Charley would get used to his new situation and come to love Kerry.

Sure.

She arrived home that night hungry and exhausted. The waistband of her skirt felt very tight. She took off her suit as fast as she could and pulled on comfortable, elastic-waist pants. Panic bubbled inside her belly. She had to decide soon. Very soon.

Jay arrived shortly after she did. He kissed her cheek, and she hoped he didn't recognize the dismay in her eyes. Over a dinner of pork chops and potato salad and coleslaw from the deli section of the supermarket, she got up her nerve to broach her concerns about Charley.

"The house is dirty, dishes all over, and he was in the same clothes, and I don't trust that boyfriend."

"Renee, stop torturing yourself. Look, if the biological mother is that bad Child Protective Services will see, and the judge will have to review the case," Jay offered.

"I wish we hadn't found him, wish I wasn't so damn good at my job," she said bitterly.

"Holy cow, I've never seen you so riled up about a case, honey. What's going on?"

"It's not fair. You said so yourself. The judge never should have given him to Kerry. He should have stayed with Grace Bennett. My God, when I think…"

"Okay, Renee, what's up? I know you. There's something going on here, isn't there?"

"Jay, don't be silly." She scooped up a big forkful of potato salad and chewed it. She couldn't meet his eyes. "It's just that I know—we both know—how ineffective any of the social services can be. And how long will it take? Jay, he said he wanted to go home. He said it over and over."

"The poor kid." He shook his head.

She looked down, heat infusing her cheeks. "I thought of calling the judge. But then...oh, Lord, Towey would have a conniption. I'd be demoted. I...can't. I just can't."

"Renee, for God's sake..."

"Never mind, Jay. I'm just venting." She waved a hand dismissively. "It'll work out."

"Sure it will," he agreed.

But she couldn't shake thoughts of Charley Pope—his pouting lip and the dirty T-shirt; the way he'd said he wanted to go home; his assertion that Kerry wasn't his mother, only a baby-sitter. His words to *her* that she'd promised to take him to his mommy. The guilt hurt so much she almost howled.

In bed that night with Jay, she felt teary and overwhelmed. Was it simply hormones racing about in her blood? Was it guilt? Was it anxiety? But she couldn't help the words from bursting out of her as she lay in the dark, in her husband's solid, familiar embrace.

"Jay, honey?"

"Mmm."

"You asleep?"

"Not anymore."

"Jay..."

"What?"

"Jay, I'm pregnant."

His big body stiffened. "What?" he asked again.

"I'm pregnant. Over two months and..."

"You're pregnant? You really are?" His voice was full of wonder.

"Jay, listen."

He put his hand on her stomach. "I can't believe it. Why didn't you tell me?"

"I...I was thinking. I..."

"Wow, this is something. This is exciting. Did you tell your folks yet?"

"No...Jay..." She swallowed, lying there in the dark, looking up at the ceiling. "I'm not sure I want to keep it."

He sat straight up, the sheet falling off him. "You're not sure you want to keep it?" he asked ominously.

"Jay, please, listen. The timing's so bad, and my job, well, you know what would happen. And then..."

He leaned over her; she tried to discern his expression in the dark, but she couldn't. "You mean," he said slowly, "you're thinking of ending your pregnancy?"

"Yes," she whispered.

"That's my baby in there," he breathed. "And you want to get rid of it?"

"No, it's not that, but I don't know if I'm ready. Jay, please, try to understand," she pleaded.

"You're thirty-three years old, you have a husband, you're healthy, you're moderately well off. For God's sake, Renee, what more could make you *ready?*"

"Jay..." Tears burned in her eyes.

"Look, Renee, I love you, and I love that baby. And if you destroy it, you destroy our marriage. Do you hear me?"

"I hear you," she said in a shaky voice. She shouldn't have told him. She shouldn't have.

"I love you, Renee," came her husband's voice after a time.

"I love you, too," she replied.

And as she lay there, wrung by apprehension, Renee broke down and cried, weeping for her ambition, hating herself for finding Charley Pope and for not desperately wanting her own baby. Hating herself and wondering if she loved the tiny creature growing within her as much as Grace Bennett loved her foster son.

CHAPTER FOURTEEN

THE FOLLOWING MORNING Luke was on a roll, just as he had been all of yesterday. He was a man on a mission. He didn't bother showering or shaving, and hadn't even done up his jeans when he appeared in the kitchen at the crack of dawn to pour himself a quick cup of coffee and tell Grace he was out of there in five minutes.

"It's time to dig up some real dirt on Daniels," he said, distracted.

"The boyfriend."

"Yeah. I've got an old acquaintance with Denver PD, a guy with Vice who worked with me on a case in San Francisco once. We got to know each other. I'm betting he'll be happy to shake down a couple of gang members. Maybe one of them will do some talking."

"About Daniels?"

Luke took a sip of coffee, sputtered at the hot liquid, then headed toward the bathroom. "It's worth a shot."

"But what if it doesn't work? What if...?"

"You don't want to know" was all he'd say, and Grace had a sudden, disquieting image of Luke beating Kerry's boyfriend up until he confessed everything, naming names, disclosing his clients—including Kerry.

She sat on the couch as the sun rose over Denver, feeling tired and restless, and she tried to force the images aside. Luke was going to do what was necessary to bust Kerry. Grace had begged him to help. She could hardly complain about his methods.

She dropped her head into her hands and fought her misgivings. He'd told her to be strong. But oh, how hard it was. The sense of utter helplessness was threatening her sanity, and nothing anyone could tell her would change that. Yesterday, when Luke had gone out early, she'd reached her parents on their way to Colorado, and she'd talked on the cell phone for nearly an hour to her father, listened to his anger, his frustration, listened to his confidence in Luke's ability to win back her child for her. It was easy for them, ex-policemen, but they had lived in a world so alien to her experience she found it difficult to judge if their bravado was male chest beating or reality. In the meantime, here she sat, alone and going crazy with the need to do something, anything, that might help get her baby back in her arms.

She went into the bathroom and stepped into the shower, which was still wet from Luke. No matter where she turned, she couldn't get away from him.

She tried to put him out of her mind and decided to dwell, instead, on what she might have done over the past few months that could have altered this outcome. Had she fought hard enough in court? Had her lawyer taken all the right steps? Perhaps losing Charley would have been the only outcome no matter what they had done.

The water sluiced down her shoulders and her back, easing her tension, but only temporarily. Nothing was going to help as long as Charley's future was in jeopardy. She put her hands on the warm tiles and bowed her head, taking deep breaths, telling herself to trust Luke, to trust her father, who would be in Denver tomorrow afternoon at the very latest. As desperate as her situation was, she forced herself to remember that not everything had been so very terrible over the past two weeks. She'd met Luke, hadn't she? Discovered a side to herself she had never suspected. She was a woman capable of unquenchable desire for a man. Not any man. *This* man. She'd changed so radically in such a short period of time she barely knew herself. Had it really been Professor Sally Grace Bennett, schoolmarmish, dowdy Grace, who'd given and taken such pleasure?

When she finally got out of the shower, she noticed Luke's wet towel, still lying in a damp heap on the bathroom floor. She couldn't stop herself from picking it up, holding it to her breast, even bending her head to draw in its scent.

She toweled herself off and was still marveling that this body, this image in the steamy mirror with the short, wild red hair, was her. Could it have been this body that had lain beneath that man and reveled in every sigh and touch? And she'd known all along that the man who'd awakened this hidden side shared none of the same feelings. He loved someone else. He loved his *wife*.

"I don't care," she said aloud, but she didn't believe it.

She'd lost her child and found love in the space of two short weeks, she thought as she dressed. What would she tell a patient who walked into her office and said, "Doctor, I'm in love with a strange man who's married and still in love with his wife"?

What would she tell her?

For one, she would tell her she was out of control, self-destructive, in denial. Beyond that, Grace had no answers. Perhaps she would tell the patient, "Great, that's great. Look at all the years you busied yourself in your work and your child. Isn't it wonderful to feel alive? Isn't it wonderful to have known love, even if for a few moments, than never to have loved at all?"

It was only midmorning when she dialed her neighbor's number, knowing Luke would forbid it, knowing that just possibly the FBI had a tap on Stacey's phone. But she risked it. She'd dumped her animals, her mail and half her everyday problems on Stacey. She owed her at least a quick call.

She never got a chance to thank Stacey for tending to all her chores, though. Her neighbor launched right in. "Oh, my God, Grace, I've been waiting for days for you to get in touch. I know maybe we shouldn't talk—I mean, God knows, we've all been following your story. Anyway, your friend from Child Protective Services came by last week, asking around about you, and we got to talking and, well, she said for you to contact her immediately. She said not to use her name, you'd know who it was."

"Did she say anything else?" Grace's heart was pounding and the hairs on her flesh rose.

"No, nothing, just that it was vital you call her."

"Okay." She took a breath. "I just called to say thanks, Stacey, thanks so much for everything."

"Oh, forget *that*. You owe me for some cat food, okay?"

Grace almost laughed.

"Now, get off the phone and call your friend, and

hey, I love you and Charley and I know this will work out. Screw the courts."

"I love you, too," Grace said, tears threatening, and then she hung up.

Two minutes later she was on the phone with Susan Moore at Boulder Child Protective Services.

"Oh, thank heavens," Susan breathed into the phone. "I was afraid I'd never hear from you."

"Stacey, my neighbor, said—"

"Yes, yes, I have something for you. I don't know how we missed it. And I can't use it myself, but..."

"What is it?" Grace was bursting with curiosity.

"It's a report. It was stuck way back in some files in the storeroom, confidential stuff. Anyway, you've *got* to see this."

"But what is it?"

"Look—" Susan paused as if thinking "—do you have a fax number or access to a computer?"

"No, no computer." Then Grace snatched up the apartment complex information card stuck on a plastic holder next to the phone. "Okay, yes," she said excitedly, "here it is, a fax number. But for Lord's sake, don't put my name on the cover sheet. Use the name Luke Sarkov. That's S-a-r-k-o-v. Here's the number." Grace gave it to her. "Oh, and put instructions on it to phone apartment 108C as soon as it comes in, okay?"

"All right, yes, I'll get this off to you within the next five minutes. Oh, wait till you see it!"

"You can't just tell me now?"

"Better that you have the whole report," Susan said. "I'll get the cover sheet ready right now. And Grace, good luck. My God, what you must have been through."

"Yes," Grace said, "it's been hell." *Except for Luke,* she thought, and then shook the notion out of her head. "Thanks, Susan, really. Thanks for doing this. I can't wait."

"Oh, and this never came from me. Okay?"

"Absolutely. I promise, mum's the word."

"I'll see you soon."

"I hope so."

"I will. I know I will. And Charley, too. Good luck."

"You're a great friend," Grace said, and she hung up.

The fifteen minutes it took for the call to come in from the apartment complex office was agony for Grace. She counted every second. Wringing her hands, pacing, chewing her bottom lip till she tasted blood. What had Susan dug up? *What?*

When the phone finally rang she leaped, snatching it up halfway through the ring. "Hello?"

"This is the office. We have a fax for Mr. Sarkov. Is he there?"

Grace had it all planned. "Oh, gosh, he's in the shower. Should I just come down for it? *Say yes,* she prayed.

"That will be fine."

"See you in a minute," she said, and she was out the door and dashing down the walkway toward the office before the woman had even severed the phone connection.

LUKE GOT OUT of his car in the parking lot of the apartment complex and felt the heat hit him. It was late afternoon, and the sun glared off the asphalt in rippling waves. He shed his summer-weight sport

coat, tossed it over his shoulder with a hooked finger
and wondered how Grace was going to take the news.
The good news and the bad news.

The first thing he'd done that morning was to get
together with his acquaintance at the Denver Police
Department. His pal Frank had once worked with him
in San Francisco on a numbers runner bust, and
they'd kept in touch. He'd explained right off that he
wasn't there in an official capacity, but he could use
some help.

"So, you're a private dick now?" Frank had asked.

"I'm doing this job for a friend. You remember
Big Bob Bennett?"

"Bennett, yeah, it rings a bell. Worked with kids,
right?"

"That's him."

"So, what's up?"

"I need the inside dope on this guy named Eddie
Daniels."

"Daniels, huh? Oh, I know him, all right. I don't
have to tell you that Eddie is Kerry Pope's main
squeeze. Hell, the whole country knows about the
Pope woman and her kid and the CU professor. Say,
you wouldn't be helping out the professor, would
you?" But before Luke had replied, Frank had said,
"No. Wait. Don't answer that. The less I know the
better."

Luke had nodded.

Then his friend had said, "I hate to tell you, Sarkov, but we've been trying to nail Daniels for some
time now. Trouble is, he doesn't make mistakes.
Never talks on the phone about deals he's involved
in, always makes his contacts with suppliers in places
we can't monitor, and so far we don't have enough

to take to a judge and get a search-and-seize warrant.'' Frank thought for a time. ''I'll tell you what. We've got one of the Mile Highs in jail right now. Arrested him for pulling a weapon on another guy in a bar. He's waiting for arraignment as we speak.''

''Has he been questioned?''

''Nah, he lawyered up so fast it made my head spin.''

''Shit.''

''Yeah.''

Luke pondered the problem. ''What if you give him a little slack, look the other way on the assault charge if he hands over some info on Daniels?''

''Geez, Sarkov, that means getting the D.A. involved, all that crap.''

''I know. But this is important, Frank.''

His pal sighed. ''I guess we can try.''

They'd driven to the city jail on Cherokee Street and waited for the gang member to be brought to the visitors' room. He turned out to be tall and skinny, with a shaved head, a beard and a loop earring in his left ear.

''Rick Boraski,'' Frank had said, ''meet a colleague of mine from California. He needs some information.''

''Talk to my lawyer,'' Rick had said, bored.

''I want to talk to you,'' Luke had replied with a steely edge to his voice.

''Shove it, cop.''

''I'm not a cop. I'm a P.I., and nothing you say to me will reflect on you. I want some good info on Daniels. It might just make things easier for you, Boraski.''

''Yeah, sure, and pigs fly.''

"Daniels. Give me some details."

"He'll kill me."

"He'll never know."

"Maybe I talk and I get zilch in return."

"My word," Frank had put in. "I'll call the D.A. today. I'll do it from here, if you want. Maybe get your beef down to felony menacing. Maybe even illegal possession of a firearm. But you gotta give us something."

Rick had thought for a time, and Luke had waited with trepidation. Not showing it, though. *Never let down.*

After Boraski had pondered for a couple of minutes, Luke had sat back and said, "This is a one-time shot, buddy. You've got five minutes to make up your mind, then we're outta here. If I were you, I'd wise up fast."

Rick looked at Frank and nodded at Luke. "He for real?"

"Oh, yeah," Frank had said.

When the five minutes were up Luke had abruptly risen from his chair. "I figured you for more smarts, Boraski. Come on, Frank, we've got other fish to fry."

They had been halfway down the corridor, when Luke heard Rick tell the jailer, "Call them back here. Hey, tell them to come back. I'll cooperate. Hurry, man."

Thirty seconds later Luke sat across from the punk again. "If you're yanking my chain, Rick, there'll be hell to pay. Now, let's hear what you've got."

Rick was sweating bullets, but he talked. "Okay, there's gonna be a big meet in a couple weeks. The L.A. Angels are driving a load of pot to Denver. First time they're trying it. They'll switch the shit for cash near Chatfield Reservoir off Interstate 470.''

"Exact location?" Frank had asked.

"That's all I know. I voted against it—too dangerous. But Eddie's a greedhead." The man shrugged bony shoulders.

"All right." Frank had sounded satisfied. "I think that'll do, Boraski. I'll make that call."

Luke had thought furiously. Two weeks was too long a wait to pin something on Daniels. Grace wouldn't last two weeks. Hell, he wondered if he could.

"Anything coming up sooner?" he'd asked the prisoner.

"Not that I'd talk about," Boraski had said coolly.

They'd left the city jail, Frank happy, Luke disappointed. He needed more and he needed it sooner. But he'd done his best. Now, to break the news to Grace. Two weeks would seem like an eternity to her.

He'd thanked Frank and returned to his car, racking his brain for new leads, new evidence trails to follow, new ways of digging out information on Daniels or on Kerry. Sure, there were steps he could take, but they all needed time. And time was Charley's enemy, Grace's enemy, *his* enemy. *Damn.*

Luke wiped sweat from the back of his neck and let himself into the apartment. In his head he was framing the words he'd use to tell Grace he might have made some headway at busting Eddie Daniels. He didn't want her to get her hopes too high, though, because the arrest was weeks off. God only knows, she'd suffered enough.

He unlocked the door, called out, "It's me," and wondered exactly when he'd become so fiercely protective of this woman. Had it been before or after the other night?

He walked down the short hall and into the living room, and the sight of her was a soft sweet blow to his gut.

Instantly, he figured something was up. She leaped up from where she'd been sitting at the kitchen table, her cheeks flushed, her eyes as bright as green gems, a look of taut expectation on her face. For a heartbeat he forgot his good intentions, and a craving to make love to her on the spot overwhelmed him. He knew, in that rush of time, that he'd never wanted a woman with such urgency. *Not even…Judith,* ran through his brain.

But Grace broke the spell as abruptly as she'd cast it. "I've got news, Luke. Oh, my God, wait till you hear!" Her smile widened, and he thought she might just jump out of her skin.

He saw then that she was holding some sheets of paper. "I guess you better tell me," he said, clearing his throat, retreating back into reality.

"Oh, where to start?" She began pacing, waving the papers. "It's all here, I mean… Oh, Luke, just read it."

He took the sheets from her. "Where did you get this?"

"Just read it. I'll tell you everything, but please, read it before I burst. I've been waiting and waiting for you."

"I can see that," he said laconically. He stood in the living room, didn't even sit, and scanned the papers.

The first thing he saw was *Confidential* stamped in red on the top. Then *Child Protective Services, Boul-*

der, Colorado. And then Kerry Pope's name and the text of the typed report. The dates in the text made him immediately aware that this report had been written when Kerry was very young.

He read on. When he was done, he looked up in amazement. "How in hell could the judge have overlooked this report?" he rasped.

Grace was still jittery, shaking her head. "I don't think he ever saw it."

"Where did you get this?"

"Oh, gosh, I called my neighbor Stacey..."

Luke lifted a brow.

But Grace ignored him. "Anyway, a friend of mine from Child Protective Services, the same lady who put me onto the underground railroad, left a message for me to get in touch, so I did, and she faxed it to me."

"And this had been in Kerry's file all along?"

"No, it was stuck away with some papers from when she was a minor. Susan—my friend, that is—found it."

Luke blew out a whistling breath. "I realize Kerry was a minor at the time of this report, but still, this should have been brought to light. The judge could have kept it out of the official transcript, but it should have had some bearing on who got custody of Charley."

He looked down at the report again. Read once more how Kerry had been living in Durango, Colorado, working as kitchen help in a saloon there. How she'd had a two-year-old baby girl. Luke did the math. Kerry would have been fifteen when she'd gotten pregnant. She'd been in high school, he knew, in Denver. But then she'd dropped out of school, and there had been some missing years. So she'd had a baby in a town in the other side of the state. And that baby, that twenty-two-month-old baby girl, had died from a fall down a set of basement steps. The coroner had ruled the death accidental.

Luke looked up from the report. Grace was watching him.

"Well?" she said.

"It was not an accident," he said quietly.

"That poor, poor baby girl," Grace said. "And Kerry's got Charley. Luke, that woman has Charley. We have to take this to the judge right away."

He thought for a minute.

But Grace was too excited to wait for his reply. "Or should it go to Child Protective Services, instead? No, that would get Susan in trouble. Maybe Natalie, my lawyer. Yes, she'll know what to do."

"Hold on."

"What? Hold on, why?"

"Look, Grace, this is good stuff, but it's only a report of an accidental death. The judge may not allow it. It's not hard evidence. You need proof that it was more than an accident." He flicked his fingers on the report.

"Okay, okay." She took a few steps then turned and retraced them. "Then we need to go to Durango." Her voice was strained, tight in her chest, full of hope and excitement and fear.

"Grace, I can go, but..."

"No, I'm going. Tonight. Can we go tonight?"

He met her gaze. What was the point in arguing? "Okay."

"I'll pack." She paused, then, "Oh, God, she has Charley."

He nodded. "Not for long."

"But what if…"

"Listen to me," he said in a steel-edged voice, "if I have to kidnap your boy I will. You believe me?"

She held his eyes for a blink of time and then said, "I believe you. I've never trusted anyone like this, but yes, I believe you."

He wanted to tell her how important her words were to him. There was a lot he needed to say. But when he spoke, the only thing that emerged was, "I'll go check us out of here," and he turned and left, wondering exactly when it was he'd become a coward.

CHAPTER FIFTEEN

GRACE AWOKE the next morning in another strange motel room, this time in the Adobe Court just outside of Durango.

They'd arrived late the night before after the five-hour drive and had trouble finding a motel at the height of the tourist season. They'd especially had trouble finding a place with two rooms. Grace had been so tired she hadn't said a word, but she had lain in bed half the night and wondered, why had Luke been so adamant about not sharing a room with her? Oh, she knew that they agreed their liaison had been a mistake. Still... And what would he have done if there *hadn't* been two open rooms anywhere in town? Would he have slept in the car, gone to any lengths to avoid being in close quarters with her? What did he think about her now—that she was loose, horny, desperate? Or did he feel something? If their love-making was a barometer of their feelings, she had to believe he cared a little. But how did she feel about him? How did she really feel?

The night dragged on, the questions assaulting her brain.

Despite the lack of sleep she rose quite early, Charley filling her thoughts and hope beating in her breast. She peeked through the drapes. Durango. Sun and stunted pine trees and red cliffs rising behind the parking lot. The whole world was splashed in dazzling morning light.

But there was no time for sight-seeing. She and Luke had work to do. God, how she hoped this break panned out.

She showered and threw on some clothes—wrinkled white stretch slacks and a green short-sleeved shirt, a much brighter green that she'd ever dreamed of wearing before. She tried to put makeup on, but her hand trembled. Her image stared back at her from the mirror—a woman with red spiky hair and no glasses, a stranger. She hardly recognized herself. Yes, there was a physical change, but something else made her study her reflection. A tautness, a fierce light from within. No longer was she a mild-mannered professor; the woman in the mirror was a crusader, a driven human being. A woman trying to save her child. And herself in the bargain, it occurred to her.

She hadn't spoken to Charley in—how long now? Two—no, three—days. She'd never before been out of contact with him for more than a few hours. What must he think? He was too young to understand why she couldn't even call him. Was he eating all right? Did he cry himself to sleep? Was Kerry watching him, taking care of him? Or would Charley fall down a flight of stairs *accidentally?*

She couldn't think about that. She simply couldn't. Kerry wouldn't dare hurt Charley, not with all the media attention. And Eddie Daniels, that awful man, he wouldn't dare, either. Plus Charley was more than a twenty-two-month-old baby. He was a smart, resourceful little boy. He'd be okay. She took a deep, cleansing breath. Dear God, he had to be okay. *Hold on, baby. Hold on a little longer.*

She called her parents on the cell phone, touching base as she'd promised. They'd gotten into Denver last night and found a spot to park the RV out past the suburb of Parker.

"Where are you?" Bob asked.

Of course, she realized, her parents thought she was still holed up in the city. "Well," she said, "hold on to your hat, Dad, but I'm not in Denver. I'm in Durango."

"Durango? And where, may I ask, is *that?*"

She filled him in as briefly as possible and heard the infusion of hope in his tone. "Holy cow," he said, "if you can get a copy of the autopsy report and maybe the police file on the death of that child…"

"I know," she breathed, "I know. Right now, though, every minute Charley is with Kerry is a minute too long. I better go and meet Luke. Give Mom a hug for me and let's all pray we're successful here."

"You call us, okay?"

"I promise," she said. "Love you guys."

She'd barely gotten off the phone, when Luke knocked on her door. They had breakfast next door at a Western-style café.

"Let's hurry," Grace kept saying. "I want to get the information and get back to Denver with it."

"The courthouse won't open for a half hour," Luke said. He looked tired, just as she did. Had he lain awake, too? Lain there in the lonely dark, thinking about her?

She cleared her mind. "I know, I know the courthouse won't be open yet. I'm just so…I'm a wreck. I'm worried sick about Charley. He can't possibly understand why I haven't come to get him." She nibbled absently at a piece of toast. "Being left behind is a terrible thing for a child, you know. It could make him distrust me, because I left him, I deserted him.'' She looked away, tears pricking her eyes.

Then Luke's hand covered hers, and her flesh burned. ''He'll be okay, Grace. We'll have proof soon.''

She closed her eyes and forced her fears down, took a breath. ''Can we go now? Is it time?''

They drove through downtown Durango, but she barely got an impression of the charming restored brick Victorian buildings and false-front Western saloons. The courthouse had just opened when they arrived, and they found the office that housed records.

Luke flashed his Metropole Insurance ID and informed the clerk he'd been sent on a job to help Sally here, a social worker, with a child abuse case.

''I need a copy of the death certificate for a Merilee Pope, deceased seven years ago—in November, that would be,'' he explained.

''There'll be a charge of $3.50 for the copy,'' the clerk said.

''That's fine.''

''It might take me a few minutes. You folks want to wait or come back?''

''We'll wait,'' Grace said.

''We'll come back,'' Luke said, taking her elbow and leading her out of the office.

''Damn it,'' she whispered, pulling her arm out of his grasp.

''Look, the woman doesn't want us in there waiting. Trust me on this. Come on, we'll walk a few blocks. It's a cute town.''

''Okay, all right. I'm just so…so impatient.''

''I know.''

They wandered down Main Avenue to the narrow gauge railroad station, where tourists waited to board the train for its scenic trip to Silverton, high up in the mountains to the north. The sun was shining, not too hot yet in the morning. Hordes of tourists filled the streets, crowded the restaurants, shopped. Grace wished—oh, how she wished—she could be a carefree tourist, too, strolling along holding Charley's hand while he asked a million questions. How he'd love the toylike narrow-gauge railroad cars. She could take him for the ride, and he'd laugh and he'd wiggle and run through the train station. Maybe he'd fall down and skin his knee. There'd be a few tears and then he'd get over it and...

Charley, she thought, *don't forget me. I'll come for you as soon as I can.*

She jumped with impatience, her skin hot, her muscles twitching. When they finally returned to the courthouse, she felt dizzy from tension.

Luke paid the clerk and took the paper she held in her outstretched hand. "Thank you," he said gravely.

Out in the corridor, Grace craned her neck to see the copy. It was slightly smudged, hard to read, the seal a circle of dark splotches.

"What...what does it say?" she asked.

"Merilee Lynn Pope, born, died. Accidental death. Head trauma due to a fall. That's it."

Disappointment made her heart drop like a stone. "But we need more than that, Luke. We have to prove it *wasn't* an accident."

He smiled humorlessly. "Give me some credit, Professor. We have the doctor's name who signed this certificate."

"So?"

"Next step. Talk to the man."

"How do we find him?" A tiny spark of hope kindled in her heart.

Luke peered at the copy. "Lousy handwriting. It looks like McDougal or McDaniels, something like that. First name Grant."

"Do you think he's still here? It was, what? Seven years ago?"

"The phone book, Professor."

There was a Grant McDougal, M.D., in the Durango listings. Grace's heart gave a glad leap. When Luke phoned his number, his receptionist proved very difficult to convince, but finally Luke got the doctor himself on the line and made a date to meet him at his office after lunch.

For Grace, the hours until the meeting dragged by endlessly. They walked around the streets; they watched the small, colorful railroad cars go by on their regular trips to Silverton, saw the trolley car on Main Avenue, ate lunch—not that Grace would ever remember what she put in her mouth. From the confidential report Susan Moore had provided, they knew the name of the saloon where Kerry had worked—the Silver Belle—but it was closed until evening. Time grated on her nerves. *Hold on, Charley.*

"Hey, this is detective work," Luke said. "Mostly it's waiting. You get used to it."

"I hope I never have to get used to it," she said. "But honestly, I'm glad you're here. If I had to do this alone…" She shook her head.

Eventually, it was time to meet Dr. McDougal. His office was small, in a renovated Victorian. There was flowered wallpaper on the walls and lots of green plants. He came out to the waiting room and clasped

Luke's hand, a thin, ascetic-looking man with a gray mustache. "Pretty far off the beaten track here in Durango, aren't you?" he asked Luke after scrutinizing his ID.

"I'm on temporary duty out of Denver," Luke said smoothly, "helping out on a Social Services case." He nodded at Grace, as if to say, *She's the social worker.*

Grace tried to smile, but she was afraid the doctor would recognize her, even with her red hair and contacts. Recognize her and turn her in to the FBI. How many lies and half-truths could they tell before someone caught on?

"This child." Luke held out the death certificate and McDougal looked down and took it. "Do you recall this case?"

After a minute he said, "Yes, yes, I remember this. Poor little girl. She was DOA at the hospital. A fall." He glanced up at Luke, then switched his attention to Grace and frowned. "Why are you interviewing me about this case now? It's the mother you should be talking to."

"Oh, absolutely. We've both spoken to the woman," Luke said.

"And?"

"She was unwilling to give us the information we need."

"I see."

"We have suspicions, and we thought you might be able to help us out."

Grace finally spoke up. "You see, this woman— the mother, Kerry Pope—is suing for custody of another child, and Social Services is checking up on her history."

The doctor stared at her. "Ms...? I'm sorry, I didn't catch your name."

Her nerves leaped under her skin, internal bullets of fire in her flesh. "Oh, everyone calls me Sally," she said, cringing inwardly.

"Sally, then," the man said, apparently far more interested in the copy of the death certificate in his hand than in a punk-looking social worker from Denver.

It struck Grace like a bolt from the blue—this sort of clandestine work that Luke engaged in day after day was terrifying, yes, but thrilling, too. She remembered for a flash her last—and final—boyfriend. Mr. Boring. How many times had she told herself she could never live life with a dull man? She'd given up the girlish hope of finding the knight on a white charger who would sweep her away, and she'd immersed herself in her professor role. Then Charley had come along, and she'd believed he was enough. But now, standing here, playing out this con, playing it out as Luke's partner, she knew with sudden clarity that she craved so much more from life. Luke had only been the catalyst in this discovery. And, when all was said and done, what did she do with the knowledge?

"All right, ah, Sally," the doctor said, breaking into her musings, "why don't we sit in my office and I'll do what I can to help. It's been years, of course, but the case is coming back. One thing's for sure, we don't get many like this in Durango."

"I bet," Luke said, exchanging a look with Grace that told her to cool it now, and made her feel as though he'd been reading her thoughts. Perhaps he had. Perhaps he knew more about her hopes and dreams and fears than she did.

McDougal led them into his office, which subbed as an examining room, also, and closed the door. They sat as if they were the man's patients, across the desk from him. Behind them was the examining table, drawers full of medical paraphernalia—a jar of tongue depressors, a thermometer in a plastic sleeve lying on a sterile towel, awaiting his next patient.

"Kerry Pope," the doctor said. "She was very young, far too young to have had a baby. She received some government benefits, I believe. I'm afraid I didn't really know her. I was the acting coroner at the time, and I recall that I only saw her once or twice. The hospital did the child's autopsy and I simply signed the death certificate."

"What did the autopsy report say?" Luke asked.

"If memory serves, death due to head trauma. But I believe the X rays showed a previously healed ulna fracture. That's an arm bone. So I was suspicious."

"Why exactly were you suspicious?"

"Well, the child…"

"Merilee Pope," Luke prompted.

"The head trauma—from a fall, the mother claimed—the broken arm…those things can all be due to abuse. Of course, I would need to review the autopsy report, but I believe it also stated there were bruises on the child's body that were inconsistent with a fall. Yes, I suspected abuse."

"Did you inform anyone of your suspicions?" Luke asked.

"I did. I sent a letter and a copy of the report to Social Services."

"And?"

McDougal shrugged under his white jacket. "By the time Social Services went to the police with the problem, Kerry Pope had disappeared. They may have put a warrant out on her, but I'm not sure. I do know she was never found. Well, until now, it seems. So she's got another child...." The doctor trailed off.

Luke nodded. "Do you think Kerry Pope hurt her own child, maybe even killed her?"

"I don't know. It could have been an accident. It's so hard to prove these things. And without proof, without the mother to question, the cause of death had to be ruled accidental."

Grace was looking down at her hands. She wanted to scream out, to jump up and yell at the doctor, but she held on to her self-control through sheer will-power. Charley was with that woman, her mind kept repeating in an endless litany.

"Would you testify in court about this case, Dr. McDougal?" Luke was asking.

"Yes, but again, I can't say anything definitive."

"Would you consent to being deposed?"

"Well, I don't see why not. Sure."

"Would you, say, make a phone call or write a letter about Merilee Pope? And it would help if you could contact the hospital for a copy of the autopsy report."

"Yes, I could do that."

"Thank you, Dr. McDougal," Luke said, rising. "We'll be in touch." He handed the doctor his card. "You can reach me at my cell phone number if you have any questions or if you remember anything else. Thank you very much for your time."

"Good luck," McDougal said. "I hope you resolve your...problem. Let me know where to send the information.'' He paused, then went on. ''If I had to make the decision, I'd be very wary of granting Miss Pope custody of a child. But it isn't up to me, is it?''

Outside, Grace took a ragged breath and stopped Luke on the sidewalk with a hand on his arm. ''Do you think he read about Kerry in the papers? He seemed to recall that autopsy report awfully quickly.''

Luke considered for a minute, his sandy brows drawn. ''He was hard to read. The one thing I do know is that he's willing to help.''

''I guess that's all that matters. I just thought… Well, if he read about Kerry, and if he gets to thinking everything over, he might put two and two together and realize who I am.''

''Hey,'' Luke said, ''we'll be long gone by then. And even if the good doctor does figure it out, so what? You heard him. He's totally against Kerry having custody of another child. Right?''

Grace mustered a smile. ''Right.''

They both tried to catch naps that afternoon before the Silver Belle Saloon opened and they could talk to someone about Kerry and her employment there. Sleep was impossible for Grace, though. Her mind gave her no chance. Her brain raced; it chased its tail in unending circles; it shrieked silently and prayed. Kerry Pope, with one child dead of some sort of neglect or abuse, had Charley, and here *she* was on the other side of the state. And Luke. Luke, *Luke*. When she wasn't worrying about Charley, she was obsessing wildly about Luke.

She was only too aware of him right next door, a thin wall separating them. He was remaining so controlled, so cool. They'd made love, for God's sake, and he'd said things… Yet now he acted as if there had been nothing between them, as if he were indeed an investigator helping out on a Social Services case. She wondered if she gave away her feelings with every word, every glance and gesture. How uncomfortable her behavior must make him feel, a silly uncontrollable female wanting more from him than he could give. Well, he covered *that* up, too.

The minutes crawled by as she lay tensely on the bed. *Charley. Luke.*

They drove to the Silver Belle at 7:00 sharp. Luke had to bang on the door before anyone let them in. The place was large—a long bar on one side, a dance floor, pool tables. It smelled of spilled beer and old wood and a sweet aroma, some sort of hickory barbecue sauce.

Luke flashed his Metropole ID. Grace guessed it looked official enough to impress the people who worked there. He asked the bartender if he'd known Kerry Pope when she'd worked here.

"Nope, I've only been here two years. Try Katrina. She's been here longest."

Katrina was about thirty, blond and as wholesome looking as her name. She wore jeans, cowboy boots, a sleeveless Western shirt and a red Stetson. She was cute.

"Oh, yeah, sure, I remember Kerry. Scrawny little thing. Had a kid. Wow, that's right. Her kid died, didn't it? Then she left—just, boom, here one day and gone the next. She was way too young to have a kid. Also too young to drink as much as she did."

"Did you know her very well?" Luke asked.

"No, not really. Just to say hi to if I saw her around town."

"Did she have a boyfriend?"

Katrina thought. "I don't know. I mean, she had the kid, right? So she must have had a man around somewhere. But I really can't recall, you know, anyone picking her up or stopping by. Just the kid."

Disappointment squeezed Grace again.

"Anyone else you can think of who knew her?"

"Let's see. Hmm, mostly they're gone—moved, I mean. I'm the oldest employee they have here. Except for Maggie. She's the bar manager. Sure. Try her. It's her night off, though."

"Maggie who?" Luke pressed.

"Maggie Winslow."

They found her listing in the phone book. Maggie wasn't home. Luke left a message on her answering machine, then there was nothing to do but grab a bite to eat, go back to the motel and try to get some sleep.

"Take it easy," Luke said at the door to Grace's room. "I told you, investigating requires patience. We've learned a lot today."

"Not enough," she murmured.

"Get some sleep," he repeated, turning to go to his room, and Grace realized in that moment she couldn't bear him to leave her alone. She couldn't spend another night tossing and turning, waiting, waiting, afraid and lonely, obsessing, wondering, so empty inside.

"Luke," she said.

"Mmm?"

His expression was blank, so neutral that she almost swallowed her words, but a terrible need made her forge ahead. She cringed at her shamelessness at the same time as she spoke. "I want to be with you tonight." *My God*, she thought, was there no depth to which she wouldn't sink?

He looked at her hard, his eyes cold and ice-blue, the double brackets around his mouth deepening. He was silent so long her skin crawled.

"I'm sorry," she began, "I didn't mean to put you in a bad position. I'll…"

"No," he said. "You're not putting me in any position I don't want to be in."

"Then you…?"

He bent his neck, his face close. She could smell him, the unique scent she'd never forget no matter how long she lived. "This might just be the stupidest thing either one of us has ever done."

"I know," she breathed.

He took the key from her hand and opened her door. She walked in ahead of him, exhilarated and afraid, knowing deep in the secret places of her heart that she needed so very much more than comfort or companionship. With every passing minute, with every stolen glance in his direction, she was falling in love with this man. How easy it was to deceive herself into believing that he shared her sentiments. The horrible, aching truth was that his feelings mattered very much. When all was said and done, if— no, *when*— she had Charley and her life back, it was never going to be the same. Not without Luke.

She stood in the middle of her room, barely able to catch her breath, and heard him close the door. Silence pulsed in the air and her heart beat furiously against her ribs. She faced him.

"Come here," he said in the dimness. Neither of them made a move to turn on the light. The drapes were drawn.

She went to him, and he held her close. She was trembling, and for a time he only stroked her back.

She put her arms around his waist and pressed her cheek against his chest. His heartbeat sounded in her ear, steady, reassuring, while hers pounded madly in her ears.

Then he tilted her face up, and his mouth came down on hers. A sensation burst within her, like a glorious drowning. She gave herself to it, not so afraid anymore. She arched closer, rising on her toes to push against him, linking her hands behind his neck. She heard him groan, a deep animal sound in his throat. Wonder filled her that she had this power, this incredible gift.

He pulled back, and for a moment she was afraid she was losing him, but he only meant to unbutton her shirt. She reached out and began to unbutton his, their gazes locked, solemn.

When her blouse was off he ran a finger over the swell of her breast above her bra. Fire licked at her belly. His shirt hung apart, his chest bare. He had very little hair. She laid a hand flat on his chest, feeling his skin, the jump of his heart, and his eyes never left hers.

He took her wrist, drew her hand up to his mouth, kissed the back of it, turned it and kissed the quick pulse. Still holding her hand, breathing hard, he said, "We don't have to do this if you don't want."

"Luke, please. I want to. I want—"

But he didn't wait for her to reply. He kissed her again, and then they were on the bed. She felt so alive, pleasure racing through her blood. His body was familiar, as if she'd known him forever, as if all the hours they'd spent together since they'd met had made them friends—no, closer. Long-standing lovers.

His hand trailed across her belly; his mouth teased

her nipples. She was taken over by sensation, arching against him, writhing, her breath coming faster. She felt herself tilt over the edge, gasping, as his fingers found the sensitive bud at her center. Crying out, her voice unfamiliar, her body bucking. Was this her? But it didn't matter.

He poised himself over her, his eyes shadowed and feral, his forehead and chest damp, the tendons on his neck standing out. He plunged inside her, and it began again, the crescendo building as he thrust into her, filling her, taking away all else, heavy on her, hard in her, until her body shook and she cried out once more. Then he shuddered in her, releasing himself, groaning, pulling her around on top of him, holding her tightly, as her tremors subsided. Soothing her as he ran one hand down her back. Up and down.

"Luke?" she breathed.

"I'm here." He kissed her cheek, her nose. "Grace, I'm here."

For one exquisitely perfect moment they were together, and he was hers alone, and nothing, absolutely nothing, could touch them.

CHAPTER SIXTEEN

THEY MET MAGGIE WINSLOW the next morning for coffee. She'd returned Luke's call promptly at 8:00 a.m., his cell phone ringing from under the pile of clothes on the floor of the motel room. Grace watched him as he got out of bed and walked across the floor nude. He was so beautiful to her she felt her heart swell.

But when she heard him say, "Thanks for calling back, Miss Winslow," she sat up, and everything came rushing to the fore: Charley, the FBI, Kerry Pope.

Luke seemed able to shut off part of his mind, the part that contained her, the part that held their relationship. He picked up his clothes, calmly dressed, felt for his room key and told her he'd meet her for breakfast in an hour.

"Okay," she said. Just that. *Okay.* As if they had not held each other and made love and said things to each other that no one else in the world could hear.

She showered and put gel in her hair so that the spikes would hold, then dressed in the dark spandex top and capri pants. Her punk look. In the bathroom mirror her eyes were huge and moist in the contact lenses, and she realized she gave the appearance of a woman who'd just spent all night making love. Well, she had. The dreamy expression and the sensitive skin would stay with her. All day. For days, she knew. Yet men were so capable of shedding the aftermath of sex. How many case histories had she studied in which women had complained about precisely that—how easily their men could discard the intimacy? But the sensations stuck with women, the immediacy of touch and feel and scent. Stuck for days and weeks and frequently for life.

Were her feelings for Luke forever?

If she concentrated on Charley, she discovered, she could get through the day better. She needed to concentrate on Charley, because *he'd* be with her for life, while Luke would be gone soon. In a few days, a week or two—did it matter?

To know how to behave with him was difficult. Things had gotten so complicated between them. She felt she was walking on eggshells all the time, unable to show him her real feelings, guilty for even considering their relationship when Charley was in danger. Her mind whirled constantly from Luke to Charley, around and around. With no solution in sight for either dilemma.

Maggie Winslow was whippet thin, her skin sunbaked and wrinkled beyond her age, which was at least forty. She wore a low-necked black vest over tight blue jeans, and sandals that revealed feet as brown as her arms and face.

"Sure, I remember Kerry. God, how could I forget? She had that darling little girl who died. Maryann? Melody?"

"Merilee," Luke said solemnly.

"That's right. Merilee. Kerry was terribly young—sixteen, maybe seventeen. She came to work that night—well, she came to say she was quitting. The night her little girl died. She was already drunk when she got there, crying and wailing. She was a basket case. And she told me that her boyfriend—I think his name was Bob something—had pushed Merilee down the stairs. She *told* me that. Okay, she was drunk, but I've listened to a lot of drunks, and this girl was telling the truth. She told me the baby was crying—maybe it was a tooth or something, and she wouldn't stop. So the boyfriend shook her, and when she cried louder, he knocked her around so hard she fell down the steps. Nice guy.''

They were sitting in a quiet corner of a coffee shop down the street from the saloon where Maggie worked. As soon as she finished telling them about Kerry's drunken confession, a terrible pall enshrouded them. Grace thought she might have to run to the rest room and vomit, but she swallowed convulsively several times and the queasiness passed.

Finally, she broke the silence. ''Kerry's with another *nice* guy nowadays, and she's trying to get custody of her biological son,'' she said quietly.

Maggie looked at her hard. ''Sure, it's been in the news. Not about the boyfriend, but about the little boy and his foster mother. The woman's still missing, isn't she?''

Grace's heart seized. Maggie knew who she was. Everyone in the whole world could see through her laughable disguise.

''Yes, the woman is missing,'' Luke said evenly.

''But the FBI's still looking for her,'' Maggie put in.

''Yes.''

''I feel bad for that little boy. Stuck with a mother

he never knew. It's a shame. I want to see a story like that come out with a happy ending, you know?''

"So do we," Luke replied. "That's why we're checking up on Kerry's history."

Maggie turned to Grace. "And you're with Boulder Child Protective Services, you said."

"Yes," Grace began, then cleared her throat before murmuring again, "yes."

"And your name is—what did you say?"

"Sally."

"Sally?"

Grace thought frantically. "Moore. Sally Moore," she said, borrowing her friend Susan's last name.

Then Luke deftly went on. "We've interviewed a lot of people so far, trying to get enough hard evidence for the judge to reopen the custody case. I've got to tell you, Maggie," he said, his eyes holding hers, "you're the closest we've come to unearthing information that the Pope woman is not a fit mother. What you've given us is invaluable."

Maggie Winslow appeared to have forgotten whatever questions she harbored about Grace's identity. She leaned forward, elbows on the tabletop, and Grace could see that her cleavage was brown and freckled and that she wore no bra. "Look, I went to the police here as soon as Kerry told me that story, but they couldn't do much of anything about a drunken girl's ramblings, especially when she'd just seen her kid die. They just didn't do much, and then Kerry and her boyfriend disappeared a couple of days later, and that was that."

"Would you testify in court if necessary?" Luke asked.

"Sure. If someone pays for my motel room." Maggie leaned back and folded her arms under her breasts.

"Would you consent to be deposed?"

"Here, in Durango?"

"Yes."

"Okay."

"Would you phone the FBI agent assigned to this case and tell her what Kerry told you?"

"Absolutely. I'd like to get it off my chest after all this time."

Luke pulled one of his cards out and wrote on the back of it. Handing it to Maggie, he said, "This number will get you directly to Special Agent Renee Paynter in Denver. She's the FBI agent in charge of this case. She's also the one who found Charley Pope and handed him back to Kerry. Would you call her and tell her your story?"

"Yes, I sure will." She took the card and studied it, then looked up. "Will this woman, Renee Paynter, believe me?"

"Oh, yeah, she'll believe you," Luke said. "In any case, she'll have to look into your allegations."

Grace was holding her breath, thinking, *This might work. This might get Charley removed from Kerry's custody.* She suddenly wanted to admit to Maggie who she was and why this phone call was so vitally important, but she didn't dare.

"You can get in touch with me anytime, day or night, Miss Winslow," Luke was saying. "My cell phone number is on the card. We appreciate what you're doing. It's going to prevent what happened to Merilee Pope from happening again."

Maggie looked at him soberly, then switched her eyes to Grace. "What are you going to do now?"

"We're heading back to Denver," Luke said. "I think we've found out what we needed here."

"I'll make that call," Maggie said. "I have kids, too, but mine are grown. I'd have killed for my kids. Still would, I guess."

"I know what you mean," Grace said. "Thank you for doing this."

"No big deal." Maggie Winslow nodded and smiled. "Good luck."

The drive back to Denver seemed endless to Grace. After she reached her parents by cell phone and filled them in on the latest developments, she sat mulling over the new information they'd gotten from Maggie. The woman's testimony coupled with correspondence from Dr. McDougal would surely carry a lot of weight with a judge. But would it be enough? And would the judge act in time to save Charley from the same fate as his poor baby sister?

Then there was Special Agent Paynter, who'd blithely handed Charley over to Kerry in the first place. Would Maggie's information convince her to ask the court to review the custody case?

She turned to Luke. "I'm so afraid that Paynter woman won't do anything," she said as they passed through Pagosa Springs. "Her job is to uphold the law. She doesn't care if Kerry's a good mother or not. She doesn't care if the judge's ruling is wrong. She's not going to be interested in a death that happened years ago and can't really be investigated."

"So you're playing the devil's advocate now? Remember, I interviewed her. She'll do something about it, Grace."

"Oh, God, I hope you're right." She stared ahead, out the car window, not seeing the mountains go by.

"I swear, if Maggie Winslow's call doesn't get things moving, I'll kidnap Charley from Kerry's house myself."

"You will not."

"Watch me," she said.

KERRY POPE WAS cleaning up after lunch. She'd made ham-and-cheese sandwiches for Eddie and Charley, and there was mayonnaise all over the table because Charley had pulled his sandwich apart, eaten the ingredients separately and left the pieces of bread smeared upside down on the table. She was always cleaning up messes lately, she thought. Dirty clothes, dirty tables, dirty towels and books and toys. Little boys sure were sloppy.

She did the dishes, wiped off the table, then sat down to finish the second beer she'd had with her sandwich. She was a nervous wreck these days, the center of attention of reporters and cameras. The beer tasted good. There was a roach left in the ashtray, so she lit that up and drew in deep, pungent breaths, feeling the familiar calming effect wash over her body.

Thank goodness Charley was busy playing with the dump truck he'd brought with him in his bag of clothes. Busy for a little while, at least. The kid cried a lot and kept asking for his mommy. Over and over till Kerry was sick of it. She'd told him a hundred times, *she* was his mommy.

The phone rang, but she didn't reach for it. The calls were almost always for Eddie. It was how he ran his business.

Charley was crawling around the living room floor, pushing the dump truck. She was grateful for the reprieve. He demanded an awful lot of attention most of the time. She had Grace Bennett to thank for spoiling her son like that.

She wondered idly where Grace was, and she harbored a small, sneaking suspicion that Charley's foster mother hadn't given up so easily; she was out there plotting and trying to figure out how to get him back.

Well, she wouldn't. Charley belonged to Kerry, and that was that.

Eddie came out of the bedroom, where he'd been talking on the phone. "You need to make a delivery," he said. "I'm busy."

"I can't, Eddie," she said. "I have to stay with Charley."

"Well, I have to drive down to Pueblo to pick up a shipment and *you* have to take this stuff out to Aurora."

"I can't, Eddie." She heard herself whining but couldn't stop. She was light-headed from the beer and dog-tired from the pot. What she needed was a nap.

"Listen." Eddie grabbed her arm and stuck his face in hers. "You live here for free with that brat of yours, so you better do what I say."

"Ouch, Eddie, that hurts."

"You can take the 4Runner. Mike's picking me up. Here's the address. Just deliver this bag and count the money."

"Eddie, honest, I can't. I'll be followed. All those reporters. You know what—"

"There aren't any outside right now. Just get the hell out of here. I'm not kidding." He let go of her arm, flinging her against the kitchen table in the process, so that she half fell, knocking chairs over.

"Eddie," she cried, getting up and rubbing her bruised arm. "What do I do with Charley?"

"Take him along. He'll be your cover. At least he's good for something."

"But I can't. What if—?"

She never finished, because Eddie slapped her hard, the shock exploding in her head. "Get going, bitch," he warned.

She was half-drunk, stoned and sobbing her heart out as she and Charley got into Eddie's car. She remembered to put him in the back seat, but there was no car seat, and it never occurred to her to fasten his seat belt. She was crying so hard Charley was scared, utterly silent, his little face pale.

"Just be good," she said to him between her sobs. "Please. Charley, just sit there and be good."

The bag she had to deliver was hidden under the passenger seat. If stopped she would say it wasn't her car, and she didn't know the stuff was there. She'd rehearsed the lines a million times.

She was heading south to get onto the interstate, which would take her out to the address in Aurora, still crying, her cheek throbbing where Eddie had hit her, when the light at the next intersection turned red. She never saw the red light or the delivery van because she was weeping so hard. All she was aware of was the rending screech of brakes, a resounding crash, metal tearing and then black, absolute silence.

RENEE PAYNTER THANKED the Winslow woman gravely, then hung up the phone and sat at her desk for a time, her brain working feverishly. Kerry Pope had had a baby girl seven years ago in Durango, and the child had died. The child had *died*.

My God.

All right, all right, she told herself, *check the facts.*
She buzzed her secretary, asked her to get Durango's
courthouse on the line, spoke with the clerk there.
Yes, there had been a twenty-two-month-old child,
Merilee Lynn Pope, who'd died of an accidental fall.

"Funny you should call," the clerk said. "Some
people were just here asking for the same death certificate."

"Do you remember their names?" Renee asked,
her blood pumping.

"Well, no. A guy, around forty, real good-looking
dude. And you'd never forget those eyes of his. Cold
blue eyes. He was with a lady; I remember she had
a red dye job on her hair. Cute. He was working for
some insurance company."

"Thanks," Renee said.

Well, Grace would never be described as *cute* by
anybody, but maybe this clerk didn't know cute from
dowdy. Much more interesting, however, was the
clerk's description of the man. *Cold blue eyes.* Hadn't
Renee had lunch with a reporter whose eyes she had
mentally noted as cold and blue?

You don't suppose...? Renee thought, but there
was no time to dwell on the coincidence. She filed
the information in a quiet corner of her mind, then
put all her concentration on the problem at hand: a
dead baby girl. Kerry Pope. And Charley. That innocent little boy. Whom Renee had handed back to
his mother.

The judge in Boulder couldn't have known about
the dead baby. He simply couldn't have, or he would
never have given Kerry custody of another child.

How could the welfare of this child have slipped

through the cracks of the very system meant to protect him? Why hadn't anyone known about Kerry's first baby? *Why?*

She had to remedy the situation. She herself, because she had precipitated it in the first place. Grace Bennett had delivered Charley into safe hands, and Renee had sniffed him out and turned him over to a woman who had no right to be a mother.

She left the Federal Building in a car from the pool, phoning Kerry's number from her cell phone as she drove. No answer. Damn. Where was that girl?

It didn't take long to get to the neighborhood where Kerry lived. She turned onto Federal Boulevard and drove, too quickly, toward Kerry's street. She'd wait in front of the house if necessary. Wait for however long it took. And then she'd grill Kerry about the dead baby till she gave in and told the truth.

A couple of blocks shy of the turn, Renee braked, seeing two police cruisers with blinking lights and an ambulance in the middle of the intersection. As her mind processed the scene, she saw a familiar black 4Runner, its side smashed in, being hooked up to a tow truck.

Stark horror gripped her. Kerry…Charley… What had that pathetic woman done now? For perhaps two minutes she was paralyzed, then she reached in her shoulder bag for her FBI badge and started toward the policeman on the scene, striding with the confidence of her position.

GRACE WAITED in Luke's car down the street from the FBI headquarters. She had been waiting for half an hour, and was crawling with anxiety. She fervently prayed that Luke was doing the right thing by going directly to Renee Paynter with the information about Kerry, but she had her doubts. Her instincts told her to get to Charley, snatch him, then run to the ends of the earth. To depend on the system that had already failed her son was futile.

They'd argued the subject all the way back to Denver, and Luke had prevailed, but when he'd parked the car, he'd put a hand on her arm.

"I'll give it a try, Grace," he'd said, "and if it doesn't work, I'll get Charley for you some other way. I swear to you I will."

"She'll know you lied to her about being a reporter. She'll kick you out of her office or she'll arrest you. She'll have you followed."

"Trust me, okay?"

She'd met his eyes, and she'd wanted to believe in him. She had to believe in him. "Be careful," she'd breathed.

It was hot now in the car, and she was sweating. Her forehead was damp; the skin under her arms and around her waistband prickled. Where was he? How long was he going to talk to the agent? Or had the woman detained him already?

She was going crazy sitting there, helpless. She'd felt nothing but helpless for the past two weeks. All the running, hiding, the long nights on the underground railroad, her parents putting themselves in jeopardy for her, Luke... Even Luke, a stranger when this had begun, had gone beyond the call of duty for her and Charley.

But where had the efforts gotten them? Charley was with Kerry. Grace's parents were living in the camper outside Denver, chewing their nails, as helpless as she was. And Luke. In her mind's eye she saw an image of him in handcuffs.

The minutes ticked by like hours, and she began to panic. He'd left her the car keys. Should she leave? She could get the directions to the campground from her dad and join them.

Desert Luke? After all he'd done for her? What was she thinking?

She'd been staring at the wide steps leading into the Federal Building for so long she didn't notice him till he was striding briskly across the sun-drenched street toward the car. Her heart gave a glad leap, and relief swamped her, but then she saw the tight expression on his face, and all her relief sank to her feet and drained away.

He opened the door and slid into the driver's seat. His face was so set with strong emotion she was afraid to ask what had gone wrong. Then abruptly he pounded the steering wheel with the palm of his hand. His outburst made her shrink away.

"What?" she dared to ask.

The keys were still in the ignition, and without looking at her, he started the engine. "There's no easy way to tell you this," he said, "but there's been an accident."

"Accident?" she repeated dumbly, her mind unable to fit itself around the word.

"Kerry ran a red light and a van nailed her."

"Kerry? But… Oh, God, Charley? What about *Charley?* Was he with…?"

"I'm afraid so," Luke said in an unfamiliar voice.

She stared into the middle distance, seeing nothing, her body frozen. Horror dug at her stomach. And then the words came as if from someone else. "Is he…?"

"God, no, Grace, no—at least he…he wasn't when Renee Paynter last spoke to the hospital."

Grace took a quavering breath. There was nothing to say. Nothing.

They arrived at the hospital ten minutes later. She'd barely been able to give Luke directions. She hadn't heard him when he'd told her Agent Paynter had gone on ahead and would be there, too. He'd punched in her parents' number on the cell phone while waiting at a stoplight, and she hadn't even heard him tell them the horrible news. She thought somewhere in her mind that they, also, must be rushing to meet them. Nothing mattered.

The only time she spoke was to say, "If Charley were…if he were…I'd know it. He's all right. He's got to be all right."

She never remembered Luke dropping her at the emergency entrance, then going to park the car. She never remembered the moment of stark terror as she ran through the big double doors and grabbed the first nurse she saw. And she never recognized the confusion on the nurse's face when she cried, "Where is my son? Where is Charley Pope?"

The first cognizant moment Grace knew was when she saw Charley sitting on a gurney, a white adhesive patch over his left eyebrow. His T-shirt had a few drops of blood on it and his knees were skinned, but he was alive. And when he saw her, he kicked his sturdy legs and held out his arms and yelled, "Mommy! Mommy, look at your funny hair! See, I got a big bandage."

She was unaware of a nurse putting a restraining hand on her arm. She was unaware of the confusion over who really was this child's mother. She didn't notice the tall, strikingly beautiful African-American woman who nodded an okay to the nurse to let her go to Charley.

She merely rushed to him and enfolded him in her arms and buried her face in his hair and held on for dear life.

Then Luke was there, and Charley was saying, "Mommy, you're hurting me. Mommy, I was in this car and there was a big bang and I bumped my head."

After a very long time, Grace finally let him go and stood back. "Charley, oh boy, did I miss you, sweetie pie," she said, her voice trembling.

"Me, too, Mommy. There was this lady who baby-sat me, but I don't like her much."

"I know, baby. I know." She bit her lower lip, wiped at her tears. Only then did she think to ask the nurse, "Kerry Pope, is she...is she all right?"

But it was the other woman who stepped forward. Immediately, Grace was struck with the knowledge of who exactly this woman was: FBI Special Agent Renee Paynter. The air seemed to whoosh right out of Grace's lungs.

"Miss Pope was knocked unconscious," the agent said, her brown eyes fixed on Grace. "She's been taken to a room here in the hospital. She's under twenty-four-hour observation for a concussion." Then, shocking Grace, she stuck out her hand. "By the way, I'm Renee Paynter."

Grace did not know what to reply. She looked at the woman's proffered hand, then slowly held out her own. How bizarre, shaking hands with the very person who'd pursued her, who'd taken Charley from the protection of his loving grandparents and darn near gotten him killed.

Behind Grace, Luke had gone to Charley's side and was listening to the child tell him about his bandage.

Renee's glance went from Grace to Luke and back again. She still held Grace's hand.

Grace swallowed and met the woman's gaze. "So what now?" she asked with what she thought was admirably forthright courage. "Are you going to arrest me?"

The agent studied her for a long moment. Then she said, "Not today."

But Grace wasn't about to let her off the hook so easily. She gathered herself up and said, "Well, you know what, Agent Paynter, I don't care as long as Charley's safe. You can do whatever you want to me, but that *woman* is not getting Charley again."

"Don't worry about Kerry Pope. She is going to end up in detox. She was a mess. She never should have been driving, much less with a child in the car. And she had drugs with her."

"And you wanted Charley to live with her?" Grace asked incredulously, but they were all interrupted when Bob and Sally Bennett arrived. Charley tried to get down from the gurney, and Sally caught him and held him.

Bob glared at the FBI woman. "I warned you," he said.

"Look, Mr. Bennett, I'll apologize for simply doing my job if *you* apologize for aiding and abetting a federal fugitive."

"Crap," he said, but his tone lacked its normal conviction.

Then the agent turned to Luke. "How did that article for *Weekly People* come out, Mr. Sarkov?"

"Oh, that," Luke said without missing a beat. "My

editor decided it didn't contain enough human interest.''

"I told that lady," Charley was saying, pointing at Renee, "see, I told her I wanted my mommy."

A pall of stillness fell over the group.

The agent broke the silence. "Well, Charley, I guess I got your mommy for you." To Grace, she added, "Goodbye. I wish you luck in court." She glanced at Charley. "He's really quite a special little boy."

"Yes, he is," Grace said, and she turned away from her nemesis and went to her family.

RENEE LET OUT A BREATH as she left the emergency room. "What a formidable crew," she murmured, and couldn't help wondering how their saga would end.

Then her mind shifted to her own troubles. The Bennett case, which she'd believed was going to put her on the fast track to advancement, would likely have the opposite result. A promotion would not be forthcoming in the immediate future, she realized. And she was surprised at how unimportant that seemed now that Charley had been returned safely to his mother.

Far more pressing, though, was her decision, her baby.

She pulled in a breath, headed to the reception desk and asked, "Would you point me to Maternity, please?" Then she walked down the corridor as if on autopilot and took the elevator to the third floor. There, she strode to where a large plate-glass window overlooked the newborns in their bassinets. Rows of babies, with name tags in pink or blue. Tiny faces, tiny hands. Soft blankets wrapped around the brand-new bodies. Some were asleep; some wailed, waving minuscule fists. All those babies, awaited for nine long months. Adored, beloved miracles, each and every one.

Renee stood there for an endless time and watched, and once a nurse came by and asked her if she needed any help, but Renee shook her head, not replying because her throat was tight and there were tears in her eyes.

Finally she went back down to the lobby and used one of the pay phones to call Jay at his desk.

"Paynter here," came his familiar voice.

"I love you," Renee said, choked up.

"Renee? What the hell?"

"I just wanted to tell you I love you, you big doofus," she said.

"Well, that's nice," he said carefully. "I love you, too. What's the occasion?"

"The occasion...? You know what, Jay? We're going to have a baby."

CHAPTER SEVENTEEN

COURTROOM C IN THE Boulder County Justice Center was very full that hot August morning. In the corridor outside, and surrounding the building, were legions of reporters and video cameras and satellite vans. Inside were the juvenile court judge, his clerk; Professor Sally Grace Bennett; her attorney, Natalie; and Grace's many supporters. So many supporters they couldn't all fit in the room.

Judge Henry Fallon had to bang his gavel several times to call the session to order; the buzz of conversation was quite loud.

Grace sat at the same table as she had all those weeks ago, Natalie Woodruff at her side. Her parents and Luke were on the blond wood bench behind her. Dr. McDougal from Durango was there as an expert witness, and Maggie Winslow, and Susan Moore from Boulder County's Child Protective Services. Renee Paynter was present, too.

Kerry Pope was noticeably absent, and she had not arranged for a representative; she had withdrawn her request for Charley's custody.

Grace was nevertheless nervous. Natalie had assured her that the judge was amenable to her custody suit. But Grace didn't trust anyone at this point. The judge could change his mind. He could remand Charley to Child Protective Services. He could even, she supposed, arrest her.

She knew the judge had called this emergency hearing because of the immediate concern for the disposition of Charley's custody, especially since the whole country was scrutinizing the judge's every decision. Also, Natalie had informed her, it was an election year, and Henry Fallon realized he had to remedy his previous, near-tragic, ruling to assure his reelection.

But the motions of justice had to be made manifest in an orderly and lawful manner.

Grace sat quietly, her hands folded tightly on the table in front of her. She listened as each witness testified, but her mind was focused on only one thing: Would she get custody of Charley?

Susan Moore testified first, giving the background to the case, how Grace Bennett had become a foster mother.

Natalie Woodruff then asked her about the confidential file on Kerry Pope she'd found.

"Yes, it was stuck way in the bottom of the box. It was so old I guess no one had bothered with it for ages. And since it was marked *Confidential,* no one looked at it. Actually, I found it downstairs where we store old records."

"What did this report say, Miss Moore?" Natalie asked.

"That Kerry Pope had a daughter in Durango, Colorado, and that the little girl, Merilee, had died of an accidental fall."

"What did you do with this information?"

Susan sat up straight and replied clearly. "I gave it to Grace Bennett."

"Why?"

"So she could prove that Kerry Pope was an unfit mother."

"Thank you, Miss Moore," Natalie said. "No more questions, Your Honor."

Dr. McDougal was next. After establishing his credentials, Natalie only spent fifteen minutes on his testimony.

"Yes, there were bruises inconsistent with a fall. And there was evidence of a previously broken ulna in her left arm."

"What conclusion did you draw from the autopsy, Dr. McDougal?"

"I suspected child abuse, but simply didn't have enough proof. The mother was distraught, and then she disappeared." He shrugged. "There wasn't much I could do by then."

Maggie Winslow was next. Natalie had her relate the story of the night Kerry had come into the Silver Belle Saloon and confessed to her.

"So, Kerry Pope told you that her boyfriend had hit Merilee so hard she fell down a flight of steps?"

"Yes, that's right."

Judge Fallon asked a question of Maggie: "Your deposition alleges that Miss Pope was drinking. 'Drunk,' I believe you said."

"Yes."

"Was she coherent?"

"Coherent enough, Your Honor. I sure believed her. In my job, I listen to a lot of inebriated people, and I'm sure Kerry was telling the truth."

"Thank you, Miss Winslow," Natalie said. "You're excused."

There was evidence from the policeman first on the

scene at Kerry's accident. Yes, she'd smelled of alcohol. Yes, there had been a paper bag of drugs under the front passenger seat. No, she had not secured Charley Pope or herself with a seat belt. Yes, the accident had clearly been her fault.

She had been unconscious when he'd arrived on the scene, so he had called an ambulance for her and the little boy. At the hospital, tests confirmed her unlawfully high blood alcohol level and the use of marijuana. He had subsequently arrested her on the grounds of DUI, drug possession and endangering the life of a minor. The driver of the other vehicle had suffered just bumps and bruises, having been properly restrained by a seat belt. Yes, both vehicles had been damaged.

"Where is Kerry Pope now?" Natalie asked.

"She's undergoing detox."

"And the charges against her?"

"They're pending until she completes the program. Then it'll be up to the Denver district attorney."

"Thank you, Officer," Natalie said.

Grace listened, holding her breath. Surely the judge could see the clear picture of Kerry that was forming. He'd never give Charley back to her, but would he give him to Grace?

Then Natalie called Renee Paynter to the stand. Renee testified as to her involvement in the case. She carefully did not blame Grace for the abduction of Charley; she only presented the facts.

"I located Charles Pope in Yellowstone National Park. He was on a camping trip with Professor Bennett's parents. As I had been charged, I returned him to his biological mother, Kerry Pope."

"You interviewed Kerry, did you not, Special Agent Paynter?" Natalie asked.

"Yes."

"Please tell the court your opinion of her."

"My opinion? I'm not sure that should go on record."

"Go ahead, Special Agent Paynter," the judge said. "I'll allow it."

Renee took a deep breath. "I thought she was immature and careless. I thought she had very bad taste in men. I thought she would probably not make a very responsible mother."

"Thank you," Natalie said. "No more questions."

"Just a minute," the judge said. "Special Agent Paynter, I have a few questions for you, but they're off the record."

The court stenographer let her hands drop to her lap. Grace frowned, wondering what this new tack meant.

"Now, I'm a county judge, and this is a custody case to be ruled on by Boulder County. I realize that it came under your jurisdiction only when Charley was, ah, removed from the state and not turned over to his biological mother in a timely fashion. What I want to know, Special Agent Paynter, is how the federal government intends to handle this now. Are you going to charge Professor Bennett?"

Grace fixed her eyes on Renee and held her breath. The FBI agent shifted in the witness chair and spoke directly to the judge. "I don't believe there are any plans to do so, Your Honor."

"I see." Judge Fallon peered at Grace. "Nevertheless, I would like to register my opinion at this point. Professor Bennett's behavior was deplorable."

Renee sat like stone. Her silence spoke eloquently.

"All right, then. I believe these proceedings are over. Anything else, Miss Woodruff?"

"No, Your Honor."

He banged the gavel once. "Reconvene court in one hour for my decision. You're all excused."

It was the longest hour of Grace's life. Her parents were all smiles, positive the judge would rule in her favor. Natalie was, too. The only person who seemed to understand her mood was Luke. He took her arm and said they were going for a walk to get away from the media.

It was hot out, but trees shaded the pedestrian path that followed Boulder Creek across the street from the Justice Center.

"What do you think, Luke?" Grace asked. "What do you really think?"

He still held her arm and dappled sunlight moved across his face as they walked. "I think you have a damn good chance."

"Oh, God, I hope so."

"And if you don't get custody of him this time, you'll try again. I know you, Grace. Eventually, you'll succeed."

"But meanwhile, Charley bears the brunt of strangers raising him. That's a hurtful situation for a child. I could point to a dozen case studies..." She halted, took a breath. "Oh, what's the use second-guessing? How much time do we have left?"

He glanced at his watch. "Thirty-five minutes."

"So long?"

He turned her toward him and tilted her face up. "Grace, listen, whatever happens to Charley, you've given him four years of complete love and security.

No one can take that away from him. Look how well he's adjusted since you got him back.''

"Yes," she admitted. "I know, but..."

"You've done your best, and it's pretty damn good."

She tried to smile. "Thanks."

"You're a brave, fine person, Grace. Charley's lucky to have you."

"Luke..." She wanted to ask what he was going to do after today. He'd promised to stay for the hearing, but she knew he had to go back to San Francisco soon. He had a life there, a job, friends, a wife. A whole complete life that didn't include her.

"Yeah?"

"Nothing. I guess, well, just thanks."

Grace was back in Courtroom C early, and she sat waiting, her heart thumping, as the courtroom gradually filled. Natalie patted her hand and gave her an encouraging smile.

Finally, Judge Fallon entered and took his seat behind the bench. This time the courtroom quieted without the sound of his gavel. Grace closed her eyes and clenched her hands into fists.

"After due consideration," the judge began, "and after listening to the testimony given by the various witnesses, and also bearing in mind the pending charges against Kerry Pope and the psychological assessment presented to me by the psychologist treating her at the detox center, I have come to my decision. Despite my reservations in giving custody of a child to a person—" he glared at Grace "—who has flirted with breaking federal law, I must agree that Grace Bennett deserves legal custody of her foster son,

Charles Leon Pope. I do declare this hearing over.''
Bang went his gavel.

Grace sagged in her chair, unaware of the commotion behind her, of the cries of delight, of the reporters rushing out of the courtroom. She felt faint, the relief so powerful it rushed through her like an ocean at high tide.

Charley was all she could think. *Charley, you're safe now.*

She barely registered Natalie's embrace, her father's raspy ''I told you so,'' her mother's joyful tears. She thought, irrelevantly, that she had to begin adoption procedures instantly, and maybe she should go to the clerk's office today and initiate the process.

At last she stood up, so many people coming up to her, shaking her hand, congratulating her. *She'd won,* she kept telling herself. It was real. She'd done it.

One of the bailiffs approached and suggested that Grace and her parents leave by a back door to avoid the media.

''Yes, that's a good idea,'' she said, the rush of relief receding. She felt weak and happy and completely unable to face cameras or microphones. She wanted only to see Charley. And Luke.

She turned abruptly, realizing Luke hadn't said a word to her. Had he left already?

But he was there, his beloved face giving nothing away. She knew him well enough, though, to realize he would never show emotion in public.

''Luke,'' she said, holding out her hand.

He took a step toward her, their hands touching, and she saw his features soften, saw emotion smooth the lines around his mouth and change the icy hardness of his eyes to a soft blue. He smiled slightly and began to say something, and she felt the electric tingle where their fingers touched.

"Congratulations," he said in deliberate mockery of strangers' words. "You did it, Grace."

She smiled back. "I couldn't have done it without you."

"Come on, Grace," her father interrupted. "We've got to get the heck out of here."

The bailiff led them quickly toward a back door of the building, she and Luke and her parents, leaving Natalie to brave the press at the main entrance. But they were too late; as Grace exited the building into the hot glare of the August sun, someone stuck a microphone into her face, asking, "Grace Bennett, may I have your feelings on the decision today?"

She mumbled something, and her father hustled her away to her car, and when she turned around to ask Luke what he was going to do now, he was gone.

Just gone, vanished.

LUKE PUT HIS John Hancock on the dotted line, dropped the pen on the coffee table and sat back. "All done," he said.

Judith let out a relieved sigh. "Well, frankly, Luke, I thought we would end up in court, especially after your last visit. Mind if I ask why you decided to give me the divorce?"

He shrugged.

"That's your answer? Lifting your shoulders and dropping them. After all this time?"

"Let's just say I got to thinking you were right. Our marriage really was over before I left the police department."

"I see."

He smiled wryly. "I'm glad you do, because I'm not sure I'll ever understand when and where it fell apart."

"Maybe there aren't any answers. Not for anyone going through this."

"Maybe not." He stood up and took a last glance around her living room, noting the vase with the dried flowers in the corner, the pen-and-ink sketch of the San Francisco skyline on the wall—both had been wedding presents. He supposed Judith was entitled to them; they'd come from her family. Everything had come from her family, and he'd thought it reassuring at the time, odd and reassuring and completely alien to his experience. Judith's family had been one of the things that attracted him to her.

"Sure you wouldn't like a drink or something?"

"No, I'm pretty tied up right now." He walked to the door, turned the brass knob.

"I should tell you," she said, following him, "I'm planning on marrying Fred sometime around Christmas. I just thought you'd like to hear it from me and not...well, you know."

"Congratulations," he said in an even voice, despite a lingering sadness. Then he gave her a chaste peck on the cheek. "I really do wish you the best."

"Thank you," she said. "And thank you for signing the papers. I know it was hard."

He didn't realize it at the time. He didn't analyze his emotions until he was driving down off the hill and turning onto Van Ness, but when he'd kissed Judith, his senses saturated with her particular perfume and shampoo, with the familiar scent of her, he'd been left feeling neutral toward her. The magic had truly died. The trouble was his head was still filled with the scent of Grace, memories of the texture of her fine pale skin, the taste of her. Even the flash of those memories was enough to cause his groin to tighten and he knew, knew deep in his soul, that he'd never—not even with this wife—wanted to touch and taste and possess a woman the way he did Grace.

He phoned her that night. Finally. He wanted to tell her so much. Tell her he'd given notice at Metropole, signed the divorce papers, that he was trying to put his house in order. He mostly wanted to tell her that his body ached for her and he awoke every night in the wee hours drenched in desire.

Instead, he said, "Just touching base. I wanted to know how Charley is adjusting." He didn't even ask how she was or if she, too, awakened in a tangle of damp sheets and unbearable dreams of need.

She spoke about Charley and the nursery school he'd attend this autumn. She said he was doing all right, but she kept expecting a backwash of insecurities from his sense of having been abandoned by her.

"Both of us will have to work through it," she told Luke. "I just thank God every night for getting us together again. And you, Luke, you and Mom and Dad and my friends. I don't know what I would have done."

"Glad I was of service," he said.

"So how's work?"

"Ah…just finishing up a few cases."

"Mmm."

Why hadn't he told her he'd given notice? Or that just a few hours ago he'd signed the divorce papers? And why in hell couldn't he spill his guts and tell Grace how goddamn much he needed her?

"Have you seen Dad?" she was asking.

"Not since I got back, but we spoke on the phone. Supposed to get together for dinner one of these days."

"That's nice."

"Uh-huh."

He guessed he couldn't say the things in his heart because his life was still a mess and he had nothing to offer her. Okay, he was a coward. But he couldn't take her sympathy right now. If...when... God, he didn't know, but *if* he and Grace ever got together again, he needed to be the man he once was. Hell, he was a cop—had been—and he wasn't cut out for anything else.

Grace was talking about how many fall classes she would be teaching at the university, and how she'd gotten a ton of mail from students and faculty and neighbors, even total strangers, all telling her how happy they were for her and Charley.

Still, did he detect a note of anxiety in her voice? Did she miss him at all? Or maybe her life was back on track and she didn't have the slightest interest in a loser.

Then another notion hit him like a blow square to the jaw. The way she looked now, with that cute hair and the new clothes and those big green eyes... Hell, there were probably a dozen men beating down the door.

Was she seeing someone? Her slim fingers touching someone's thigh, his hip, tracing fire down his belly?

"Luke? Are you still there?"

"Ah, yes, I'm here. Bad connection, I guess."

He almost hung up, almost missed her words.

"You know, Luke, nothing has changed in how I

feel about you. I want you to understand that you'll always have a place with me and with Charley. Always," she said, so straightforward, so honest, so *Grace,* that he was unable to reply. Later, he tried his damnedest to recall just what he had mumbled in reply and could only remember something like *"Thanks."* He'd gotten off the line as fast as possible. Done in. Ashamed of his cowardice. Blown apart at what a useless waste of a man he'd become.

The next morning, after a sleepless night, he considered the idea of eating crow and making another visit to San Quentin, following Grace's advice to offer Manny Morelli a deal. God, but he hated crawling on his knees to that creep. Then he thought, *Yeah, pride goes before the fall,* and he'd taken the fall and yes, pride had gotten him into this untenable fix. So, could he really swallow that pride?

He drove to San Quentin that same afternoon and sat at exactly the same table across from Morelli in the visiting center of the minimum security prison.

"Well, if it isn't Cool Hand Luke. What can I do for you today?" Morelli smirked.

Luke almost got up and left. But then he thought, *Five minutes, you can swallow your pride for five minutes.*

He offered Morelli a deal. "I'll speak to the D.A. and the parole board, which I believe meets to hear your case in a month. I put in a good word for you, you sign an affidavit swearing I wasn't involved in police corruption, and we both benefit. Well?" Luke held the man's gaze.

A long minute passed. He knew Morelli wasn't going to go for it. He just goddamn knew it.

But then, amazingly, Manny Morelli nodded.

"Okay. I'll get my lawyer to draw up a legal document that'll clear your name, Sarkov. But we don't exchange anything till I see a letter from you to the parole board."

"It's a deal," Luke said, his heart beginning to pound. "You've got yourself a deal, Morelli."

They even shook on it.

It took better than a week to get both letters together, and some hefty lawyers' fees, before Luke had the sworn affidavit from Morelli to present to his former captain.

The meeting was awkward.

"So, Sarkov, how's it going?" the man asked, his eyes not quite making contact with Luke's.

"Fine, it's going fine. I wanted to give you this affidavit. I could have released it to the papers, but let's say I still have a misguided sense of loyalty."

He handed the envelope containing Morelli's statement to the Vice captain. The man pulled the paper out, unfolded it and read it, two vertical lines between his eyebrows. It seemed to take a very long time for him to finish. When he finally lowered the paper to his desk, he looked at Luke and nodded, more to himself than anything else.

"Okay, so what were you thinking I'd do with this?" the captain asked, drumming his index finger on the paper.

"I was thinking you'd put that in my file, along with a letter stating that I'd quit the force for personal reasons. A copy to the police commissioner would be nice, too."

The man considered. "Say I do that, Sarkov. You going to make trouble for the department?"

''No trouble,'' Luke said. ''I just want the record set straight. I want my name cleared.''

''Sounds like a deal to me. I'll tell you, though,'' the Vice captain said, ''if you reapply to the force you'll be turned down, okay? I understand why you kept silent. I know you did it for your fellow officers, but times are changing, Sarkov, and the thin blue line is a dinosaur as far as this department is concerned.''

Luke said he understood. What he didn't say was that he knew—and so did the captain—that there was no closer bond than that of fellow cops. The thin blue line of silence and loyalty was always going to be there.

He spent the next days finishing up at Metropole, and on a Friday afternoon just before Labor Day he left the downtown offices for good, walking out into the fresh breeze blowing up the hill from the bay and whistling to himself.

Free at last, he mused, hands in his pockets, strolling along the busy streets. He was free at last.

And he owed it all to Grace. To the words she'd said to him on the drive to Denver. To the strength of her convictions and her bravery in the face of seemingly insurmountable obstacles. She was his rock.

And now, he thought as he jaywalked across the street, dodging cars, now just what was he going to do with his hard-won freedom?

CHAPTER EIGHTEEN

FALL SEMESTER CLASSES at the University of Colorado began shortly, and as usual, Grace was so busy that the last days of summer flew by.

Then there were the nights. Once Charley was in bed, she had time to catch her breath. Time to think, to rejoice in so many aspects of her life. The adoption papers had been filed, and she'd been assured there were no hitches. Susan at Child Protective Services had even told her that Charley's adoption was on a fast track.

Susan had called that morning to relay the good news. "By Christmas you'll be his legal mom."

And Kerry... Between the FBI, in particular Special Agent Renee Paynter, and Denver Social Services, Kerry was in a rehab program, a lengthy one. She'd finally made it through detox and sent a message via the system to Grace, apologizing for the hell she'd put everyone through, promising to get straight and stay that way. She also said that she'd like Charley to know about her one day, when she was ready. Of course, only time would tell if Kerry could overcome her problems. Grace often thought what a tragic life Kerry had led. But there was always hope. Hadn't she herself learned that unequivocal truth?

She sat in her living room, Whiskers in a cozy ball next to her on the couch, Hazel stretched out in her lap, Charley's toys scattered from one end of the room to the other, and she marveled at the resilience of human beings when faced with seemingly impossible odds. That day in Courtroom C when the judge had ordered Charley taken from her had been the low point of her life. She hadn't been able to see the future. She hadn't been able to think straight. Yet she'd survived, and beyond that, she'd prevailed.

And how could she forget she'd had Luke's help?

She was thinking about him, her eyes closed, conjuring up his face, trying desperately to cope with her love for him, when a rap at her front door startled her out of her musings.

"Gotta move, Hazel. Come on, fatso," she said, easing the cat off her lap.

It was Stacey. "Hey, neighbor," Grace's friend held up a bottle of wine, "how about a social hour?"

"You don't have to twist my arm." Grace pushed open the screen door and held it for Stacey, then went to fetch two glasses.

"You've been so busy lately," Stacey called. Then added, "Oops, sorry, is Charley in bed?"

Grace reappeared. "Oh, don't worry, he sleeps like a log. Once he goes to sleep, that is."

Stacey used a corkscrew Grace provided and opened the wine, poured two glasses and sat on the couch next to the cats. "We haven't had a heart-to-heart since you got home," she said, tickling Hazel's chin. "I want all the gory details of your great adventure, and I especially want to know about your new look. Are you going to stay short and red?"

Automatically, Grace touched her hair. "I don't know. What do you think? I mean, I like it, but is it too much for Professor Bennett?"

"Good God, no. It's perfect. After all, this *is* the twenty-first century. No reason a professor can't look a little punk. But there's something else." Stacey leaned forward, her wineglass in both hands. "You seem, well, radiant, you know, glowing. Am I missing something?"

"Of course not." Grace glanced away and took a sip of her wine.

"Bull. You're an awful liar. Did you meet someone on your adventure?"

"Stacey, really that's…"

"Private, I know. But tell me anyway. After all, you owe me for feeding these dumb cats and paying your first-of-the-month bills. Come on, fess up."

Grace bit her lip. "Okay. Yes, I met someone."

"*All right!*" Stacey beamed. "Tell me everything, every last juicy detail."

"You're sick."

"Hey, just think of me as your shrink. We'll reverse roles—how about that? It'll do you good."

Maybe it will, Grace thought. Maybe talking about Luke could free her of her futile obsession. Or at least help her to come to grips with it.

So she told Stacey the story, from the first time she'd met Luke at the Chinese restaurant till he'd pulled the disappearing act.

"Did you, you know, sleep with him?"

"That question is off-limits."

"So you did."

Grace couldn't help a smile, remembering. Oh, you bet they'd made love.

"So, have you heard from him? I mean, is he coming to visit?"

"He phoned me from San Francisco."

"And?"

"And nothing." Grace shrugged eloquently. "He said he was trying to get his life in order."

"So, what does that mean?"

"I don't know. I could guess, but with Luke, it's hard."

"Mmm. Just that one call?"

Grace nodded. She didn't want to think about it, much less hash it over with Stacey. How many hundreds of times since she'd last seen him had she gone over and over his words in her head, searching for meaning where maybe there was none?

"That bastard. God, *men.*"

"He's not like that."

"Oh, really?"

"Honestly. It's just that he's got problems of his own."

"Doesn't everyone?"

"These are big problems." And then Grace told her how Luke still fancied himself in love with his ex-wife. *"Wife,* I mean. The divorce…isn't, well, wasn't final." She deftly omitted most of the ugly details of Luke's departure from the police department under a shadow of suspicion, but she did tell Stacey that he'd quit the force and now found himself lost without his calling.

"Sounds like he was right—he ought to get his sh…stuff together."

Grace couldn't help laughing. "You sure hit that nail on the head. And I wish I would have said those exact words to him." She paused for a moment, thinking, then she said, "He's a very special person, but he has some unresolved issues. He was an orphan, and it's colored his whole life. He has trouble trusting people.''

''Wow, you picked a good one.''

''Oh, Stacey, he's really wonderful, but...''

''Has he talked to your folks, you know, about you or anything?''

''I've been afraid to ask. My mom would tell me everything, but Dad... He wouldn't say a word. He and Luke are too much alike in that respect.''

''So, Luke is history and you're still in love.'' Stacey took a long drink. ''Great, huh?''

Still in love... ''Yes, great,'' Grace concurred. But was he history?

''Well, you'll get over it. In time, you know—'' Stacey shrugged ''—you'll forget what he even looks like.''

But late that night, alone in the darkness of her bedroom, Grace knew she'd never stop loving him. She only prayed that her newfound strength would sustain her. But she didn't know; she just didn't know.

Once classes started she settled easily into her routine. Charley, too, settled in at nursery school with more ease than she would have imagined, given the trauma of their separation only a few weeks ago. She kept a close eye on him, nevertheless, and knew she was overly protective, but that was okay—they both needed the reaffirmation of their bond. She'd even consulted one of her psychology professors, now retired, about Charley, and he'd given her some warning signs to watch for, things like reversion to infantile behavior, bed-wetting and such. But so far Charley seemed normal.

After the first week of classes, Grace made a decision. Well, she thought, driving home with Charley in the back seat, she had made two decisions. First, she was going to get her hair cut again and the roots touched up. The second-year students loved her new look; Charley liked it; she liked it. Second—but more important, she thought, as she turned onto her street— she was going to get in touch with Luke. Difficult as it was sure to be, she needed to tell him how she felt. If she didn't she'd always wonder. She'd lie in bed at night when she was eighty, for God's sake, and still try to figure out how her life might have changed if she'd made a single call.

But that call was going to be impossibly difficult.

She must have been preoccupied with thoughts of Luke and his wife, and so very much more, because when she parked and got out and opened Charley's door, she never even noticed the red Subaru convertible parked across the street.

"Sweetie," she said to Charley, "grab that small bag on the seat...no, the smaller one, that's it, and don't squash the bread. Here, I'll get the car door."

It was Charley who first saw him. He was sitting in the golden evening light on the top step of her porch, knees splayed in his blue jeans, hands clasped in front of him. He was so still he could have been a statue.

"Mommy! Look! It's Luke! Hi, Luke!" Charley raced up the sidewalk, short legs pumping, the bag containing the bread crushed to his chest.

Luke? Grace whirled around, almost stumbling in her shock. "Luke?" she mouthed, and she blinked, not trusting her eyes. Then she could only stare, unable to move, two plastic grocery bags in her hands, her purse slipping off her shoulder.

It is him, ran wildly through her head, as if her eyes could not be right.

His voice came to her out of an invisible fog of confusion. "Hi, kiddo," he was saying to Charley, then he rose slowly, one hand patting Charley's head, ruffling his hair, the other liberating the squashed loaf of bread from Charley's tight clasp.

"I'm in nursery school," Charley was gushing, "and my teacher is Miss Pangborn, and well, see, my friend Billy is spending the night and Mommy says we can camp out in the backyard if it doesn't get cold. Mommy? Is Billy coming tonight? Mommy?"

But she barely heard. It was as if her brain had ground to a halt and frozen, stuck on a single thought: *He's come back.*

While she fumbled for control, tried to feel her feet beneath her, he came down the walk and took the groceries out of her hands. His touch, the mere sensation of his flesh on hers, sent molten waves of joy though her veins.

"You want these in the kitchen?" He held up the bags, one in each hand.

"What?" she got out, a hoarse whisper. She cleared her throat. *Luke, here.* "What did you say?"

"Should I put these in the kitchen?"

How could she have forgotten those eyes, or the smile that was shy and tough and self-mocking all at the same time, and the strong lean lines of his face? How could she have forgotten how beautiful he was?

"Grace?"

"Ah, yes, the kitchen."

"Come in!" Charley was calling, "I'll show you. Mommy? Can I have a cookie?"

Somehow she found her feet and followed Charley

and Luke inside. A thousand times. She'd played this scene in her mind a thousand times, and yet now that he was here, actually *here,* not a single word or gesture or thought came to her.

"Want the milk in the fridge?" Luke asked.

"These are my favorite cookies," Charley said, his eyes the size of saucers as he pulled the cream-filled chocolate cookies from the plastic bag. "Mommy? I won't spoil dinner. I promise. Mommy?" He could have devoured the entire bag for all Grace knew. How many times had she dreamed this scene, silently mouthed the words they would speak to each other?

"Got a beer?" Luke looked at her, his eyes taking her in hungrily—or was she imagining the whole thing?

"Ah, yes, behind the eggs, I think." She took a breath. "Luke? What…what's going on? I can't believe… I mean…"

He found the beer and popped the tab open. "What's going on," he said, "is that I'm unemployed. I quit the insurance company. Pretty much quit everything."

"But…?"

There he was. As big as life. Right in her kitchen. "A lot's happened since I phoned. And hey, I'm sorry I didn't keep you up-to-date, but…" He shrugged. "What can I say? I'm a jerk."

"That's okay," she whispered, dazed.

"That I'm a jerk?" A corner of his mouth lifted in a smile, and her heart leaped in her chest.

"No, no," she said, half-aware of Charley and the cookies and milk now spilled on the counter, "that isn't what I meant. I just mean that I understand."

Then the words tumbled out. "Are you divorced? Did you…?"

"Yes," he said. "It was final—" he looked at his watch "—about two hours ago. California time, that is."

"Oh."

"And I took care of that other thing—the mistake, shall we say, on my record. Not that the department wanted me back, but my record is clear. That advice you gave me about how to deal with a certain incarcerated gentleman—well, it worked. I was thinking…"

"Thinking?" He was so close…two, three, feet away, taking up half the kitchen, so handsome. She could practically feel the heat radiating from him, smell his special scent. In a minute she was going to faint.

"Can I watch TV, Mommy? Luke, you want to watch with me?"

"Ah, thanks, kiddo, maybe later."

"Okay," Charley said. "*Power Rangers* comes on next. You can watch that."

Luke said, "Sure why not," and Charley bounded out of the kitchen making his car sounds, "Broom, broomm!"

"Hey…" Luke turned back to her and his features took on a grave expression. "I'm no good at all this communicating, explaining, okay?"

"Yes, I mean, okay. Sure. But…"

"I phoned the Denver PD and they're reviewing my application. It looks good."

"You'd be working in Denver? You're moving to Denver?"

"Just let me get this out, okay?" He didn't wait

for her reply. "I'd like to be here, Grace, here with you and Charley. On the phone, well, you said…"

"I still mean it," she blurted out. "Oh, Luke, more than ever. I…I missed you so much. I…" Suddenly, her eyes widened. "Do you love me?"

And then he laughed. "Isn't that what I just said, Professor?"

"No. No, you did not." Her heart felt like a bird's wings beating against her rib cage.

"Well, I do. Okay?"

"You do what? Say it, Luke, I need to hear the words."

She took a step closer. And another. And she reached up and touched his face with her fingers. They were trembling. "I love you," she whispered.

He turned his head into her hand, then found her palm with his lips and kissed it. "I love you, Grace. God, how I love you," he said against her skin.

She kissed him, kissed him gently at first and then with such feeling her knees began to weaken. And then she pulled away and studied him through tears of joy.

"Should we, ah, ask Charley?" he said.

And Grace laughed, drinking him in with her eyes. "What do you think he'll say?"

"That he wants me to watch *Power Rangers* with him."

She nodded, moving back in his arms to lay her head on his chest. " A complete family," she murmured, and she closed her eyes and listened to the strong beat of his heart.

MAITLAND MATERNITY

Where the luckiest babies are born!

In April 2001, look for

HER BEST FRIEND'S BABY
by Vicki Lewis Thompson

**A car accident leaves surrogate mother
Mary-Jane Potter's baby-to-be
without a mother—**

and causes the father, Morgan Tate, to fuss over a
very pregnant Mary-Jane like a mother hen. Suddenly,
Mary-Jane is dreaming of keeping the baby...and the father!

*Each book tells a different story about the
world-renowned Maitland Maternity Clinic—
where romances are born, secrets are revealed...
and bundles of joy are delivered.*